The Realms Series

Book Four

Giant Country

Emory R. Frie

For *Dad*, who makes me laugh and taught me to think.

Thank you for making me *strong*.

Dusk has dawned, I hear its call,
above the world I've watched it fall;
I smell blood and I smell bone,
and I smell fear coated in gold;
Grind your bread and bake their teeth,
and death will come while you're asleep;
I will rage. I will rage.
Fee-Fi-Fo-Fum

'Til the mountains crumble down,
and oceans become heaven's crown;
Land sinks low, the gold runs dry,
and when these bones rain from the sky;
'Til the giants fall to myth,
and none remains to journey with;
I will stand. I will stand.
Fee-Fi-Fo-Fum

I will stand for my homeland,
for nowhere else could bear my hand;
I will stand by friend and kin,
we share the gold under our skin;
I will stand 'til my death comes,
and as my soul greets sky and sun,
I will sing, I will sing,
Fee-Fi-Fo-Fum

-The Giants

Chapter One

Fee-Fi-Fo-Fum,

I Smell Blood

Walls of stone and iron stood firm under the thunderous uproar that reverberated throughout the room. Normal foundations would've crumbled in its chaos. Mead and whiskey splashed over oak and brass tables. Crimson wine stained the floor, rippling pools in the cracks.

The giants had not gathered like this since the sabotages began. Since the harp had been stolen right from under their noses. Since the goose stopped laying eggs.

Now, as voices began to drop so others could be heard, it became clear there was a common thread through each major gathering.

"Sightings are increasing."

"They're getting sloppy!"

"They're getting bolder, not sloppier."

"This is the talk of weak-kneed cowards," spat a giant with too much bone in his hair and too little hair on his chin. "We're bigger than them, stronger than them! And we've let them scurry around like rodents in our halls—"

"They don't fear anymore, you dumb lout," shot a greying giantess, jabbing a muscular arm at him. "Sit down before you keep speaking things you've dreamt up in nursery beds, pretty boy. Or else *you* want to go scrambling after an enemy you can hardly rest your eyes on?"

"Unlike you, old hag, I wouldn't have any trouble crushing a belowlander under my heel once I come across one."

"I'd like to see you try! You'd trip over your own hair before you'd get ten lambs close to one of them."

The young giant lunged at her with a shout, trying unsuccessfully to wrestle her to the ground. Giants surged forward to pry them apart. As soon as they wrenched him away, the giantess sent a blow to his jaw with her imbedded brass knuckles. "Go home and take off those bones until you've earned them, you knee-knocking lump of clay."

Across the room, another voice howled above the others, "It's been over a year, now! Who's to say the Giant Slayer will return at this point? Perhaps he's scampered off for good."

"And good riddance to him!" whooped someone with tankard raised.

"Don't be daft," reasoned another. "He's bound to return sooner or later, mark my words. Either our leverage or the gold will do it, else that foreign witch makes certain it's so."

Mention of the witch sent a new stir, one that escalated after the mention of the Giant Slayer. Deals with witches made spines shift, but deals with *foreign* ones caused aromas of fear to mix with the steam of anger in the room.

Doubt became product from the discomfort of fear.

"How do we know she'll keep her side of the bargain?"

"Who's to say the deal's intact?"

"So long as we do our share—"

"And after that, what then?" bellowed one with long dreadlocks and a voice that carried over others around him. "We do our part, maybe the witch does hers, then what? Will we be controlled by this foreigner like dogs, or merely smite out like sheep for slaughter?"

Angry shouts roared up around him, rattling the shields and bones on the walls.

Bolstered by the appraisal, he exclaimed, "You all know it is true! If we work with the witch, we have given ourselves over to her mercy. Since when have we giants been willingly reliant upon a foreigner?!"

A sense of unified agreement settled into the commotion. The giant's chest swelled at the approval. Feet slamming up onto a wooden stool, he stood over the crowd. "We don't need this ambiguous deal."

Tankards smashed against each other before they were downed.

"We are *giants*!"

Fists pounded the air.

"Down with any foreign witch who dares to think she has authority over us!"

Gears locked into place and churned in such metallic chorus that it killed all other sound in the room. Great brazen doors opened wide. The air vibrated in anxious anticipation.

Then all fell silent.

He was a looming shadow in the doorway, reeking of menace. "Do I hear *doubt* in your voices, giants?" his voice rolled across stone, low and foreboding.

None dared respond in frozen wait.

At last, the figure moved forward, footfalls heavy and intentional against the stained floor. The crowd parted for him as he approached. Chainmail clattered under a cloak of furs. War hammer and jagged sword hung from his leather belt, humming with every thump against his thigh. It was like the souls of the slain were singing.

"Do I smell *fear* pulsing through your trembling hearts?" Dark hair bound by silver brackets and twisted braids fell over his shoulders. Grey leaked into his short cut beard and thick eyebrows. "What reason have you in feeling such dejection? Were you not long ago roaring in passion and agreement for that which you question now?"

Under his gaze, giants bowed their heads or dropped their eyes. The iron ring about his brow proved his authority. His eyes of blue and brown proved his dangerous will.

"I have promised you protection, hearth, and home," he continued, stepping further into the crowded room. "Have I not made good on my promises?"

Whispers of assurance batted at his ears.

"And yet, it is not enough." He turned to face them as a whole, anger lit behind narrowed eyes. "Justice. Revenge. Peace and ease of mind from those who would do us harm. I have failed you in this, as those before me failed to eradicate an escalating danger to our kind. We banish those who threaten these values. We cower on this side of the mountains which we cannot cross. We treat an enemy barely tall enough to reach the common giant's knee as if they are rocks in our shoes. For years, we have let the belowlanders stay on their side of the mountains, failing to treat them as a formidable opponent. Generations of neglect for this feud have come back to stab us in the back in the form of one boy. One boy who lit the match for an apocalypse threatening our very species! One boy whose nightmarish reputation has plagued a country he has no right belonging to!"

Giants leaned forward and stepped away, hanging on his words, wary of his clenched fists and bruising voice.

"The Giant Slayer, as you so eloquently call him," the Giant King growled, "has proven to be a warning of our impending extinction if we continue as we have: merely breaking bones, snuffing raids, fortifying an already doomed castle. Which is why we have the deal with the foreign witch."

Though anxiousness came at the mention of their reluctant agreement with the witch, no giant dared to raise any doubts before their king.

Gripping the carved handle of his war hammer, the Giant King gave a frustrated scowl. "Are you of such cowardice, you gentle giants?! Is your memory so easily lost? Your famed Giant Slayer has absorbed the golden egg! The gold of this country flows in his veins, shoots through his bone and muscle. He is bound to this land. Longing will grow to such strengths it will drive him mad, and he will come crawling back into our arms. And when he does, his bone shall be wrought, the witch will receive her payment," hefting his war hammer in the air, he bellowed, "and we shall have our revenge!"

Uproar erupted, rebounding off the walls. Alcohol flew into the air. Fists punched the sky. Staffs and feet pounded the ground.

Then the Giant King lowered his hammer to point directly at the one with long dreadlocks. "As for you, faithless coward, do you dare challenge me with your loose tongue? Or do you surrender from your falsehood?"

Grimacing, the giant slowly stepped down from his stool. He cut off a portion of his beard with a knife and proceeded to bare his wrists, as was custom. The Giant King nodded, accepting his surrender.

"Does anyone else question my authority in this matter?" he questioned, scanning the crowd with hammer still raised before him.

When no challenge arose, the exclamations fell to a rumbling chant. Feet stomped in rhythm as the chorus grew louder: *"Fee- fi-fo-fum. Fee-fi-fo-fum. Fee! Fi! Fo! Fum!"*

Chapter Two

See How They Run, See How They Run

Water splashed up around Jack Caldwell's ankles as he sprinted through the creek, the others following close as his heals. His heart pounded heavily. Muscles burned as he forced them to work in ways far too familiar yet long unused. Running took a different art form in this land.

Stay light on your feet.

Don't let the tremors in the ground throw you off.

Speed is crucial.

Never even consider tripping and falling.

Don't be afraid.

Don't be afraid.

He wanted to scream it to the others, but he dared not waste his breath on words. He was still readjusting to it, this kind of running, this kind of weight in his bones, this kind of flow in his blood. If he opened his mouth, he could lose steam.

At least the others managed to keep up.

Another quaking thud rippled through the earth. Kai Ødegård nearly lost his footing because of it, catching himself at the last moment. The next jostle caused Alice Liddell's knees to lock. She cried out from the shock, but kept going.

He led them along the edge of a river. The rushing water drowned out their footsteps and panting. Even so, they were far from safe. They had to run. They had to hide.

The current rushed faster beside them, toiling in white water rapids. Someone shouted behind him in alarm. At just the right moment, Jack slid to a stop, pebbles skittering over the ledge of a cliff. A waterfall roared beside them, tumbling into the abyss of mist below.

"Now what?" Red Daim questioned, catching her breath faster.

Breathing heavily and unable to answer, Jack walked along the cliff's edge. He jumped.

Wendy Darling yelped, and Kai lunged for him.

"Careful! It's a steep drop."

Alice's face appeared over the edge. "You little twit."

Jack looked up at them from the ledge two meters below. It was a narrow path down the cliff, unnoticed to anyone who didn't know it was there. He beckoned them to join him quickly.

The path fell away every ten paces before they had to lower themselves to a ledge just below where they stood. It went on like that, back and forth, descending from ledge to ledge. When the rumble came again, it sent rocks and dirt spraying down into the mist. Jack pressed his back to the mossy cliff face. His arm shot out protectively in front of Red, who was right behind him, to keep her back from the edge. They stayed like that until the shaking settled.

Nearly half way down the cliff, the path stretched out behind the waterfall and broadened to a more comfortable width. Jack tried to calm the nostalgia

14

threatening to rise in the back of his throat. The mouth of a cave opened beside them, invisible behind the plummeting water. It was too short to enter without ducking. Only Wendy didn't have a problem walking through.

Inside, the cave instantly broadened into a spacious room. The small opening prevented much water from dampening the shelter. Numb, Jack walked deeper into the darkness. He felt around for the indention, hands running over rock. Fur hit his fingers. He didn't flinch as he tore away the covering, exposing dry wood and finding flint in the back. He left the lengths of rope in the back.

When he returned to the others with his treasures, his hands were shaking. He dropped the wood to the ground. Wordless, he stared at his hands. Why were they shaking?

Kai took the flint from him gently. Nodding gratefully, Jack shoved his hands in his pockets. But the tingling was all over now, subtle but present.

Sparks flicked from flint to wood. Kai blew softly on the small flame when it caught, light growing. It illuminated the cave more than it should've. Jack's stomach clenched at the sight. Tendrils of gold webbed through the glistening rock walls. The gold never bothered him before. Now, it winked at him. Taunted him.

The others stared in awe. They didn't know.

"It's beautiful," Alice whispered.

Jack huffed, muttering, "Home, sweet home."

He trudged back to the nook where he'd retrieved the wood. Two furs and one woven blanket remained inside. Brushing away a spider and relocating a small lizard, Jack took them out and shook them off.

"I only have three," Jack explained, passing them to the girls. "One of them was a giant's dishtowel."

Kai shrugged as if the cold didn't even bother him. Sometimes Jack wondered if his resilience was due to his being a Swede or spending so long in the Snow Queen's realm. Or maybe it was all an act.

When Jack handed Red the dishtowel, she stared at it in her hands. He prepared himself to counter her refusal. Instead, she whispered, "You were here with Harry and Jill."

The lump was tightening in his throat again. He nodded, turned away. "Yeah, this was where we camped out for a while."

Instinctively, his gaze ran over the names carved into the wall. There were two lists. One was their signatures, the first act of vandalism the trio performed upon their arrival to the cave. That had been Harry's idea. They had to leave their mark somehow. Little had he known their mark dug up gold and blood.

The hit list ran just next to their names. Most were crossed out: Cormoran, the first giant he'd ever killed; Cormelian, the vengeful giantess; Blunderbore, keeper of treasures; Gogmagog and his wicked daughter Alba; and last was Galigantus, a master of human torture, the reason for Jack's inevitable capture. Jack touched the last name, the one that had yet to be crossed out: Nozrok, the Giant King. The one in all of his nightmares. The one who killed…

"Are you alright?"

It was Wendy who asked. He cleared his throat with a shrug. "Yeah. Yeah, I'll be alright."

16

But he felt like he could see them at the edge of his vision. There was Harry retelling their daily adventures, waving his hands as if they were puppets. Jill was there too, giving Jack a knowing look that questioned if her brother remembered that they were all there for the said adventures. They vanished if he looked their way. His throat tightened. He would never have that moment again.

He took a stone from the floor and crossed off Jill's name. His hands were still shaking.

Not feeling particularly chatty, Jack settled himself by the fire and lay with his back turned to his friends. The unseen back of the cave glittered like stars. But it was only gold.

It was only gold.

He set off with Alice early the next morning, leaving Kai watching the cave—they were the only ones awake. Of the weapons they'd brought from the Enchanted Forest, Jack took the bow and arrows while Alice grabbed the knives. They left their swords in the cave, hoping they wouldn't need them.

On the way up the cliffside, Alice asked, "So what are we looking for?"

"Food."

"The running kind?"

"Why else do you think we brought these?" He gestured to the bow and arrows strapped to his back.

"Grandeur?"

Jack shook his head with a laugh. "Don't expect an easy catch; everything is used to hiding. They're accustomed to hiding from giants, though, so they're practically deaf to anything else. We should get pretty close without notice."

"Anything mystical?"

"To you, maybe. They're strange little beasts, quick on their feet, climbing up and down trees, hiding in plain sight." He glanced back at Alice. "They're known here as *squirrels*."

"*No.*"

"And not the talking kind either."

"You're full of all sorts of curiosities."

"I am an anomaly."

Alice rolled her eyes, letting him help her up the next ledge. "Is that all?"

Jack shrugged. "We usually stuck with squirrels, fish, rabbits—sorry."

"They don't talk?"

"No."

"I'll try not to think too much on it."

He skirted across a thinned portion of the path. "There's sheep if we catch a flock, but they're always manned by giants. Goats stick close to the mountains. Both are unnaturally large, some bigger than horses."

"Are the rodents unusually sized, too?"

"Only slightly."

"Alright; continue."

"Watch out for boar, they've got wicked tusks. The deer do too, but you hardly see those."

"Deer with tusks?"

"Perfectly normal." He climbed another ledge, but Alice didn't need help with that one. "Some sort of dog— they're called dholes—and then these weird puma-looking

18

things live near the mountains, but they stray every so often, so be wary. And then the bears. Do not approach them at any cost."

"Noted."

"They will eat you."

"Doubly noted."

They reached the top, the waterfall toppling over the ledge beside them. As Jack helped her up onto solid ground, Alice at last broached the obvious question.

"And the giants?"

Jack tried not to shiver. "They don't have great eyesight; can't spot many details. So, if we come across any, hide. And whatever you do, do not be afraid."

"If this is a question of bravery, I can assure you—"

"It's not a matter of bravery; it's a matter of fear," Jack interjected, more serious than he'd been all morning. He fought past the pressure building in his chest. "They can smell fear."

"They can *smell* fear?"

Jack nodded, stooping by the river to wash his face off and let water run down his throat. When he looked up, Alice was chewing on a leaf. He didn't ask.

"Any kind of fear?"

"As far as I know."

"I can't promise anything when it comes to heights."

"You realize you just scaled a cliff *twice* without batting an eye, right?"

She didn't say anything. No snide remark. No rolling eyes. Nothing he expected. She just looked confused, as if he'd just said that her eyebrows were missing. As if she'd lost something.

By the time he stood up, prepping his bow and arrow, Alice took the leaf from her mouth and asked, "Is that why you try to be so funny all the time? To push away fear?"

"Who says I'm trying?"

"Oh, you know, *voices*."

"I'm hilarious. And you're crazy."

"That's a matter of opinion."

"I get worried about you sometimes."

"So do the voices." Alice took out a knife for each hand. "Let's go get some squirrels."

Deciding not to question her, Jack led her into the woods and away from the waterfall, praying they wouldn't run into any giants.

They managed to get two squirrels and some wild peas that Alice assured would not damage the boys' sitting muscles—whatever that meant. As he'd predicted, they hadn't seen hardly any other animal besides a rabbit that scampered away before they could get close.

The others were awake by the time they got back. Wendy sat outside the cave, legs dangling over the edge of the cliff. She smiled when she saw them and followed them inside. Red was pacing. Kai was stoic. Both perked when they entered the cave.

Jack didn't look at the lists on the wall this time.

"Good, we're all awake," Alice stated as she plopped the squirrels and peapods on the floor. "Now, can we actually talk about what happened back in the Forest?

20

Then we can go on to this place and what we do from here."

Red pressed her lips together, nails digging into her arms. Jack suppressed the urge to go up and put his arm around her. But without much prompting, Red explained how she had averted from Alice's plan back in the Forest: how she'd slipped away with Esmeralda; how they faced Carabosse; how Quasimodo and the witch had killed each other. Her hands were still stained with blood. She hadn't had the chance to wash them yet.

Wiping away tears, Wendy approached her and kept her arms around her in a long hug. Red wasn't crying, though. Not now. Not like back in the fortress after the wolves had escaped, and he held her as she cried into his chest, trying to keep her from blowing away, trying to protect every piece of her that was breaking. He wished he could tell her that he was still here for her. He wished he could tell her a lot of things.

The others filled in the blanks for Red, Wendy speaking of Isbjørn and Grimrose, Alice and Kai assuring Red of her friends' safety. Jack made sure to bring up the Huntsman's stuck leg in the ground.

"And the third?" Red asked, looking up at each of them. "Who was the third to die? Are you certain everyone was accounted for: the gypsies, the knights, the royals?"

Alice shrugged. "Unless someone was internally bleeding—"

"Didn't you see his face?" Kai spoke up, hands busied with separating the peapods.

Red frowned. "Fang?"

"That was the face of a man who just lost everything."

Jack looked at his friend, but he didn't raise his head. He'd seen the ring before; Kai had showed him back at the Facility. It was the only thing they hadn't taken away from him. It reminded him what he was fighting for. Who he was fighting for. The ring swung from his neck, a band of black silver with the texture of a meteorite. Jack appreciated that it wasn't gold.

Ready to move on, Red asked about the giants, the country, any possible threats, any possible humans. At first, he relayed what he'd told Alice, about the animals and the giants' ability to smell fear. But at least there were no dragons.

Red leaned forward. "How big?"

"Easily fifteen meters. We'd be like… like…"

"Squirrels?"

"Sure; we're like large squirrels in comparison. Thanks Alice."

"Anytime."

"They'd kill any one of us without a second thought if they ever got the chance," Jack added, forcing himself to look at the names scratched into the wall.

"Are there any other humans?" Red voiced, repeating her previous questioning.

"The giants call them belowlanders." He rubbed a peapod between his fingers. "They live on the other side of the mountains. The giants want to destroy them. They want to destroy the giants."

And so it goes, he thought to himself.

"The belowlanders see that they only have two options here: escape or conquer. For the first time in eons, there was a way out of this land, and I destroyed it." Jack shrugged, hiding the shiver that shot down his spine at the memory of taking axe to beanstalk until his palms bloodied. "They don't like me very much. The feeling's mutual."

"How long were you here?" Alice asked.

"About two years. We wanted adventure, treasure, to make a difference." He sighed, "Then we just wanted to go home."

Wendy locked eyes with him, a silent suggestion. Something churned in his veins. It was time to mention the gold in his blood.

"There's something else you should know." Jack lowered his gaze to his hands. "The giants have a way to torture you unlike anything else. They use golden eggs from a sacred goose to poison your blood." He remembered the pain coursing through his veins, gold choking him from the inside as the metal took hold of his heart and the country claimed his mind. "Whatever you do, don't get captured. If you are, give them whatever they want. Tell them anything, do anything, but do not let them put you through that torture… It never stops."

Wiggling over to his side, Wendy put a hand on his arm and leaned her head against him. He patted her hand in appreciation. Red was looking at the gold ore in the cave walls as if picturing arteries throbbing with gold. The way his did.

When Alice asked who was in power here specifically, Jack pointed to the only giant's name on the wall that had no mark run through it. "Nozrok is the giants' king. The belowlanders follow a man called the Fiddler, but they don't claim him as king."

Thinking of the Giant King brought back memories of golden pain and Jill lying dead on the floor. Were her bones decorating Nozrok's hair now? Or did they leave her to rot while her brother watched from the cages that swung above? He didn't want to think about it.

"I know who the Master is," Alice spoke.

She turned to Kai who refused to look at her. They didn't need to hear anything more.

"We've been wrong before," he said lowly.

"I'm not wrong now."

The air charged, waiting. Jack never suspected the Master to be in this place. Giants hated foreigners, and the belowlanders had no outside resources. But he wasn't sure he was ready to realize the Master's identity. That meant they'd have to face her sooner.

Alice held up the pocket watch. "We should leave. We have to end this."

"No."

Four pairs of eyes fixated on him as if they weren't sure he'd actually spoken. But Jack didn't take it back. His fingers were shaking.

"I'm not leaving," he said. "I've got to find Harry, get him home. It's the only thing... I can't live with myself unless I try to get him back."

"We have—"

"You did it for the Hatter," Jack countered before Alice could get a single protest out. To Kai, he added, "And you would do the same for Gerda. If you want to go, then by all means. But I have to stay."

Stay. The word put a weight into his bones that forced his hands to stop shaking.

Kai's silence could cut stone.

"I promised you that we'd get your friend back," Red spoke gently, resolutely. That's all she needed to say that she was staying. He couldn't help the slight smile of gratitude and relief.

Wendy squeezed his hand. "I'm not going anywhere."

Alice narrowed her eyes, pocket watch still in hand. Who knew what kind of things were buzzing around in her head? "She's been pulling our strings this whole time, watching where we run when she prods us. She's the reason we're here. The *master* puppeteer," she said forcefully, making every point stand. Her words lingered. Then she slipped the pocket watch under her shirt. "I suppose we can wait a bit longer to draw back the curtain."

Jack raised his eyebrows.

Alice shrugged. "It's hardly been a month since we started searching after Wonderland; excluding Neverland. Who knows how long we spent there."

A lump formed in his throat. Taking a deep breath, he faced Kai. Of all of them, he was the one who would risk the most in staying. Without a word, Kai tossed aside his peapods and left the cave. Jack followed.

The waterfall roared, deafening, spraying them in a fine mist. Drops clung to the hair on his arms. Kai raked both hands through his hair, growling words he couldn't make out.

"You know I can't understand you when you go all Swedish on me." Jack cracked a smile.

Kai wasn't amused. His glare turned on the waterfall as he rubbed his scarred jaw agitatedly. Jack's smile waned.

"Look, Kai—"

"You are asking me to choose between my…" He gnashed his teeth in frustration.

Jack sighed, choosing his words slowly, "I know that stopping this master is very important to you."

"I couldn't care less about the Master if she wasn't…" He whipped towards him. "You know what lies on the other end of that blasted pocket watch?"

"I know."

"You know what awaits there? *Who* awaits there?"

"I know."

"You know how important that is for me!"

Jack bowed his head. "You've waited a long time."

"I've waited longer than the lot of you!" Kai cried, icy eyes blaring right through him. Jack stood frozen, afraid to move unless Kai snapped. Fists clenched, Kai turned away. "And now…"

Silence stretched between them. Jack's hair hung in wet strands over his brow. Kai's clothes clung to his skin. He knew how difficult this was, the gravity of what he was requesting.

Jack remembered when the Facility first brought Kai as his roommate, how hard and angry he'd been. Kai hardly spoke to him at first. When he did speak, it was Swedish under his breath, which made Jack think he couldn't understand English. Then the nightmares would come, vivid and butchering. Jack would wake up screaming. After one of these nightly terrors, Kai spoke to him for the first time.

"Who do you see in your nightmares?" he'd asked, voice gravelly.

"Too many faces."

"Me too."

Jack shifted now, pleading, "Are you staying?"

"Of course I'm bloody staying."

Chapter Three

The More She Saw, The Less She Spoke

Wendy saw the first giant.

While Kai and Red went out for food and firewood, and Alice bounced ideas back and forth with Jack over the plan he tried to formulate, Wendy decided to climb to the bottom of the waterfall. The thrill was intoxicating. She hugged the side of the cliff, going from ledge to ledge like a goat. The path had stopped a little way below the cave. But she never minded the danger. Climbing was as close to flying as she could get now... besides falling. This was safer.

She reached the bottom without breaking any bones, skirting the edge of the river the waterfall fed with pounding mist. Large rocks emerged from the riverbank. Moss crawled up their sides in furry tendrils. Water wove through clusters of rock as if the river desired the feel of stone between its fingers. Fish gleamed under the surface, flicking between the maze of rocks so often it was a wonder they didn't get lost.

Nimbly, Wendy leaped onto one of the mossy rocks. Trout drifted lazily below. Sunshine leaked from the cloudy sky, glistening on the water. She frowned at the sparkle. Fish scales caught the light in golden reflections.

And the stones, they glittered brilliantly all around her, laced with golden veins, gold bleeding through moss.

Did this whole country thrive from gold, or was it infected with it? Jack described the gold in his blood as torture. Did that mean this whole land ached with it? Or was it like a drug, feeding this place but disagreeing with any who wasn't used to it?

Wendy wondered if the trees held gold as well.

She stood on her perch, ready to leap back to shore. Her breath caught in her throat.

The bear was like nothing she'd ever seen before. Thick fur wet with dew grew from iron mesh and flesh, steel claws jutting from massive paws, copper framed eyes of gold pinpointed on her. Saliva dripped from jaws filled with mismatched metal teeth. Its mass could easily challenge a polar bear—she would know.

Fear clutched her chest. The bear huffed, lumbering forward two steps, blocking any way back to shore that didn't end in between those razor teeth. Wendy wondered how far she could swim before the massive beast caught her. How fast could she climb up the cliff before she got out of reach? Her heavy heartbeats said *not fast enough*.

The bear lunged forward with a roar of grinding steel. She jumped. Claws raked across her arm and she hit the water. Her back slammed against the bottom of the river; air rushed from her lungs. Ears ringing, she scrambled to get up for air. She broke the surface coughing, adrenaline telling her to leap away quickly. The roars were chaotic now, but no bear came boring down on her.

She crawled back to her feet, looking over the boulder. The bear was wriggling wildly as it was lifted into the air. Wendy stumbled back. A giant, great and terrible in every way, wrestled the hybrid bear as it wailed in his grasp. Arms wrapped around the beast, the giant had the bear facing out against his torso. He broke the bear's sternum with a sickening crunch. Life drained from the beast's golden eyes.

The giant slung the limp body of flesh and metal over his shoulder. Wendy's heart pounded in her ears. With a frown, the giant sniffed the air, gaze sweeping over the river. His eyes landed on her, rusty brown pools she couldn't tear her eyes away from. Dread dripped over her bones and froze her muscles.

They can smell fear.

But even if she managed to shove away the fear now, it would do no good. The giant saw her. If she didn't think she could run away from the metal bear, she didn't stand a chance against this.

He huffed, arm wrapped around his catch. Then the giant turned away and trudged into the surrounding woods. The ground shook under her feet and sent ripples through the water.

Hesitantly, Wendy climbed back onto the boulders, hands pressed against the gold washed moss. Fear ebbed away.

The giant had left her alone.

But after everything that Jack had told her, that made no sense at all.

When she tried to recount the story to the others later that day after an agonizing climb back up the cliffside with her injured bicep, Jack instantly expressed his doubts about the whole situation. He insisted the giant didn't see her. He swore that the fear came from the bear. But she related again that the giant had held eye contact, and that the bear was already dead by the time he'd smelled the air. That the giant saved her.

"No, he spared you," Jack persisted. He was trying to make her understand what he did, she could tell. There was a strange wrinkle between his eyebrows that reminded her of her brother John when he'd try to lovingly tell her that something she believed wasn't as true as she claimed. She never cared for wrinkles, but she respected them. They tended to hold wisdom, even if it was misplaced.

"Not that I'm not thankful he spared you from becoming bear chow," Jack continued as Red bandaged Wendy's arm to the best of her abilities with their limited supplies. "But giants do not *save* humans. This one was probably just bored or lazy, satisfied with his catch and not up for another. Giants are merciless, but not stupid."

Wendy didn't respond, letting the subject drop. But she wasn't convinced. Maybe giants were dangerous and bloodthirsty. She was familiar with those things. But one of them had saved her. Didn't that mean something?

Chapter Four

If I Don't Hurt Her, She'll Do Me No Harm

The black Wolf trotted through the underbrush, rabbit clamped in her mouth. It was so large her jaws were growing sore with the awkward size. She'd only ever seen a rabbit so large in Wonderland—but he also wore a waistcoat and had the mind of a man. A foul smell filled her nostrils from the wet carcass. Rain drummed against the ground. It seemed the sun was a rarity in this place, always hiding behind clouds or rain. Though the ground was moist and mud coated her paws, at least the earth was used to the dampness so that it didn't flood or sink.

Fur bristled on the base of her neck. The Wolf stopped, ears flicking to the low growl that rumbled through the patter of raindrops. Her muscles tensed.

Amber eyes gleamed in the dim light as the creature stalked toward her. Lips curled back in a vicious snarl. The dhole was smaller than her, red fur shot through with gold, dark at the end of its nose and bushy tail. Tufts of matted hair stuck out at every angle, a sure sign of agitation. She noted the ears pressed flat against its head, the ribs that stuck out from thin sides, how the skin stretched over a skeleton. But it was the eyes that made her cautious. Eyes lit with savage madness.

The Wolf twisted her nose, realizing the dhole's crazed desire for the rabbit she held. She bent her knees to prepare for the inevitable attack.

She noticed the rabid foam just before she did anything that landed the two canines in a fight. It was yellow, dipping. There were few things more dangerous than a desperate, rabid predator. Even if she could kill it, she would not risk the chance of herself becoming rabid.

Carefully, the Wolf surrendered her catch. She backed away slowly, never letting her gaze drift from the rabid dhole. It didn't take long for the animal to throw itself at the prey, ripping the rabbit apart. With the dhole distracted, the Wolf bounded off, putting a great distance between herself and the infected animal before she slowed.

Alice was waiting for her by the river, blonde hair hanging in wet strands. "How many?"

Red shifted form, uncovering three muddy rabbit from a hole under a nearby tree. "There were four." She scowled at the woods behind her where the dhole was feasting on her last catch far away. "Help me skin them, will you?"

Alice produced a knife. "That's what I'm here for. And the onions; I found some along with a few mushrooms."

"Mushrooms?"

"They shouldn't be poisonous. I stole them from the squirrels."

Red huffed a laugh, her previous annoyance gone in an instant. She threw her friend a limp rabbit. Catching it, Alice went to rinse the mud off in the stream. Red was a little surprised when Alice took out the carcass and immediately went to break the skin around the ankle, revealing some knowledge in skinning rabbits. It seemed unnatural.

"How do you manage to stomach it?" Red asked, proceeding to pull the skin off her own rabbit.

"What do you mean?"

"Because of your friends back in Wonderland; the White Rabbit, the March Hare?"

Alice shrugged, yanking the skin from the creature to expose the pink body beneath. "White used to talk about the difference between those like him and Doe and March, and other animals like this. They have souls, like us. You can see it in their eyes—it's *different*. Like you."

"Me?"

"When you're the Wolf. I can still see you in your eyes. It's not the same as another wolf, one that doesn't change into a tall, black haired, warrior woman."

Red laughed and shook her head, but didn't bother to argue.

Alice used her knife to remove the extremities, lips tight. She didn't look up at her. "My father taught me this."

Rain washed down her face. "So did mine."

"Was it to teach you a lesson?"

A shiver ran down her spine. Red imagined a younger Alice, one who unabashedly spoke of talking animals and flowers and rabbits in waistcoats. She imagined her father, the drunk, the broken man whose daughter reminded him of the wife he'd lost, whose daughter had gone mad in his eyes. She could just picture it: her father teaching Alice how to skin rabbits. To teach her a lesson.

Red shook her head, because their lessons were different, their fathers were different. "No."

They didn't bother to gut the game yet, leaving that for when they got back to the cave. But Alice made sure to fold the heads and feet into the pelts, just in case they were to make stew later. If they had a pot.

Red took the last rabbit to skin. Blue eyes watched her solemnly in the grey rain.

"What do you think about Jack?"

The question caught her off guard. Heat crawled up her neck. "What about him?"

A grin spread across Alice's face, but she continued, "He isn't sleeping. At all. I've had to force him to eat anything when we're talking through his plans. Otherwise, he doesn't take a bite. And as far as the plans go for saving Harry..." She shook her head. "I'm worried about him."

"He's just trying to make things foolproof."

"He's covering up his fear of losing someone else by obsessing over this plan of his," Alice persisted. "Do you remember back in the Forest? When Esmeralda told him about his fear of history repeating itself?"

She did remember. *Your fear takes the form of a giant pouring sand down your throat from an hourglass.* It was a haunting image. She wondered if the sand was gold.

"You know Jack; he doesn't plan like this. He makes an outline and fills in the blanks as he goes," Alice continued. "He's going mad. And I know mad. It's a slippery slope, and when madness is linked to obsession... You've seen the Queen of Hearts."

With a sigh, Red relented. "What do you want me to do? I won't tell him to stop."

"I'm not asking that. I want you to talk to him. Figure out what's going on. Get him to take a break, eat something, sleep. And push him to turn whatever plan he makes into action. We've almost been here a week. We can't stay here forever, not when there's a war on the way."

Red stood with skinned rabbits in hand. "Why me?"

Alice cocked her head. "Because he'll listen to you."

She huffed, shaking her head as she walked away. Mud squished under her feet. Her ears burned.

"I'm not blind, Red," Alice called after her. "And neither are you."

"You're mad."

"But not blind!"

Red didn't bother to reply.

Jack was alone, and he wasn't. He'd outlined the giants' fortress on the floor long ago. He used to only have three stones to maneuver, but he added two so as to represent them all. But every map in his head felt vague, incomplete. He couldn't hold a plan for more than a few moments before a giant emerged or Jill lay dead on the floor.

Looking over it, the fortress looked like a wheel. There were four towers within and connected to the double walls, each holding a different kind of fortified cell. One was the treasury, a room with gold and jewels and bones. Another held a smithy and arsenal—it smelled constantly of metal and fire. Then there was the prison, a place of torture and hanging cages. Lastly, the centermost tower with the mead hall, throne room, and *real* things of value: a goose, a crown, and a harp.

Jack shook his head. No, not a harp. They'd stolen the harp. That's what got them into this mess in the first place, the thing that changed the game. The feat that finally got the giants' attention.

But it didn't earn his name.

The Giant Slayer.

He threw his rock against the wall so hard it chipped. Pressing his fists to his pounding temples, he dropped his head on his knees. Angry tears burned his eyes. He shoved them away with a sniff.

"Hey."

Jack was quick to compose himself, jerking his head up and pulling a grin. "Hey, Rubes."

She sat next to him, handing him the rock he'd thrown. "You dropped this."

"It slipped."

She gave him a look that made him feel like she could see every bit of him behind his smile. Right down to the gold and the screams and the body count he was responsible for.

"You want to tell me what's wrong?" she asked.

"Yes." But he didn't say anything else. His throat tightened. His smile was hard to keep up right now.

I promise I'm a happy person, he told the himself over and over. But it was hard to remember in times like this, in this place, with memories he'd laid to rest long ago resurfacing. Ghosts don't stay buried when they're laced in gold.

"I didn't know," Red spoke again, gentle, "about the gold in your blood. Why did you never tell me?"

He shrugged. "I denied it for as long as I could. Wasn't until that wizard told me it was there that I couldn't ignore it any longer."

"I see it in your eyes," she disclosed. "I never noticed before."

"I guess neither of us were looking hard enough."

She looked away. "Is it permanent?"

He wished he had a different answer. He wished he could say that the side effects were meaningless, that he only had a little torture—enough to haunt him but not enough to scar him. But he couldn't lie. Not to her, not to himself.

"Most people who go through that kind of torture only get it once. They only need it once," Jack explained, remembering golden eggshells littering a stone floor. "It lingers in their veins, a mere trace barely detectable. But what the giants did to me wasn't torture. It was punishment."

"How many?"

He shook his head. "At least once a day. For a week. The stuff is probably all the way in my bones."

Red was silent for a long time. Jack studied her face, her lowered green eyes, her drawn brow. He appreciated that there was no pity. Concern, perhaps, but nothing as uncomfortable as pity.

He leaned over and bumped her shoulder. "Why are you really here?"

Bottle green eyes looked up at him and he had to catch his breath. "We're getting worried about you."

Jack passed a hand over his face with a sigh. "Alice sent you?"

"You've been mulling over a plan for days."

"So she did send you."

"Is this about Jill and Harry?"

"No. I mean… Yes, but no."

"Care to specify?"

"Rubes…"

"Tell me what's wrong."

He huffed, but he didn't tell her about the bodies at the end of every dead end to his multitude of discarded plans. He told her why they were there.

"Last time I broke into the giants' fortress," Jack began, "we were going in to steal the golden goose for the belowlanders. We'd done it before, the three of us, when we stole a magic harp. There wasn't supposed to be any issues since it was so easy before. I should've known things never go the same way twice." He rolled one of the rocks in his hands, as if the action might calm him. "We were forced to retreat and Jill was captured. Harry and I wanted to go back for her, but the belowlanders refused to help us. So while they abandoned ship, Harry and I went back in to get Jill. We were too late." The rock fell from his grasp. He bowed his head. Everything in him felt so heavy, so weak, as if the gold inside was weighing him down. "Harry didn't see her. I tried to tell him, but he didn't believe me. He went back, and the giants were coming, and I… I left. I climbed down the beanstalk, Nozrok followed me, and at the bottom I managed to chop the bloody thing down. But Nozrok managed to get back up before it fell. And now there's no way in or out of this place except for Long Ears' pocket watch. Unless you happen to have some magic beans on you?"

Red ignored his question, so he shrugged it off as rhetorical.

"We aren't Harry and Jill," she whispered.

He fought the lump in his throat. "That's not what I'm saying."

"It's what you're thinking," she insisted, as if she knew what he was thinking. "It's not the same, Jack. No, none of the rest of us have fought any giants, but we can take care of ourselves if you let us."

"I know," Jack admitted, rubbing the back of his head. "But…"

"No arguing," she scolded, hitting his shoulder as she got to her feet. "You're always better with improvisation; so the next time I talk to you, you'd better have a plan of action. Got it?"

He laughed, but relented.

He wished she wouldn't leave.

Chapter Five

Goosey Goosey Gander, Whither Shall I Wander?

Kai stood watch while Wendy was following a theory in the tree above and Alice collected peas and mushrooms near its base. He was perfectly aware of Wendy's talent for climbing, but this was ridiculous. The closest branches were far above their heads, a height he couldn't dream of reaching. But Wendy shook off her shoes and instantly started up the trunk. He often questioned if her ability to fly was really tied to that little talisman she'd lost.

Alice held her findings in her shirt like a pouch, flipping her blonde braid over her shoulder as she approached him. "So, Kai," she began, a sure sign of the line of questions to come, "what's it like there?"

He didn't bother to ask where she meant. "Cold."

"I figured as much." She chewed her lip. "What can we expect?"

"I have no idea."

"I'm serious."

"As am I." Kai remembered the world he'd left behind well, but he couldn't imagine it would be the same world he would return to.

41

As if she could read his thoughts, Alice tried again, "Well, how was it when you left? Who was there? What was there?"

He worked his jaw, wondering how to phrase what Alice was searching for. "There were three witches, but the most powerful of them called *Häxan* worked for the Snow Queen. A group of nomadic robbers roamed the southern mountains. Between the mountains and the Snow Queen's castle lay a forest where... I don't know how to explain... people of earth?"

"Like nymphs and dryads?"

Kai hesitated. "Not exactly. They were humans, but they bound themselves to an aspect of nature, like a tree or river. It gave them prolonged life and magic beyond my comprehension."

"Interesting. Anything else? Besides the obvious frozen devil?"

"Some of the animals were *more* than just beasts, like your friends in Wonderland. But not quite the same." A chill ran down his spine. "And then there was Frost."

Alice raised her eyebrows. "Frost?"

"I was right!"

Kai looked up where Wendy was peering down at them from her high perch. He'd nearly forgotten she was still up there.

"Right about what?" Alice questioned loudly up at her.

"The tree," Wendy shouted down, "its bark and leaves are webbed with gold."

"You had to go that high to figure that out?" Kai asked.

"This way is more fun!"

Kai shook his head but smiled.

"This whole country is thriving on gold," Wendy continued, lowering herself to the branch below. "Where does it come from? Is it poison? A living organism? Something as basic here as water?"

"You're starting to sound like Alice."

Alice just shrugged without denying the statement.

"What do you think, Alice?" Wendy asked.

For once, she had no questions. "It's a drug; beneficial if used properly, toxic if otherwise, and addicting either way."

"But drugs often have antidotes, don't they? If we can figure out its counterpart, then maybe—"

The ground shook under his feet, and Kai's knees buckled. Leaves showered down. Wendy clutched tightly to her branch.

"We need to go!" Kai hissed as another quake rumbled the woods. He pressed Alice against the tree to minimize their chances of being spotted.

Wendy didn't climb down. Instead, she pointed ahead. "Look."

Kai whipped around, shielding Alice, hand flying to his sword. A stampede of massive sheep thundered through the woods ahead, creatures that towered even at a distance. Behind them ran four giants holding long crooks in hand. Bleats and laughter echoed in his ears.

The three remained transfixed as the shepherds and their flock disappeared with only the broken earth and a cloud of dust in their wake. The giants never saw them. They were gone before fear even had the chance to set in.

By the time Kai blinked away his daze, Wendy was on the ground beside him. She looked at him as if what they'd just witnessed proved a point.

They can't be all bad.

But Kai wasn't completely convinced. It was one thing to see a giant gentle around his own kind. But when any group of people, no matter how seemingly docile, comes in contact with someone they've been taught is an enemy... There's no telling what would happen. In a way, Kai didn't expect the giants to behave any differently than humans would. Which is what scared him.

Alice was glaring at him. She revealed the harvested provisions in her shirt with annoyance. "You squashed my mushrooms."

*****

Nozrok sat seething in a silence that could cause stone to crumble. Golden spheres piled high on the other end of the room, a radiance in the glum. A gilded cage sat beside the mound of eggs. Inside lay a goose, grey with sickness and depression. Her feathers should've been gleaming as everything else around her. Instead, they were chipped, molting, dull. Her bill became more opaque every day. Murky yellow eyes remained half closed.

The goose was dying.

Nothing could be done unless they recovered what was stolen.

A pitiful squawk shot like a needle through the silence. Nozrok's spine snapped straight, inspecting the goose with wide mismatched eyes. Not another sound was uttered.

The doors burst open. The Giant King's gaze turned to glare instantly.

"I am not to be disturbed when—"

"Don't use that tone with me!" the broad jawed giantess snapped. Her thick yellow hair looked like straw in comparison to the gold that surrounded her. Hard eyes glared right back at him.

"I will not be spoken to in such a way."

She scowled. "I'm not some gentle giant for you to kick around. If you don't watch your tongue, I'll cut it off."

Nozrok groaned, rubbing his temples with thumb and forefinger. "Why have you come, Yldaa?"

Pressing her fists to her hips, Yldaa revealed, "The prisoner is causing trouble again. It's been too long since the last dose."

His eyes flicked to the goose again, but nothing had changed. She wasn't bothered by the intrusion. She wasn't bothered by anything anymore besides her great loss. Then his gaze landed on the pile of golden eggs. Even if the mound was great, it was still dwarfed in comparison to what it used to be. What it could be.

But unless they kept the prisoner under control, then their leverage would crack. Months of carefully lain foundation would be wasted. Fear had to be bred, nurtured, cultivated until it became a useful weapon. An asset. An advantage. The prisoner was almost there. Then he would have all the information he needed to right the wrongs done to his people. He would fulfill his promise. It only took time and patience, two things that were wearing thin in his mind.

The prisoner needed a fresh dose.

There were so few left to spare.

It was with great hesitation that he said, "Wait a few days for the pain to dwindle. Then we shall inject it fresh. Unless there is momentary relief, there is no consciousness of pain. And pain breeds fear; and fear is our weapon."

Yldaa huffed. "Have it your way. And save the laments for your woeful drunks craving the motivation."

Nozrok said nothing as the giantess turned on her heal and let the heavy doors swing shut behind her.

Sinking back in his chair, Nozrok dug his knuckles into his jaw. The goose remained silent. It sifted thoughts of revenge behind his brown and blue eyes. Perhaps the famed Giant Slayer would come for the goose again. Perhaps he'd come for the prisoner. Perhaps he'd come for the Giant King himself. But he would come. It was the only thing that Nozrok was certain of.

*****

As they explained their adventure earlier, Jack listened with concern. Two giant sightings so close together in the same area… He hoped it was coincidence. But somehow this safe haven behind the waterfall didn't feel so safe.

Alice was pouting over her bruised mushrooms. Somehow that did not surprise him. But Wendy's fascination with the gold that infected the country; he only needed to wonder about it for a moment before he realized. She was looking for a cure. For his cure. As sweet as her intentions were, Jack hated to think about informing her of the impossibility of her search. Especially in front of Alice. She'd probably say something about how nothing was impossible or some other motivational madness. Despite either of their potential persistence, the gold was permanent. It made him heavier than he looked.

Then Kai mentioned the sheep, and Jack's gears started turning.

"I've got a plan."

Alice leaned forward, mushrooms completely forgotten. "Really?"

"Everything's probably going to go wrong."

Kai grunted, "Good. That's how we work best."

Jack flashed his friend a grin. "How do you feel about riding colossal sheep?"

"My favorite pastime."

"Glad you're bloody staying, then."

As they gathered around the map on the floor, Jack explained his outline of a plan to get in and out of the fortress. It involved massive sheep, lengths of rope, and a lot of prayer. Throughout the process, Jack drilled into them the most important aspect of the plan, "Remember, the key is *no fear*."

No fear.

Chapter Six

On a Cold and Frosty Morning

Step one: Find the bloody sheep.

Jack forgot the sheer magnitude of distance a giant and his flock could travel in a matter of hours. Thankfully, that large of a crowd left footprints, so it wasn't too hard to follow them. Never mind the fact that Kai had a tracker's eye and Red had a Wolf's nose. Those two led the rest of them along.

Before they had left the cave, Jack had lingered beside the names written in the wall. Fingers traced the markings his friends made long ago. He swore to himself that the only name to be crossed off now was Nozrok's. Harry would be saved. He had a long life to live.

Unsure if he'd ever return to this cave again, Jack said a silent thanks to the memories and farewell to the ghosts that clung to the stone. Wendy had silently slipped her hand in his. He let her lead him away.

They reached the dozing flock well past midnight. The shepherds left a bonfire crackling. Three lay asleep, their snores loud enough to keep any predator at bay. Jack knew one was keeping watch. So long as they kept to the shadows, they wouldn't be seen.

Jack led the others up to the edge of the gargantuan sheep. The creatures weren't bothered by their presence. If any of them tried anything too threatening, it would only take a cry to summon a stampede to crush them to bits. Jack didn't want to think about possibly dying the same way his parents had.

Silently, he motioned for the others to come closer. Kai approached with the rope wound around his chest like a sash. Jack took the end to prepare for executing the plan.

Then the sheep started bleating.

Jack whipped around to find Red backing away with her hands up defensively. "I swear, it was an accident!"

"What did you do?" he accused in a whisper.

"I barely touched it."

"The thing is at least five times your size. *Barely* wouldn't have caused it to cry."

"Then what—?"

Wendy hushed them sharply. The wakeful giant stirred, stood, scanning the flock with narrow eyes. Jack instantly hastened the others to get down. Shadows masked them well there. So long as the sheep didn't make noise again, and there was no fear...

The shepherd settled down again after several long heartbeats.

When Jack rose to a crouch, Red whispered, "What's wrong with them?"

"Maybe they don't like you," Jack responded, wary gaze on the giants beyond the flock.

"It's the Wolf," Alice spoke up softly. She was touching the nearby sheep as if to test her theory. "It has to be. They sense a predator."

"I'm not going to hurt them."

"They don't know that."

This time, Kai hushed them with a look. He passed the mantel to Jack the same way, putting him on the spot. Jack thought quickly, recalling Red's observation about his improvisational skills. Well, if this was how the plan went askew...

"You can follow as the Wolf," Jack determined. "Don't exhaust yourself, but stay as close as you can. The rest of us will go as planned."

With only a hint of hesitation, Red nodded in consent. She met his gaze. He didn't mention that he wasn't sure how she would get into the fortress alone. But if any of them could find a way, it would be her. They both knew that. He tried his best to convey a message of good luck before she looked away.

As quietly as possible, Jack and Kai helped tie Wendy's arms and legs around the closest ewe's middle. She had to pull her hair up so it wouldn't hang before she hugged the fuzzy underbelly. Cloth was wrapped around her forearms to prevent rope burn. The thick wool hid the ropes easily. From a giant's eyelevel, she would be undetected.

Alice was next, her limbs longer but still invisible under the strong sheep. Kai and Red had to help Jack with his sheep. The padded ropes dug into his wrists and ankles. Nothing about this was comfortable. But at least it didn't take much muscle to hold on.

He watched as Red helped Kai under his steed. They had to pick a larger one that wasn't as bothered by Red's presence so she could help with the ropes. Once Kai was secure, Red stepped back with a silent promise to free them once they got inside the fortress. She melted into the Wolf and disappeared into the night.

Now all that was left was a long, excruciating wait for morning and the discomfort that was to come.

*****

Nozrok suspected an invasion.

According to a cook, two blacksmiths, six shepherds, and eight witnesses, sightings had doubled in the past three days alone. They were getting braver. They were becoming fearless. This fact alone troubled the Giant King. If the belowlanders were starting to eliminate their fear as completely as giants themselves, that crippled the giants' advantage. They may never see them coming.

Every nerve spiked, muscles tense. If the sightings were to be believed, then the belowlanders were getting their bearings. Only Jack and the rest of his trio ever got close to knowing the fortress' layout. Nozrok assumed they knew more than he'd ever care to admit. Now the belowlanders were scouting the grounds, clearly planning something.

He racked his mind trying to determine what they were planning. An invasion, yes, but for what purpose? They would never attempt to wipe them out directly—it would take every one of them to stand a chance. He knew they would never abandon their haven across the mountains so completely. Besides that, they already had the harp in their possession. That was all they would need to ensure the giants' eventual extinction. Unless they had yet to discover they held such power.

Perhaps they were after the goose this time. Surely they wouldn't dare. They wouldn't be so senseless as to try for another heist of such magnitude. Yet the thought ate away at the back of his mind. Their boldness was troubling. He shouldn't underestimate them.

"*Toog!*" he thundered, rising to his feet.

The giant who loped in had a knotted face and one arm longer than the other. Scars in his skin and human bones in his hair proved how great a warrior he was. "My king," Toog said, baring his wrists to show submission. There was a growl in the back of his voice, a permanent wound from when a belowlander tried to slit his throat. The attacker's skeleton decorated his neck now.

"Double the guard around the goose," Nozrok ordered. "No belowlander is to get within ten lambs length around her."

"May the gold eat me alive should I fail you, my king!" swore the warrior. Baring his wrists once more, Toog left to carry out his orders.

Assured of the goose's safety, Nozrok began to settle when his crown started to burn. He hissed between his teeth. Knuckles paled. Quickly, he threw the iron band from his brow and watched it clatter across the floor. Pain pulsed through his temples. He frowned as it glowed amber before it cooled once again.

Smooth satisfaction and anticipation dawned on him.

"Welcome home, Jacky."

*****

Step two: Hang on for dear life.

Of all of Jack's brilliant ideas, this was probably the worst of them. The journey was one of the most

52

uncomfortable experiences he'd ever had. He didn't even want to think about the pitstops.

Every bump made his muscles ache. His wrists and ankles burned despite the fabric wrapped around them to keep the rope from rubbing too much. Sparingly he let his head hang, risking a good kick in the head. Otherwise, his face was pressed to the sheep's fuzzy underbelly.

Whoever said that sheep's wool was soft was wrong.

It all worsened when it started to rain. Jack tried not to choke from the stench. There was no helping the mud either.

He hoped that Red was keeping up. Even if he could look back to check on her, it took every ounce of his energy to hold tight to his ride. At least he didn't have to worry about fear. Everyone had to be too jostled or too exhausted to fear. And he was pretty sure that the wet wool and mud could mask any smell.

Step three: Arrive at the fortress in one piece.

Jack suspected something was wrong as soon as he heard the shouting, the screeching metal, and that was all. It was too quiet. They stopped too soon.

Then the shepherds started counting off their flock. Not a good sign. If the giants noticed the ropes around their sheep's bellies, then everything would go downhill.

Or if they heard the sudden squeal beside him.

Blasted bloody...

Jack tried to hush Alice who was dangling upside down under the sheep next to him. The ropes around her arms had slipped off. She'd swung down so hard that her eyes watered. A lump formed in his throat. It didn't even matter if the giants heard her or not. Now, they would most definitely see her.

The sheep were already bleating as the shepherds moved through the flock.

"*Alice, get up,*" Jack hissed.

She looked up at him briefly. He saw it. The fear, just a tinge of it. He wished he could help her as she tried to swing back up to the sheep's chest. But there was nothing he could do. The sheep squirmed in discomfort.

"What in iron, stone, and clay...?" rumbled the hollowed voice above.

Jack wanted to scream for their attention. *Take me instead!*

Then Alice was gone.

So, with a deep breath, Jack closed his eyes and went against all trained instinct within him. He thought about the others tied underneath the sheep, unsure what was going on. He thought about Jill's body sprawled out on the floor. He thought about the axe in his hands as he chopped down that blasted beanstalk piece by piece, every pounding heartbeat, every drop of sweat. Lastly, he recalled the stampede that swept across the valley, the child's screams in his ears, the battered bodies. He'd run from that, too. There was too much fear.

He felt it slip into his bones. It didn't mix well with the gold in his blood, but he let it encapsulate him. Heartbeats pounded in his ears. His breath grew short, quick; palms sweaty.

"There's another one!"

Jack felt himself torn from the sheep's stomach. There was a sharp whistle.

He couldn't stop shaking before he blacked out.

Chapter Seven

If Wishes Were Horses, Beggars Would Ride

Jack woke up with stiff muscles, a splitting headache, and the sudden realization that he was on a chopping block. Startled, he struggled to sit upright. Alice sat beside him with legs crossed. She seemed strangely calm; wouldn't even look at him.

"Two hours."

"What?" His voice sounded like it was rushing toward him from a great distance. It made his headache worse.

"People only faint for more than a few minutes if they've been drugged," Alice spoke. "You were out for two hours."

"My head hurts too much for this."

She shrugged, as if he was merely proving a point of hers.

Pinching the bridge of his nose, Jack tried to shove the pounding in his ears away. But the noise only sharpened, shaving off the fuzzy edges to form distinct voice. It wasn't in his head.

Jack narrowed his eyes and raised his head. There, by the fireplace where an iron cauldron stewed, was a giant whose grey beard was so long he had it braided and tucked in his belt. His voice was grainy, pitchy, and all together unpleasant. What's more, he was alone. That didn't prevent him from feeling chatty.

"… got wool in their ears. Mark my words, those mountains are haunted," the giant grumbled on, wringing his knobby hands. "There are gears in the ore. They move on their own."

Shaking his head, Jack tried to make sense of where they were and why they were left completely exposed without restraints. Pots and jugs hung above them. Spoons and knives lined the countertop. The chopping block they sat on was clean, though clearly used due to the cuts in the wood.

The rest of the room held three chairs—one occupied by the elderly giant—around the lit fireplace. Their swords were propped by the mantle as if ready to tend the fire. Shutters sealed the only visible window. Three doors; that made four possible exits, excluding the chimney. It was everything he didn't see that made him unsure. One outburst from that old giant could summon others instantly.

Rubbing his temples, Jack muttered, "Why didn't they tie us up?"

"They did."

Before he could protest, Alice revealed the coiled ropes in her lap. She must have slipped them off while he was passed out. Which meant she had the opportunity this whole time to escape without him.

He put a hand over his heart, feigning appreciation. "You waited for me?"

"There is that," Alice admitted, "and I've been listening to Thunderdell."

Jack frowned. "The old giant?"

"It's been quite intriguing."

"And he hasn't noticed you sitting here untied this whole time eavesdropping?"

"He's blind, or close to it."

Jack didn't like how easy she was about the situation. The curious tilt in her head, the casual nature in her voice. She was too comfortable for someone caught by giants. Not that he himself felt particularly nervous. It was like falling into memory, familiar if not comfortable. He was reminded of how things remained similar, and still sharply aware of how things could never be the same.

He furrowed his brow suspiciously. "You haven't talked to him, have you?"

This time, she actually looked at him. She pulled a smile that wasn't at all reassuring. "He said he likes talking to his food."

"Alice..."

She laughed. "You have no faith in me."

He didn't think her joke was funny.

With a hiss through her teeth, Alice shook her hand violently and cursed that Hatter of hers for being careless with his needles. At least there was some justice in this world.

"I've always liked a bit of human flesh on my toast," the old giant rambled on. "Brings me back to my childhood. Bones in the bread, flesh in the butter; just the way me mum made it."

Jack's stomach rolled over. He felt the urge to get out of there as quickly as possible.

"I know how to fix your plan," Alice spoke after she'd recovered from whatever phantom pains she had. "The shepherds were talking earlier about taking the flock to the fortress this afternoon. They only stopped here for supplies and to check in on Thunderdell. We just have to get back to the sheep as we did before—there's less chance of them checking for stowaways a second time around if they think they've caught everyone already."

"And if they notice we're missing?"

"We just need to put something in that pot. I was thinking a spoon or a dishrag. Or both."

"Why would we—oh." Jack tapped his nose. "*Blind* giant. Got it. We trick him."

"He'll think we fell into the pot trying to escape. No one will know the difference until they taste something funny in the stew."

"Brilliant. Just one thing: where do the doors lead?"

Alice pointed them out, explaining which two led outside and which went to a spare room. The back door would be the best option, since that would lead them to the sheep's pen. Jack was thankful that at least she was observant.

"Right then," he nodded, getting his feet under him, "let's go."

While he struggled to stand without falling, Alice sprung up like a rabbit light and quick. She held tightly to the ropes as she snuck across the counter to grab a dishrag or spoon, or both—whichever she preferred. Jack thought about grabbing a knife himself but thought better of it. One of them should keep their hands free, and it didn't look like it was going to be Alice.

By the time she joined him with dishrag and rope wrapped around her waist, the spoon strung through her belt, the blind giant was singing.

"*I smell blood and I smell bone, and I smell fear coated in gold,*" he croaked.

Jack grimaced at the sound. "He sings worse than Kai."

"I didn't know Kai could sing," Alice whispered.

"He can't; that was my point."

"*Grind your bread and bake their teeth, and death will come while you're asleep.*"

"How cheery."

"Don't get distracted." Jack urged her onward until he felt that they could both climb down the cabinets. If he was alone, perhaps he would take the risk and jump. But he knew how Alice felt about heights, even if recently she seemed to be losing that particular fear.

"*Fee-Fi-Fo-Fum.*"

They made it down to the floor without dropping the spoon. Jack hoped the giant was poor in hearing as he was in eyesight.

Approaching the fireplace—and, consequently, the old giant who thankfully stopped his singing to talk to himself—Jack went to retrieve their stolen swords while Alice prepared to throw their diversion into the bubbling cauldron. He took a sword in each hand victoriously. He didn't even trip over the rug when he returned to Alice positioned by the pot.

"Ready?" he whispered.

She didn't answer. That's when he noticed she had frozen, staring up at the old giant incredulously. He started

60

to remind her about not getting distracted when he caught what the giant was saying, what made Alice suddenly alert.

"Since when do giants trust witches, or any foreigner, to solve all our problems?!" The old giant spat into the fire like the words tasted foul in his mouth. "In my day, witches were banished to the mountains like any other criminal. Now we're trusting one to crush our rats for us. What young knee-knockers are making the decisions these days? Sending traitors to haunted mountains as if they die there, trusting foreign witches with not a flake of gold in their blood…"

The words were admittedly strange, but Jack didn't like the look in Alice's eyes as she listened to them. He took her arm. "It's not what you think."

She raised an eyebrow. "And what am I thinking?"

"You think this has something to do with your Master Puppeteer, but as I've explained to you before, the giants would never make deals with humans, not even magical ice women."

"Woman. There's only one."

"I don't need your sass right now."

"Jack," Alice implored, leaning closer, "if I could ask him a few questions—Don't look at me like that. He's blind; what harm could he really do?"

"Scream."

"Alright, fair enough. But don't you hear what he's saying?"

"He's talking *to himself* about witches and moving mountains and eating us as a delicacy. The giant is crazy!"

"Listen, I know crazy—"

"And I know giants," Jack snapped. "Don't think you can reason with him. Their hatred for humans runs too deep."

Alice narrowed one eye, a sign that she was probably about to do something stupid. "How much do you really know giants?"

Working his jaw to keep the agitation down, he huffed. "Just throw your spoon into the pot and let's get out of here."

He took the dishrag from her, bent his knees, ready to toss it into the cauldron above their heads, ready to give a shout as if they were falling in the boiling stew.

Then Alice cupped her hands around her mouth and shouted, "Hey you!"

"Blasted bloody..."

The giant startled, looking around for the voice with a frown.

"Big guy!" Alice kept on to get his attention. "Let me ask you someth—"

"Don't listen to her," Jack interjected in a panic. "She's eaten too many strange rotten mushrooms—the contagious kind, you know. We'll all probably be catching her crazy soon."

She gave him a look. "Do you know where your mouth runs sometimes?"

"Do *you*?"

"They've escaped!" the old giant exclaimed, his tongue getting so tangled up he had yet to reach a dangerous volume. "Show yourself, you insignificant speck!"

Grabbing the spoon from Alice and giving her a hard glare, Jack screamed. Once she surrendered a cry herself, he threw the items into the pot. Thankfully, it splashed enough to spill over the side.

They went dead silent.

The giant groaned as he stood, grabbing a ladle to fish around the pot. Jack pulled Alice back silently. If things went south, they'd have to make a quick escape. At least she was keeping quiet.

A wrinkled grin spread across the giant's face. Gleefully, he started cackling. "The little vermin fell right in! Drowned faster than a fish."

Alice frowned, whispering, "That doesn't make sense."

Jack hushed her.

As the giant stirred the stew with grotesque pleasure, Jack gave Alice a boost to reach the door handle and they snuck outside.

The problem with wishing was that it only worked with stars and flowers, and neither were at her disposal. For three hours the Wolf waited faithfully near the sheep's pen, daring not to wish, holding onto every scrap of trust she could muster, fighting against fear for her friends' lives.

She was focusing so intently on keeping under control that she didn't notice Jack until he was right before her eyes. Relief flooded through her in tidal waves.

"Rubes," his whisper carried over to her as he knelt in the long grass around the fence. "I need your help. I can't do it on my own."

Stealthily, she waited until she was beside him to change form. Red looked over his muddy hair and clothes, the raw skin showing through the cloth around his arms, the gold flecks that shone so brightly in his eyes she wondered how she'd never noticed before they arrived in this place. He wasn't injured. He was here.

"I got Alice back on," he explained under his breath. "They're taking the flock to the fortress soon. This was just a detour."

He led her to an ewe centered in the flock to avoid being seen. Red didn't bother to remind him about the problem she posed in touching sheep. Instead, she worked diligently to get him attached to the animal's belly, ignoring the aggravated protests that came with every touch. At least the shepherds were not around.

As she worked the knots, he reminded her of where they would be taken when inside the fortress. He had no doubt that she would make it in past the walls. The confidence he had in her didn't go unnoticed.

When she finished, she lingered by his side hesitant to leave again. Her hand cupped his as he gripped the ropes.

"Rubes…"

She squeezed his hand. "Don't get caught again."

With that, she left.

When afternoon came, and the shepherds emerged to take their flock onward, the Wolf followed as close as she dared until the wood thinned and the fortress towered overhead. Instinct and shadows showed her the way inside.

Chapter Eight

Take One Down, Pass It Around

With improvisational plans, Jack supposed something was bound to go sideways eventually along the way.

He couldn't stop thinking about that blind giant. The things he'd been saying, something about it set Jack's teeth on edge. But he knew it was all wrong. For one, mountains didn't move, and they certainly were not haunted. That was only a tale told to explain why no giant could survive crossing the mountain range. Only the belowlanders knew the way through. Jack had never seen the pass, but he had heard of it. It was the most precious secret held by the belowlanders.

For another, the giants hated witches, foreigners, and humans. No giant would ever associate with one who was all of the above. But he knew how enticing that was for Alice. She wouldn't let that one go until she was certain of it herself.

Maybe it was just the singing that made him uncomfortable. Chills shot down his spine. He hated songs like that, the kinds that should stay in nursery rhymes and bedtime stories. *Fee-Fi-Fo-Fum...* He was plagued by them.

At least now they were back on schedule.

As they passed through the first wall, Jack felt his heart steady and stomach tighten. By the sound of it, the fortress was anything but empty. This was it. They couldn't afford any fear now.

Anticipation began to leak into his bloodstream. He was so close to Harry, and now he was actually considering the realities of their reunion. It had been over a year since Jill died, since the beanstalk fell, since he left his friend behind. How much torture had Harry gone through? How much gold sifted through his body? Would he be remotely the same man? And once they rescued him, what then?

Jack shook his head. None of that mattered; not now, anyway. They would find Harry, and they would get him out of there. Beyond that, he had no plan.

A moment of stillness passed. The sheep grew anxious. Foul air filled his sinuses before he could hold his breath, and just as quickly they were past the second wall and in the slaughterhouse.

Which was not where they were supposed to be.

The flocks were usually taken to a pen in the innermost courtyard for later distribution. This was new. Maybe it was for security. Maybe the giants were craving mutton tonight.

Breathe. Think. No fear.

Sweat tickled his neck. The wool and ropes were agitating against his sore arms. He couldn't get down without help, and he could only hope that Red would find them before the giants did.

By the time he realized who was beside him, Kai gave a low groan and wrenched his left hand free. Instantly, he swung down and nearly knocked his head on the ground.

The sheep shifted in annoyance. Kai's feet were still fastened to its sides.

Jack laughed despite himself. How many times was someone going to hang upside down under a sheep?

Kai glared up at him.

The flock shifted. Panic hit like a rock.

"You couldn't wait one more minute?"

Jack broke into a grin as Red appeared beside them. She looked tense, her eyes bright. But at least she was here, safe.

Quickly, she untied Kai's feet. He fell with a thud flat on the ground. The sheep shuffled away, nearly stepping on him in the process.

When Red helped Jack, she released his ankles first so that he could land roughly on his feet when she untied his arms. As soon as he hit the ground, his calves burned painfully. He feigned a smile so Red would continue on to find the girls. Once she was gone, however, he grimaced and knelt next to Kai who still lay on his back. They remained still to rest their aching muscles.

"This is the worst idea you've ever had," Kai grumbled.

"Glad your bloody staying?"

"Everything hurts."

"You've never been one to complain."

Kai gave him the nastiest look, but Jack knew he wouldn't hold this against him.

Seeing the girls approaching out of the corner of his eye, Jack offered his friend a hand up. They both stood with a groan to meet them. Not surprisingly, Wendy didn't seem much affected by the ride save for the wool in her hair. Alice rubbed her arms where the rope burned her skin.

"How'd you get in?" Jack asked Red whose shoulders looked stiff.

She tried to explain, "I think someone else is—"

The ground vibrated, cutting her off. Grinding gears churned as a door was eased open. Distinct hums of, "*Fee-Fi-Fo-Fum*," echoed from an unseen butcher.

Instantly, they ducked into the shadows. Jack gestured for the others to follow as he led them through the flock. Before they broached the outside where the rest of the fortress awaited them, he met each of his friends' eyes, trying to convey the most important message he could give them:

Remember, no fear.

The fortress was shaped like a wheel with two rims and three spokes. Thankfully, there was nothing above ground level except for lookout posts on the towers and a fortified room in the central one, and anything below ground was a wine cellar or holding cell for giants themselves. The advantage and drawback as far as they were concerned were the spokes. The advantage held because they connected each of the towers for a faster passage between them with less chances of getting caught up in the traffic occurring in the rims. However, the disadvantage was the fact that the shortcut passed through the centermost tower, the riskiest one to enter due to its valuable contents upstairs. Yet this was the only option they had.

When Jack and the others emerged from the slaughterhouse, they found themselves in the tower containing the treasury—opposite to the tower with arsenal and smithy, as well as, most importantly, the prison tower. At least this was the least inhabited of the lot.

It didn't take long to sneak into the passage. The wind filtered through large open windows where brass tree branches spilled in from the courtyard outside. Pillars and pedestals provided easy places to hide. Gears that climbed up the walls, long forgotten and now left for decoration rather than use, were the best if they needed to blend in. But to hide in plain sight required complete obliteration of fear. A single whiff of it could be enough to draw a passing giant's attention.

Jack reminded himself that this was nothing complicated. They would sneak past the mead hall, get to the dungeons, free Harry, and leave this place for good. It was a simple plan, but simple plans hardly ever went wrong. At least that's what he told himself.

Reaching the end of the hallway, he felt the ground tremble slightly. He hissed a warning to the others, grabbing Wendy's arm to pull her back from the line of sight. They pressed themselves flat against the wall. Alice squeezed between two gears. Kai stood just behind the pillar, Red just beside him.

Jack heard them walking by the passage in the tower beyond. Voices came in and out of earshot. A shadow fell over his eyes as his stomach tightened. He hated this place. The sooner they got out, the better.

With the giants seemingly gone, Jack indicated for the others to wait until he was certain the coast was clear before they entered the tower. He slid down the wall until he could tell that the way they would be going down was free of giants. Quickly, he darted over to the other wall to check the opposite direction. Best not to have anyone coming at their backs immediately.

This time, he heard them first with voices like thunder and metal. He shot his friends a look, cautioning them to stay still and hidden. Kai frowned but kept a hand around Red's wrist to keep her from taking off after him.

It sounded like a large group, which meant they would pass without getting distracted easily. Jack would be invisible despite his being in their line of sight. Too many times had he hidden right under a giant's nose. He wasn't worried.

The giants rounded the corner, and Jack's chest felt heavy as his locked eyes with the brown and blue gaze of the Giant King. Anger and vengeance coiled up inside. This was the murderer who haunted his nightmares, the shadow that followed him down the beanstalk, the uncrossed name written in the stone wall. Every nerve in him wanted to enforce his title of Giant Slayer on this one foe.

A smile spread across Nozrok's face.

Jack ran.

The tower was circular, so he couldn't run for long lest he risk leading the giants to his friends again. Every breath came with each heartbeat like a powerful drum. Feet flew over stone as it shook underfoot. Only Nozrok followed him now, sending the others to find any more intruders that may have come with him. Besides, this was personal for them both.

Darting into the open mead hall, Jack ducked under benches and long tables to force Nozrok to take the longer route around them. He saw the door more by instinct than vision. Quickly, he scrambled onto the farthest table in the room, launching himself toward the handle and driving the door open.

Bulking shadows filled the smaller dark room as the door shut behind him. This was a sort of cellar between the mead hall and throne room, a place for easy access to its alcoholic contents brought up from the stores below. Jack nimbly scampered up a ghostly tablecloth, muscle memory kicking in. Reaching the top, he hardly took a second to breath before taking off again down the table and around used beer steins. He leapt off the edge without hesitation and collided with a shelf. Glass clinked as he pulled himself up among the wine bottles.

The door creaked open, light filtering into the cellar. Jack held his breath and slipped into the shadows. He took care to move soundlessly between the standing bottles as tall as he was.

"*Jaaaaaack.*"

The taunt echoed in the musty air. His stomach tightened, but he refused to be afraid.

"Come out, come out wherever you are."

He didn't have far to go before he could lower himself behind beer barrels. He'd always hated the taste of alcohol. It never agreed with him, and the smell always reminded him of this place.

"Aren't you a little old to be playing hide-and-seek?" The voice came again like gravel rolling down a hill, "I'm not much into games."

Steadying his breathing, Jack dared to pause and look at his surroundings. Nozrok still stood in the doorway blocking the light. There were two other doors. Jack knew the second one would lead a way out into the hallway right outside the passage to the prison tower. All he had to do was make it there, slowly but surely.

Nozrok shrugged. "Alright, I'll play. But I can't guarantee how much you'll enjoy the outcome."

His arms ached as he lowered himself to the ground one shelf at a time, always keeping a bottle between him and the doorway. Finally down, he ducked behind the barrels.

"I wonder what we'll do to you once you're mine again, Jacky. Would you like another egg to swallow? I know you must crave it. It's why you keep crawling back into my hands."

There was an expanse of nothing but shadow between two stacks of barrels where the door to the throne room was sealed. Taking the risk, Jack bolted across silently. He waited behind the second pile, calming his rapid heartbeats. Only another shelf of bottles and stack of barrels to go before he reached the way out.

"Maybe we'll grind your bones like the old songs say. How satisfying that would feel, crushing a femur under your skin and muscle while you writhe."

You are bloody disgusting, Jack thought as he painfully climbed the alcohol laden shelves.

"Perhaps we'll do to you as we did to your friend. Justice would be served, eh, Jacky?"

His blood ran cold.

"What was her name again? Jill?"

Shaking himself out of his stupor, Jack wove through the bottles. Muscles trembled with bitter anger. He knew Nozrok was getting closer, only talking to distract him. But he didn't want to hear Jill's name in the giant's mouth. It made his stomach churn.

"She screamed your name, Jack," Nozrok went on. "Over and over again like a mocking bird. Even as we lacerated her muscles to keep her from fighting back, she screamed for you. We drowned her until we silenced her, and even then you could see it in her eyes. She thought you'd come for her, Jacky. But she was wrong."

Anger grew hot in his chest despite his attempts to stay calm. As he paused behind the brandy bottles, a bone shifting chill overtook him. He turned to find those mismatched eyes watching him, a bottle in the giant's hand.

"Whose name will you scream, Jacky?"

Nozrok hurled the bottle at him as he scrambled out of the way. Glass shattered, wine splashing. Bottles toppled over as Jack sped down the shelf. Barrels rose up to meet him, stacked high between him and the door that meant his escape. But Nozrok was ready for target practice. Another spray of alcohol crashed above him.

"You claim the name Giant Slayer, and you flee from me like a coward," Nozrok mocked, the anger behind his voice raw and blistered.

Jack leaped up and caught the edge of a barrel just as a table slammed into the shelves behind him, causing the whole thing to collapse. He hung by his fingertips. Biceps burning, breaths coming in short hisses, he pulled himself up slowly.

"I think I'm just about done with our little game, Jacky."

Pain splitting down his arms, Jack rolled onto the top of the stacked barrels just in time to see Nozrok lift one of his own above his head. He shot to his feet, ready to jump out of the way.

The giant roared, barrel dropped and splintered on the floor. Beer washed over the stone floor. Jack scrambled to the edge of the barrel to see what was going on.

Something black and drenched in beer was latched onto Nozrok's ankle, blood in her teeth. It took Jack only a moment to realize it was Red. Cursing loudly, Nozrok jerked away from his attacker. He rounded for a kick, but she dodged him, sliding under his foot and ripping at his other calf.

Heart racing, Jack dashed across the barrels and kicked off into the air, limbs wheeling. His aim was off and he slammed right into the door, the handle bruising his abdomen. Air rushed out of his lungs. But he latched on tight, plunging down forcefully. Unlatched, the door eased open.

Jack dropped. He would've landed painlessly enough if it hadn't been for the beer. Pain shot up his legs upon impact, and his feet slipped out from under him. He sharply knocked his chin on the floor. Gasping for breath, he forced himself up. At least he didn't bite his tongue off.

The ground shook violently as Nozrok landed flat on his back. The Wolf scampered out of the way as the remaining shelf fell over onto the giant. Glass littered beside splinters. Wine mixed with beer and brandy. The Wolf was drenched in all of it.

"Rubes!" Jack shouted. He didn't have to call twice.

She was beside him in a flash, shifting form to help him shove the door closed. He wanted to wrap her in his arms and thank her for coming to his rescue. Instead, they turned on their heels and ran down the passage that would lead them to the prison tower. He never looked back, but he knew she was right behind him.

After the giants had chased after Jack, Alice had to keep Kai from running after him. She knew that he was leading the giants away from them, giving them a chance to escape. But there was no holding back Red. Once she was gone, they could do nothing but run the other way.

They didn't get far before there was a shout somewhere behind them.

Wendy frowned. "What was that?"

Vibrations traveled up her shins. The giants were coming. She had a feeling they were after them this time. They sped up the pace, careful in case they ran headlong into more giants. Which was exactly what they did.

Nearly running right past the guarded door, Wendy had to pull Kai back behind a pillar in the wall. Alice peaked around at the giants that stood so intently. The door looked heavy, made up of every metal she knew.

"That must lead to the goose," Alice whispered.

Kai was watching behind them for the giants in pursuit. His jaw was so tight, a vein pulsed in his temple. "We have to go."

With a nod, Alice pointed to the other side of the hall. "There's a passage here."

"Is that where we're supposed to go?"

She shrugged. "Only one way to find out."

"I thought you knew the map."

"It's a lot bigger in person."

"What about Jack and Red?" Wendy asked, concerned.

"They'll be fine," Alice assured. "We'll meet them at the prison."

Bracing themselves, they shot across the hall as fast as their legs could carry them, hitting the passageway long before the giants could follow behind. The temperature steadily rose as they ran. It smelled strongly of burning iron.

Alice had a sneaking suspicion that they were going the wrong way. It was too late to turn back now.

Chapter Nine

Morning Bells Are Ringing!

Ding, Dang, Dong

They didn't stop running even as they plunged into the maze that was the prison tower, Jack in the lead. The set up was designed to confuse any belowlander that may escape, with false passages and doors that led to nowhere and gears that clicked constantly overhead. But for Jack, who knew the tower's secrets well, the quick turns provided easy hiding places and the noise above muted their pounding footsteps. It wasn't until they hit a door with screaming birds inscribed in the metal that he stopped. Breath rushed in and out of his lungs. Red was hardly winded at all.

Recovering his voice, Jack scrunched his nose. "You smell like beer."

"I'll forgive you for that because you're tired and not thinking straight," Red replied as she wrung the alcohol from her hair.

"Really, *really* bad beer."

That earned him a punch in his aching bicep.

Slowly, his heartbeat steadied to normal pace. Red attempted to squeeze more liquid from her clothes. She didn't seem injured from her fight with the Giant King. Any glass he saw was only stuck to her blouse, easy to brush away. Then she made a face, stuck her fingers in her mouth, and produced two halves of a bloody molar.

"That's never happened before," she muttered.

"Are you alright?"

She looked at him, wiping away the concern on her face instantly. "I guess his skin was tougher than I thought."

Jack cocked his head. "Was that a joke? Are you making jokes, now?"

Rolling her eyes, she tossed the broken tooth aside without further comment.

Instead of making another complicated jump for the handle, he gave Red a boost to open the door. She landed far more gracefully than he had earlier—his bloody chin proved as much. Cold hit as soon as the door popped open. Jack fought back the eerie memories that clung to the room beyond. Taking a deep breath, they slipped inside.

The only light in the room came from a single torch on the wall, flickering, casting long dancing shadows. Rusty chains creaked at the very breath of a draft. From the ceiling hung cages, empty of anything living, each dangling at different lengths. A dusty skeleton bleached with time stared down at them from its suspended prison, long arm swaying back and forth. Jack wondered how it managed to stay together. Then he noticed the gleam as the bone caught the light. He looked away, but the image remained. Gold held the bones together.

Red sniffed the air and she twisted her hair into a tight braid. "No one's here."

Shaking his head, Jack motioned for her to follow him. They crossed the room straight for the black iron door. There was no doorknob, no way to get it open; only a window large enough to get a cage through.

"What is it?" Red asked, hushed as if the very nature of this place called for nothing louder than a whisper.

Jack placed a hand on one of the copper feathers that leaked down the metal door. "A torture chamber."

"Why the window?"

"Easy transportation with minimal resistance," he explained, remembering the sound of chains in friction as the cage was lowered into the other room. "And so the others can hear the screams."

Today, it would serve another purpose.

Upon his request, Red pressed her ear against the seam where the door met the ground. She waited with eyes closed, listening. She gave a nod. "Someone's in there."

His heart leapt to his throat. "Is it him? It has to be him."

She gave him a sideways look. "I'm a wolf, not a gypsy. I can't see through walls."

"I know, I know." Jack puffed his cheeks, calming himself.

Pointing to the window above, she asked, "How do we get up?"

He didn't explain. The chains used to maneuver the cages were hooked to the wall, some dangling just within reach. He started there. Scrambling up the lowest hanging chain until he was level with the hooks, Jack pulled one free beside him. It wrenched out of his grasp immediately and a cage crashed on the floor.

He froze stalk still.

When no one came, he lowered himself to the ground. Red didn't look happy about the commotion.

"What were you thinking?" she hissed.

Instead of answering, he pointed to a cage that hung close to the suspended chain. "Could you climb up there, grab that chain to hoist me up in this cage, swing me over to the window, and lower me down the other side?"

She made a face. "Then pull you *and* your friend back out again?"

"Yeah, pretty much."

Red shook her head with a sigh, but he could tell she was holding back a smile. "Just give the chain a tug when you're ready to come up."

Excitement burst through his chest. He squeezed her arms in gratitude, then scrambled to the fallen cage while she retreated to the metal ropes. Holding his breath, he watched her as she climbed.

Passing the hooks, she crossed her feet around the chain and climbed hand over hand like a sloth until she reached the pinnacle. From there she shimmied down to the cage and slipped inside. She latched the door open, preventing herself from being trapped. It didn't take long for her to reach the dangling chain and begin to pull.

Jack held on tightly to the bars as he was carried up. Estimating the right elevation, he called for her to stop.

"Rubes."

"*What?*"

He licked his lips, but his words tasted wrong in his mouth. The muscles in her arms were tense, her knuckles white. Her long, black braid hung over her shoulder—he always liked it when she braided it like that. When she looked down at him, he smiled. "Don't let go."

Tearing his gaze away, Jack began to swing. Back and forth, down for extra lag, then back and forth again. Metal screeched. In one hand he held the cage bars, while the other he kept outstretched, ready to catch the window ledge. He missed twice, the third time sending him spinning as the cage hit the door. On the fifth attempt, the rim nicked the window and Jack latched on. His muscles burned as he pulled the cage through the opening. With one last look at Red, he was lowered into the torture chamber.

At first, he saw nothing but blackness beyond a covered lamp sitting on an empty table. The cage clanged against the floor before he expected it. It jostled his feet and made his knees lock.

"*Blasted bloody...*" Jack hissed, stumbling off the cage.

The breathing stopped him dead in his tracks.

Squinting, he tried to see through the surrounded darkness. "Hello? Are you there?"

As his eyes slowly adjusted, he could make out the figure rising across the room. The dim light caught striking blue eyes. Gold shot down every vein in them.

It hit him like a blow to the stomach. He could hardly breathe.

"Is it you?" he gasped, throat tightening fast.

The voice was scratchy, painful, but unforgettable. "Jack?"

Bewilderment pounded against his ribcage. "You're real."

Jack's stupor was blown away in exhilaration. He rushed forward and wrapped his friend in a tight embrace, never minding the filth and frailty and impossibility he held.

Jill.

He pulled back and held her at arm's length. Taking her in from her tangled hair to her bare feet, he couldn't control the building excitement he had at the sight of her. "I can't believe it; you're alive!"

Her eyes shone, her voice only a croak, "Jack…"

"And all this time," he squeezed her shoulders, confirming her presence, "I thought you were dead. But here, here you are: *not dead.* I can't believe it."

"You shouldn't be here."

She seemed so afraid. He took her hand, trying to reassure her. "Don't worry, I'll get you out of here."

"You don't understand."

"It's alright; I have a way out. They'll never touch you again."

Her chin quavered, tears trailing down her cheeks. Gently, he started to pull her toward the cage, toward freedom.

Jill jerked away, shuffling back. "No, Jack!"

Heavy tension pressed between them. Confusion swelled up inside. "What are you doing?"

"You gave to go, Jack."

He frowned at her harsh plea. Maybe something in her didn't believe this was happening, a sense of denial built up to defend herself after over a year of captivity. He could only imagine the torture she underwent in this room.

"Jill, it's alright," he assured. "I'm here to get you out of this place. You can trust me."

She stood planted firmly where she was, gold infused eyes hardened and glassy.

"Come on, Jill."

"No." She looked around as if expecting monsters to form from shadows. "Go, Jack. You have to leave."

"Not without you."

"Get out of here!"

Desperation festered, his chest getting tighter. "I'm not leaving without you."

"You have to."

"I thought you were dead."

"Jack…"

"*I thought they killed you!*"

"Jack, listen—"

"No," he snapped. "I'm *not* leaving without you."

"*Jack!*" Jill shouted, every word like a dagger thrown at him. "You need to leave, now."

She didn't know what she was asking. She couldn't know. She was delirious, tortured, broken. She didn't know that she was asking him to do the very thing he regretted most in his life. "Jill…"

"*NOW!*"

The lump in his throat was almost too much to bear. Every time he blinked, he expected to see her lying dead on the floor again.

"I can't," he muttered, voice breaking.

She sniffed, backing up against the wall. "Then you leave me no choice."

Before he could comprehend what she was saying, a rope materialized in her hand. Jill pulled. Panic hit as bells sang chaos in the air.

Rubes.

Feet heavy, reluctant, Jack backed into the cage and rattled its chain. Numbness tingled between his ears. All he could ask was why. But she wouldn't even give him that satisfaction. She just stared at him, golden tears running down hollow cheeks, as his cage was lifted into the air.

He left her alone again.

Everything about it hurt.

Emptiness settled in his chest. Subconsciously, he maneuvered the cage through the window and held on tight as he plummeted to the ground. The chain snapped taunt. The impact nearly threw him off, but thankfully he was already so near the ground he could just slip down.

The ringing in his ears didn't subside until Red was right in front of him. "What happened? Where's Harry?"

He shook his head. The banging bells pounded against his muffled mind. Shining crimson caught his eye. Red's hands were slick with blood, raw and wounded from the metal. Hard determination set despite the emptiness.

He grabbed her hand and ran out of the dungeon.

Chapter Ten

You Can't Catch Me

Breathless, they stumbled into the tower and instantly Alice groaned, "Borogove."

The smithy pulsed with heat and uproar. Giants filled the room, hammering steel and fashioning iron. Despite the chaos, Kai felt a sense of elation. Where the others jumped back in alarm, he heard the harmony with every pounding shockwave, the hissing of white-hot metal hitting water to cool. The scorching heat was enough to singe the hair on their arms. Kai never minded the heat of it, not in his apprenticeship nor his professionality as a blacksmith. Something in him missed plunging tongs into the forge, the weight of a mallet in his grip, the ringing against the anvil, even bearing the heavy leather apron scorched from work.

The layout was familiar to him, so he led the girls through with confidence. None of the giants working noticed them, the protective masks they wore blocking out anything else but the projects they focused on. Kai yanked Wendy away from a shower of sparks, letting the embers hit his skin instead of hers. He didn't mind the burn. It was better than the cold he'd also grown used to.

They flew past a female giant manipulating a sword into shape, bare handed to feel the hum of the metal beneath her palms. He led them around a craftsman fitting diamonds into a crested breastplate. Pliers nearly hit Alice as they slipped off the worktable. Thankfully, the magnifying spectacles the giant wore prevented him from seeing her dodge out of the way as he retrieved his fallen tool.

It wasn't until the heat was at their backs that Kai heard their intruders crash into the smithy. They sprinted through the open doorway just in time. Daylight swallowed them up. They were between the inner wall and the outer wall, and this was where the true tumult met them. Giants traversed in every direction. The noise skyrocketed to chaos beyond the chorus they left in the tower. But they were invisible in the crowd.

Before their pursuers could follow them out, Kai grabbed the two girls and pulled them behind the crates stacked just outside the smithy. Stone felt cool against his back. He hushed Alice's oncoming inquiry, pressing them into the shadows between wood and wall.

A swarm of giants thundered out of the workshop beside them. Weapons were brandished, at the ready. In the hubbub they encountered, they split up in search of the intruders. Kai had an arm around Wendy and a grip on Alice's wrist. They waited like that even long after the giants disappeared.

Chest heaving, Kai began under his breath, "We need to—"

Something cut him off, a clamor sounding above the noise of giants in motion and beyond the pounding of hammers against metal. The bells were like an alarm. It set off everyone into immediate action.

He steadied his breathing. "We need to get out of here."

"There's a gate between here and the prison tower," Alice whispered, "and a mill just beyond the wall. It's a central point if the others made it to the dungeons. If Jack's map is right, then it shouldn't be in the way of any wandering giants."

"Can you lead us there?"

"I can try. It's not the first time I've been smaller than everything else around."

He admitted that, aside from Jack, Alice was the only other one privy to being shrunk down to the size of a doll. Her plan seemed like the best option besides, given the circumstances. With a nod, Kai let her take the lead again. His scar throbbed with each heartbeat.

Checking their surroundings, Alice trotted on with Kai and Wendy behind her. He hoped the others managed to get Jack's friend out safely.

Red could only assume that Jack knew where he was going. He had said nothing since she'd lowered him into that torture chamber, and now he wouldn't release her hand as he pulled her through the prison tower into the chaos outside. She hardly got a breath before they went straight into the stable. She didn't tell him how his grip hurt her skinned hands. The blood between their palms was slick, but she held tight. He seemed like he would crumble if he stopped now.

There ground trembled underfoot. Even if they hadn't spotted them yet, giants were in pursuit. Without thinking, they jumped into the closest haystack. Red's eyes began to itch. She squeezed them shut and held her breath.

She forced herself not to move until she heard the hay rustle as Jack emerged from the hiding place.

She gasped, instantly aware of her irritated throat and itchy arms. Before she could suppress the urge, she sneezed.

"*Gesundheit.*"

"Sorry," Red muttered, nose stuffing.

He raised an eyebrow. "I didn't think wolves got hay fever."

She sneezed again. First the sheep couldn't stand her touch, then she got a bath in alcohol, followed by her losing her tooth and skinning her hands, and now she had hay fever. "This day is getting on my nerves."

But Jack didn't laugh like she expected him to. Instead, he beckoned her onward to find their escape route. Shaking her head, she trotted after him.

"What happened back there?"

"We needed a place to hide," he said without breaking stride. "I didn't know you had hay allergies."

"Not that." She failed to grab his full attention, so she decided to just broach the obvious. "What happened in the chamber?"

He stopped dead in his tracks, but he wouldn't look at her. Concerned, Red approached him gently, trying to figure out what could have happened. Either Harry wasn't there anymore, or he found something worse.

"Jack," she prompted, "talk to me."

He shushed her.

Agitation festered in her chest. She clenched her fists against her sides, crusty blood cracking in her palms. "Fine, don't—"

His sword was out in a flash, and then he was gone. Stunned, Red would have followed sooner if she didn't sneeze again. A yell hit her ears. There was such rage and pain that she couldn't believe it was Jack. By the time she caught up to him, he was in the heat of combat.

She cursed herself for not sensing an intruder sooner.

Metal sang. Blows were thrown by fists and knees. There was no pattern, no technique she could discern from either Jack or the masked man. It was as if they made it up as they went. Like child's play, but with swords and fury. That's what held her back from intervening. One false move, and she could hurt Jack instead. Even so, she readied herself in case of an opening.

Something sharp touched her right below the ribs. Instinctively, she snatched the attacker's wrist before the dagger could penetrate her liver. Her other arm was wrenched painfully behind her back. She couldn't pull the dagger away without hurting herself. It didn't matter how strong she was; the angle was just right, and she didn't know if the blade was curved.

"Here I thought a *wolf* followed me inside," a woman's husky voice snickered in her ear.

Red laughed, discomfort tightening her tone. "You're not wrong."

"Any last words before I kill you in front of your boyfriend there?"

"Yes, I should warn you: this is going to hurt."

With a twist and clench, Red felt the bone crunch under her hand. The attacker yelled in agony. She threw the dagger away and yanked free of the woman's hold.

Instantly, she ducked a swing at her head before popping up and bashing her elbow into the woman's nose. A sharp kick bruised her ribs. Red returned the blow with a knee to the stomach and jab at the throat. Gasping, the woman stumbled back and fell on the floor.

Red quickly retrieved the fallen dagger and stood over her opponent, careful not to get close enough to get easily kicked in the shins. Onyx eyes glared at her, but wisely she didn't move. The woman held her broken wrist tightly.

Nose itching, Red sneezed.

Swords still clashed between Jack and the masked stranger. Something fueled Jack's aggression, something burning and throbbing that Red couldn't pinpoint. Whatever it was, his opponent hardly stood a chance against it.

With another burst, Jack bashed their blades together so hard that the stranger's fell out of his grip. Jack kicked him to the ground, everything in his stance leading to a lethal strike. Red held her breath. He froze, blade hovering a breath away from the man's throat. The scarf that masked the man's mouth and nose had slipped, revealing a face as stunned and petrified as Jack's. Neither of them moved but for their heaving chests. Tension leaked out of Jack's shoulders.

"You?" was all he could manage.

The man grinned, one side of his mouth rising higher than the other. "I knew you'd come back."

Exhausted, Jack's arm fell limply to his side. The man was quick to his feet, catching him in an embrace.

Confused and hazy, Red could do nothing but watch. She was afraid to move.

Jack's voice was muffled against the man's shoulder, "I thought I was too late."

"Who, you? Never!"

Red coughed.

Pulling away, the two men noticed them for the first time. The woman frowned in annoyance, eyebrow raised over downturned eyes. Red didn't blame her. The hay fever was slowing down anything that might understand what was going on.

Jack shrugged, pointing to the man. "Harry."

"Giant Slayer," the other man said, indicating for the woman.

A sense of relief washed over her. So, the chamber was empty—that's what was wrong. At least Harry wasn't dead. But she could've sworn she heard someone in there...

The woman looked Jack up and down with tight lips, scrutinizing.

"Oh, right," Jack added hastily, "this is Red."

Harry turned that wide smile to her. His eyes were the kind that hid nothing behind them and promised he could be trusted. She instantly liked the man.

In turn, he introduced the woman, "This is Spider."

Her eyebrows shot up. "Spider?"

"That's my name; don't need to go repeating it," the woman huffed.

"What kind of name is *Spider*?"

"What kind of name is *Red*?"

Before she could retort, the ground quaked and bits of hay fell from the rafters. Red tried to fight past her congestion to figure out how far away the giants were but failed despite her efforts. Her head felt worse.

"We need to go," Harry stated, anxious but strangely excited. "Shall you follow me, then?"

"What's the plan?" Jack asked.

"Just like the old days, friend." He smiled cockily—so similar to Jack that Red could've sworn they were related. "River rafting."

As the two started off, Red helped Spider to her feet, returning the dagger. "I guess this means we're on the same side."

"You're with the Giant Slayer?"

"Yes."

Spider glanced sideways at Jack, eyes narrowed, hugging her broken wrist to her chest. "We'll see, then."

Water pounded in their ears with each turn of the mill's gargantuan wheel. It hadn't been so hard to make it there. With the giants so distracted trying to find them around the fortress itself, no one bothered to check up on the waterways. The grate had a hole in the bottom, easy to squeeze through. Once the three of them reached the mill itself, they felt relieved if not safe.

Being the smallest, Wendy was elected to investigate their surroundings, searching for hiding spots or possible escape routes. Alice and Kai remained on the lookout for the others.

The grass there was taller than she was, making it easier to leave a trail. Hopefully there wouldn't be giants around to notice. Broaching the river, the grass gave way to stone and metallic mounds that leaked into the riverbank.

Wendy perched on one of the gold veined rocks. If she spotted danger, she could easily leap into the grass and out of sight.

Before her, the river stretched wide, white crested rapids rolling through a speedy current. Even a strong swimmer would find this monster difficult to cross. She couldn't tell where the water came from beyond the fortress, but it ran away from her into the woods.

She made a face and sighed. She was hoping to find something helpful, a way to escape quickly from the fortress. Certainly, they could travel along the riverbank, diving into the grass if they needed to hide. But the terrain was uneven and slick, making it impossible to run. She also had no idea what condition Harry would be in after his rescue. Would he be able to run? There still remained the issue of being spotted.

Cautiously, Wendy stood to have a better look around. Two giants walked the opposite direction in the distance, circling the wall. She had no way to discern if the mill was empty. She didn't know enough about them to know if they operated without manual labor or not.

Despite everything, though, she was still determined that not all giants wanted to destroy humans. She remembered how the shepherds laughed together yesterday. It reminded her of times she'd spent with her family; her parents, her brothers before they grew up, the Lost Boys back in Neverland. If giants were capable of laughter and love like that, then why shouldn't they be capable of forgiveness?

Her stomach clenched. Was she being hypocritical in even thinking something like that? How often did she assume a pirate wanted to kill her before he lay eyes on her? Did they not do the same to Lost Boys? The repercussions of feuds, it seemed, was to make the enemy appear as good a monster to excuse your actions of hatred and violence. Whether she wanted to or not, that seed was deep within her. It would take time to go deep enough to dig it out. Even then, would she ever eliminate the immediate reaction against pirates? How could she blame Jack for his against giants, then?

Feuds are weeds, Wendy discerned. *Once it's grown roots, it's harder to dig up; and it's far easier to spread.*

For reasons unknown, she wondered at something she'd noticed when trying to escape unseen between the double walls. Maybe it was the thought of her brothers or the Lost Boys that brought it to mind. Still, the question would not leave her:

Where were all the children?

Not once throughout the entirety of their run through the fortress did she see a child. Perhaps with the height difference she hadn't noticed. Even so, something about it bothered her. She would have to ask Jack about it when he returned.

Movement caught her eye in the water below. Something was stuck in the river. Just past the mill's wheel, three large objects were toiling and wagging back and forth on the current. They were tied to the bank, but far too shabby to be boats.

Before she could investigate, she heard her name called sharp and quick so as not to be noticed. "Wendy!"

With a final look at the strange rafts in the water, she returned to the spot where her friends waited for her. Kai pointed out the figures charging their way. She sighed in relief. At least they were alright.

"Who's that with them?" Alice voiced curiously.

They could only assume it was Harry, but at this distance it looked like there were four of them running their way instead of three. As they got closer, it was harder to deny this fact. They ran in the open field, completely visible.

"They're going to get caught," Kai murmured.

"*Borogove.*"

The earth trembled beneath their feet. A horde of giants appeared in the distance, bounding towards them at full speed. Wendy felt her heart skip a beat.

One of the figures started shouting something at them, but the angry giants drowned out her voice. She recognized Red.

"What?" Wendy cried, cupping her hands around her mouth.

In the next instant, a strange man with shaggy hair caught up to them first, shouting, "She said, *get on the rafts!*"

He bolted right past them. It wasn't until Red came by also that they snapped out of it and joined the group in running through the tall grass to the riverbank. Though the rafts were wiggly, they were close enough to make the jump. The man—Wendy could only assume this was Harry—waited by the ropes, attaching a large satchel to his back securely.

"Get on!" he hastened.

A woman emerged, arguing, "We can't fit all of these people on."

"We can, and we will." There was a look on Harry's face that finalized the discussion.

With only a moment's thought, Kai leaped onto the farthest raft and latched on. Shaking the water from his face, he beckoned someone to join him with assurance that he'd catch them. Wendy took that as her queue. She landed beside him, filling their small raft. The water was biting and anxious to pull them in. But Kai secured his arm around her, and she instantly felt safe.

The woman jumped next, but as she went to grab the edge her grasp slipped. A hasty move forced her to use her injured wrist. Her face contorted in pain. Before the current could sweep her away, Red planted her foot on the first raft and launched herself at the second, grabbing hold of the edge and snatching the woman's broken wrist. Both were thrown into the river, but her grip anchored them.

Red gave a guttural cry, fighting the current and straining to pull the both of them back on the raft. A thud jostled them. With only his feet on the wet plank, Jack used both hands to lock onto Red's arm and heave the two women back up out of the river. The raft sank halfway in the river with the three of them on it. But at least now they weren't drowning.

As Alice secured herself on the last one, Harry pulled a knife and cut them loose, sending the rafts bounding down the river.

"*Harry!*" Jack yelled, helpless.

As they picked up speed, Harry started running down the bank alongside them, ahead of them. The giants were nearly to the mill, yet to discover their escape. Swiftly, Harry sprang off a boulder and flew out into the river. He crashed onto the raft beside Alice. Nearly slipping off from the impact, Alice had to help him back up quickly. By then they were well beyond the giants' line of sight.

Shaking water off his face, Harry gave a thrilling shout of laughter as the three overcrowded rafts washed down the rapids, the fortress far behind them.

Chapter Eleven

Row Your Boat
Gently Down the
Stream

Jack couldn't feel anything. He was beyond cold at that point, numb to the water that soaked him clean through. Every so often someone would cry out when their leg scraped against something beneath the surface. Not Jack. A fish could've eaten his toes off and he wouldn't even notice. It took all his willpower to keep his blanched fingers locked on the raft as they charged down the river. His teeth wouldn't stop chattering, though.

It didn't help that the raft he rode was the heaviest. Each bump in the rapids left them spewing water.

The small waterfall nearly caused Spider to slip away again. His arm shot out, pinning her down. She honestly looked like she wanted to kill him, but she let him hold her despite the nasty look she'd thrown him. At least his reflexes weren't as frozen as he felt.

Behind them Wendy went flying, giving a cry between surprise and joy as Kai dropped beneath her over the waterfall. He had to fish her from the current when they splashed down. Coughing and sputtering, *she* didn't throw any nasty looks at Kai when he secured his arm around her.

The rapids that followed sent them spinning. Around and around they went until Jack thought his head was going to explode from nausea. Apparently numbness didn't prevent dizziness by any means. By the time they were wrenched free from the swirling rapids and he fought the urge to vomit, Jack noticed the missing raft. He cranked his head around, but for the life of him couldn't spot it.

"*Harry!*" he screamed above the roaring river. "*Alice!*"

Water exploding, they burst from beneath the surface gasping for air. Harry gave a shout of adrenaline. Alice didn't look so amused.

The current increased, and the rapids grew larger. It didn't take long before Jack had to hold his breath as their own raft went under. The whole situation seemed to sour Spider's mood.

It hit him then why the current was moving so fast. But he didn't know how to stop this thing. He didn't know how to get everyone back to shore. He couldn't even manage to open his mouth wide enough for his teeth to chatter, much less shout a warning to the others.

He'd gone over one too many steep waterfalls to enjoy the plunge.

Just as he could make out the drop off in the distance, a blast of water ignited before them as something shot up out of the river, stretching between the riverbanks to form a barrier. They hit the net headlong, forced to a stop.

"Oi!" Harry exclaimed. "Perfect timing."

"This is the plan?" Alice gasped, exasperation thickening her tone.

"Brilliant, eh?"

A rope splashed beside them. Harry snatched it, passing it back so the rope snaked between the three rafts. Jack held tight to his bit as they were pulled closer to shore. The going was slow, strenuous. Eventually, Harry looked back at them.

"We may be testing Brann's strength here," he confessed. "Let's give him a hand, eh?"

Hand over hand, Harry started to pull him and Alice along the rope to quicken the process. But the rope kept slacking with the weight. So, Kai remained on his raft with Wendy, pulling the rope taunt so the others could get to shore faster.

As they worked, Jack noticed the man standing on shore holding the rope's end. He was tall and broad with a week-old beard and thin layer of hair on his head. Something was tattooed up both arms. When they reached the shore, he realized they were black flames crawling up from his wrists.

Harry and Alice were the first to crawl up the bank. Here it wasn't a steady climb but a lip at the river's edge. Red, Spider, and Jack had to wait for their turn.

"What's this?" the man questioned, arms strained holding the rope. "You know you were supposed to bring back a goose, not hostages."

"They're not hostages," Harry corrected, shaking the water out of his shaggy locks. There were tiny braids threaded through it. Jack wondered who did that, because there was no way Harry did that himself. "I ran into a friend."

"Five of them?"

"Is that how many there are?"

Alice nodded, shivering, making sure the pocket watch was still safe and concealed.

Harry shrugged. "Ah. Well, no matter; just get them ashore."

Holding onto the rope, Jack tried to keep the raft steady as Harry helped Spider out of the river. Red went next, helping him up. He never felt more wet than when he emerged from that water and collapsed on the ground.

Over him, Harry's face appeared. "You alright, friend?"

"Remind me never to go river rafting with you again," Jack heaved.

Harry laughed at that.

Soon, Kai and Wendy were being pulled ashore— not before Kai got a slap in the face from a jumping fish. He couldn't get Wendy to stop laughing at that until they were well on solid ground.

Releasing the rope, the man inspected Spider's wrist in concern. "What happened?"

She jerked her arm away. "Broke it."

Yep, that settles it, Jack diagnosed. *She's a straight-up sourpuss.*

"Wendy, your leg."

Twisting around, Jack followed Alice's gaze where he found dark blood blossoming from a tear in Wendy's pants right at the shin.

She looked down at it, noticing it for the first time. "Well, would you look at that…"

Kai wiped off his wet face. "Let me take a look."

"Patch up quick," Harry said. "We've got to get out of here before the giants catch up."

With a request for help, he walked off with Alice and Red following close behind. They disappeared somewhere in the woods. Groaning, Jack rolled over and finally got to his feet. All he wanted was a nap right now.

Retrieving his satchel, the man tossed a roll of bandages over to Kai. Wendy's wound wasn't deep, but it bled considerably. She must have scraped it on a rock or branch in the river. After cleaning her shin, Kai carefully wrapped the bandages around her leg, squeezing her shoulder fondly as he stood. She smiled in thanks.

As the man busied himself in setting up a brace for Spider's wrist, Kai leaned closer to Jack. "What is going on, *bror*?"

"Honestly, I'm still trying to figure that out myself," he admitted.

"Do you know these two?"

"Still trying to get names down."

He picked up the slight tremors in the ground. The giants were still a distance away, but Harry was right: They needed to get out of there.

The others returned swiftly, four beasts in tow that were larger than horses. Jack felt his stomach clench. The last time he saw beasts like this, they were running away from him with belowlanders on their backs, abandoning Harry and him to rescue Jill alone.

Wendy voiced the obvious, "Are those goats?"

"Mountain goats," the man affirmed.

She raised her eyebrows at him. "I stand corrected."

Harry beckoned them forward hastily, no doubt feeling the same tremble in the ground as Jack did. The beasts were oversized shaggy rams, curled horns tipped with gold. Iron rings looped through their nostrils. Strange double-saddles were strapped to their backs for the ready.

It was the leaves that shocked them into hastening forward. They showered down like an omen, urging them on, reminding them of the enemy at their heels.

Jack climbed one of the beasts himself, pulling Red up behind him. Thankfully, the ram was too nervous about the impending giants than having a wolf on its back. She wrapped her arms around his waist. Something in him warmed.

The man attempted to help Spider up who promptly ignored him as best she could. Taking the lead, Harry brought Alice with him. Kai and Wendy were the last to climb on the final ride. Rams anxious, they took off.

Hissing a curse, the man turned his goat around to cut the net down. When the giants did at last reach the area, there was no trace of human disturbance to be found beyond the waterfall plummeting to the rocks below.

*****

The shout of the Giant King was enough to make the mountains tremble.

"He was right here!" he bellowed. "*He was right here!* And you let him get away?"

The giant before him cringed, an expression which made Nozrok even angrier. This sorry excuse for a guard had been charged with keeping security tight around the inner wall during the invasion. No human should have been able to slip past his defenses so unnoticed. Yet, somehow

Jack had made it to the most central point of the entire fortress without any alarm. By chance alone did Nozrok find him in that passage. The boy should've been handed over on a silver platter. Instead, here they were. He pressed his fist to his bare brow. The Giant Slayer had again slipped right through his fingers.

His wrath controlled under a steely glower, Nozrok asked, "Is there anything else you wish to inform me?"

The giant fiddled nervously with the braids in his beard. Surely a giant put in such a position would hold himself without ticks of weakness. Respect lowered for him with every second that passed.

"There is speculation—"

The doors burst open, cutting the guard off. Toog loped in and bared his wrists before him. "My king."

His attention instantly shifted. "What of the goose?"

"She is safe," the warrior informed, voice butchered. "No belowlander breached her room. All eggs are accounted for."

Relief stemmed the hot anger inside. At least history would not repeat itself this night, a reminder of the night in which they'd lost another prized possession. The goose was just as irreplaceable as the harp. For now, he was glad that one was safe.

He huffed out the last of his steam so only the cold remained in his tone. "Gath," Nozrok turned to the guard once again, "what is this speculation you speak of?"

Gath's eyes lowered, but at least he did not reek of fear. "My king, there is speculation that sometime during the invasion and our search for the Giant Slayer, there was another belowlander who managed to sneak in."

Narrowing his eyes, Nozrok waited for him to continue.

"This other belowlander," Gath rushed, "we believe he managed to steal the crown and escape during the chaos."

Silence thickened as his words sank in.

Nozrok had not worn his crown since its burn informed him of Jack's return. It had been here, in this very throne room. Frustration and rage boiled in his chest.

In one burst of uncontainable demand for punishment, his war hammer was in his fist as Nozrok smashed it into the side of Gath's face. His shout of anger ripped through the quiet. Blood splattered the stone walls. Gath stumbled away, maimed but alive. That was as much mercy as he would ever receive from the Giant King for this.

*****

That large satchel tapped against Harry's leg rhythmically as the mountain goats trotted along. Something about it drew Jack's attention. He couldn't think of anything that would warrant a bag so big. Yet Harry didn't seem to have a problem toting it around. It must not weigh as much as it looked.

On the rams, they covered ground quickly. The going was bumpy, but Jack didn't feel the need to complain after a morning of being tied to a sheep's belly. He made a mental note never to do that again.

The journey didn't provide much room to chat, though Jack did pick up on one conversation that Harry and Alice had. As usual, she had a question.

"Why not just ride horses?" she asked, unable to stay on long before she needed to hold onto Harry's waist.

"Ironically enough," he replied, "the only horses here are ponies. They're not too good at getting people over the pass—though they can be used as pack animals sometimes. Hence, the goats."

Jack felt a chill go down his spine. There was only one pass Harry could refer to, and that was the passage through the mountains, the one that only belowlanders knew how to find. Despite his sudden dread, he didn't turn around. Surely Harry didn't mean to take them to the belowlanders. He was smarter than that. If Jack stepped foot in that place… He didn't know if they would kill him or slap him in shackles, but either way a fight would inevitably break. Even Harry's charm couldn't prevent that.

Something in the way the hooves beat against the earth made Jack's mind drift into a haze. Everything that happened that day didn't feel real. The sheep nightmare, the elderly giant who wanted to eat him, facing Nozrok again… At least Red didn't smell like alcohol anymore; the river rafting was good for something. And there was Harry right in front of him, leading them on like a glorious ram-riding Viking. He wasn't caged or broken. It was as if he'd never been captured at all, never needed rescue, never knew his sister was still inside that torture chamber.

It was the first time he thought about Jill since he left her behind. Did Harry know that she was alive? All joy he had at seeing his friend again leaked away. Gold eyes haunted him. Bells rang in his ears.

Jill was alive.

But something in him knew she wasn't the same.

They stopped late into the night completely exhausted. As Red left alone with promises of food, the man struggled to build the fire since it rained that morning. Jack watched the woods silently. He wished he'd volunteered to go with her, but he knew that she preferred to hunt alone. She didn't want any chance of someone else seeing the Wolf before she was ready.

Before long she returned with a small boar over her shoulder and a cut on her brow.

"How the blazes did you manage to get that?" the man proclaimed.

With a shrug, Red dropped the boar. Its tusks gleamed in the firelight. "I'm a good shot."

"It must have just had a scramble with a dhole when you found it," Spider observed, taking the boar by the tusks to pull it towards her for butchering. "There are teeth marks here in the hide."

"If you say so."

Jack settled by the fire, arms propped over his knees as he twisted tufts of grass in his fingers. Stars blinked down from overhead. It was one of those rare nights where the sky was clear, and the constellations shown brilliantly like diamonds. They felt so close, as if he could touch them from the treetops. He remembered trying once with Jill and Harry. They'd just climbed the beanstalk, thought they could actually hold the sky in their hands if they stretched far enough. But stars were fickle. They always remained just out of reach.

Red sat beside him, green eyes reflecting silver and fire. When they were in the Enchanted Forest, he had overheard her telling Wendy a story about the stars. She spoke of a little girl who strove to become light despite the darkness she saw in herself. He wondered why she still only saw the shadows while he saw flames.

The boar roasting over the fire, the man looked around at them with open hands. "Care to tell me who you are, now?"

Four heads turned to Jack. He gave a small nod, as if they needed his consent. They knew just about as much as he did in this situation.

Beside him, she cleared her throat. "I'm Red."

Spider frowned. Man, could she hold a grudge. But the man got excited, stating, "Oh, I get it. *Red*, like blood and rage. That's clever. I can see that being intimidating."

Red raised her eyebrow uncertainly. "Uh, thanks. I hadn't thought about it that way. It's actually just my initials."

His face dropped in uncomfortable disappointment. Spider merely huffed.

The others gave their names quickly without comment on how intimidating their names might have sounded. Even Jack's didn't get the same reaction, though the man's spine stiffened at the sound.

"I had a brother named Jack," he muttered darkly, rubbing the fire tattoos on his forearms. When Alice asked what happened to his brother, the man said, "He wasn't quick enough..."

"This isn't about your brother, Brann," Spider interrupted, irritation in her rough voice.

"Brann?" Kai raised his head with interest. "That's an unusual name."

"More unusual than *Spider*?" Jack scoffed.

Kai ignored him. "It means *fire*, doesn't it?"

"You know Norwegian?" Brann questioned, earning an eyeroll from Spider beside him.

"A bit."

Jack hoped this didn't mean Kai would start going trilingual on him with his new fellow Scandinavian pal. It was hard enough trying to figure out the Swedish. Kai tried to teach him a few times, but the extra phonemes caught him off guard and he struggled with remembering vocabulary.

"I take it that none of you have killed a giant," Brann assumed.

His eyes dropped, though he heard Harry chuckle across the firepit. It wasn't his fault though. Even Harry didn't know what really earned his title.

Alice folded her hands in her lap and cocked her head. "What makes you say that?"

Taken back a little, Brann explained, "Your names. When you kill your first giant, you change your name to something fearsome, ironic, or memorable. When I chose mine, I did so because as a child I used to fear fire since my brother was swallowed up by the flame. But it is also relentless, destructive, powerful—What are you laughing at?"

Harry shook his head in amusement, laughter growing. "You haven't connected the dots yet, have you?"

Brann's brow scrunched in confusion.

Holding out his arm, Harry exclaimed, "This is Jack Caldwell, my friend. Jack, as in the feared and renowned Giant Slayer."

109

The man's eyebrows shot up, wide eyes turning to Jack. "You are?"

He didn't respond. Grass ripped in his hands. His spine itched, skin getting hot. He never considered himself claustrophobic, but he imagined this is what it felt like.

"You're the Giant Slayer?" Brann continued in awe—Jack wished he would stop staring at him like that. "You're a legend! You're even more famous than Silver Blood."

"*Hey*," Harry scoffed without a trace of offense.

Brann leaned forward curiously. "Tell me, how many giants have you killed?"

"The better question," Spider interrupted, eyes narrow, "is how did you return? Everyone knows you disappeared down a beanstalk over a year ago without so much as a leaf remaining upright."

"An old man gave us a lift," Jack said simply. He rubbed his hands together. It was getting harder to breathe. "Excuse me."

Rising to his feet, he left without any destination but *away* on his mind. Both Red and Kai made to follow, but Harry waved them off. "No, let me," he insisted, walking after him.

The last thing Jack heard was Brann mutter in confusion, "Old man?"

It wasn't fear, not really. He knew what fear tasted like, and though this was close, it was too hot to be considered fear. This was iron in his mouth and fire in his skin. There was dust and woodchips filtering through his lungs. Maybe this was just a different kind of fear, the kind that came in his nightmares.

Away from the firelight, Jack leaned against a tree with arms crossed over his chest. He thought he saw a tusked deer in the woods, but it was too dark to be sure. Above him, the clouds were rolling in. He pushed his sleeves up his forearms, wondering if Nozrok really did lacerate the muscles down Jill's limbs. Maybe that was why she was cooperating with them. She couldn't escape, and they drowned her in gold. She had no choice.

His breath eased. The ringing in his ears faded away.

Footsteps crunched behind him.

"Hello there, friend," Harry spoke casually. He leaned against a tree across from him in a similar manner. "So, did an old man really bring you here?"

Jack shrugged. "More or less."

"No beanstalk?"

"Not this time."

Harry sighed, lips screwed up in contemplation. His hair was longer than Jack remembered, shaggier, and the braids were new. There were scars on his face now. One sliced his eyebrow in half, another ran down the side of his nose. Then he saw it, the telltale flecks of gold in Harry's blue eyes. Jack's stomach clenched at the sight. He didn't need to ask to know his friend had the cursed gold in his blood.

"You want to tell me what's going on?" Harry inquired. "Where you've been? Why you're so down?"

"I don't want to talk about it," Jack admitted, "not here, not now."

"Fine then. We can talk about it when we're all safe."

111

"*Safe?*" The word came out sharper than he intended. It was like a joke in his mouth, one he couldn't bring himself to laugh at. "Where are you taking us that's *safe?*"

The smile in his eyes faded. "You know where."

"Yeah, I know where. It's about as safe as the giants' fortress." He worked his jaw, irritated. "Since when do you work for the belowlanders?"

Harry pushed off the trunk, arms crossed, brow raised. "I thought we weren't going to catch up until we crossed the pass."

"They *betrayed* us. Don't you remember? After everything we did for them, they hightailed it on their funny looking goats at the first sign of trouble. That means something, Harry. They can't be trusted, and they're certainly not safe."

"They saved my life!" he exclaimed, throwing his arms out in exasperation. "That also means something. I wouldn't have escaped alive if it wasn't for them."

"You wouldn't have been there in the first place if it wasn't for them."

"No, I wouldn't have been there if we hadn't climbed that *blasted bloody* beanstalk."

Jack clamped his mouth shut, heart pounding. He wanted to throw the evidence in his friend's face, show him Jill, show him the repercussions of the belowlanders abandonment. But Harry was right. None of them would be here if they hadn't climbed that beanstalk. And whose fault was that?

Harry sighed, arms dropping to his sides. "I don't blame you, friend. Not for anything. Climbing that

112

beanstalk may just have been the best and the worst thing that's ever happened to me."

Without another word, he left Jack alone.

He frowned at what Harry said. Something didn't sit right. After all this time and everything they'd been through, what could possibly have made this the best thing that's ever happened to him?

Chapter Twelve

Take the Key and Lock Her Up, My Fair Lady

"It is time for another dose."

"We have only just withstood an invasion, a theft."

"And did you think it would have no effect on her? She is getting restless."

"We should wait a while longer—"

"No, Nozrok, now!" Yldaa demanded, her voice echoing in its intensity.

Nozrok narrowed his eyes at her fury. When he assigned Yldaa with the position to oversee the prisoner, he deemed it the perfect justice after what the prisoner had done to her father and sister. They had found Gogmagog and Alba's bodies on the rock beaches of the cloud sea, stoned and drowned. Never before had a giant been drowned by a human. The stories called her the Siren. To this day, they didn't know how she achieved it.

Now, he wondered if charging Yldaa with such a position provided her the motive to abuse her authority.

"If we hit now, we may yet wrestle the belowlanders' location from her," Yldaa persisted. "She could have information about the crown."

"It is stolen," Nozrok growled. "What more is there to know about it?"

"Either way, she needs a new injection. Not tomorrow, not next week—*now*."

Sighing deeply through his nose, he turned to the other giant in the room. "What do you make of this, Uzfra?"

Uzfra coughed into his knobby fist uncertainly. He looked between the both of them from behind massive spectacles and a bulging nose. As an elder, he had coils of gold and silver in his grey beard and steel implanted in his knuckles.

"I agree with Yldaa," he confessed after much pondering. "The Siren has been cooperative before. Given the proper persuasion, perhaps she will reveal the belowlanders' location, tactics, plans. She's sure to have more information on the Giant Slayer and Silver Blood that could help us. I know as well as you how valuable the eggs are with their decreasing numbers, but if we are to abide by the deal, we must retrieve the crown. It pains me to say, but it is worth the sacrifice."

Yldaa crossed her arms triumphantly.

Jaw set, Nozrok acknowledged their correctness by walking past them and out the door. His eyes darkened. Behind him, Yldaa and Uzfra followed close at his heels. Guards standing at the embellished door parted before them just long enough to pass.

Reaching the upper floor, Nozrok eyed the goose as he selected a golden egg from the stack beside her cage. She didn't even flinch at his presence. When he left, his bitter heart hardened.

The prison tower was now under tight security, guards funneling in and out like clockwork. It didn't take long before the door inscribed with screaming birds swung open with a bang, rattling the cages that dangled from the ceiling. A skeleton crumbled to the floor.

Nozrok shouldered the final door open, slamming it shut once Yldaa and Uzfra entered behind him. The Siren scampered to her feet, backed against the wall.

"No, please!" she cried. "I've done everything you've asked."

Silent, the Giant King watched in a deadly glower as Yldaa grabbed the girl and threw her on the table. Her legs failed her instantly. Grimly, Uzfra uncovered the lamp for better light. The Siren crawled as far as she could away from them.

"What more do you want?" she squealed, breathing heavily. She could not retreat any further back.

"The belowlanders' location," Nozrok growled.

"I've told you before: I don't know. I was never there!"

"You were in contact with them for years, aided them in their acts of terror against the giants. You've confessed this."

"They never told me *where* they were."

Yldaa slammed her fist against the table, jostling the girl violently. "We'll see what you have to say after a proper injection."

"No, no! I... I... I overheard something about a pass," the girl stumbled over her words, "through the mountains."

"We know this already," Uzfra acknowledged solemnly.

"That's all I know! A pass through the mountains, a view of the clouds..."

"Fine, then what of tactics?" Yldaa demanded with a hiss. "How do the belowlanders operate? What more can you tell us about the Giant Slayer and Silver Blood?"

"I've told you everything I know! How many times..." Her face blanked and she sat up straighter, the first sign of offense she'd pulled in months. "*Silver Blood?* Why are you asking about Harry?"

Yldaa clamped her mouth together, grinding her teeth. Nozrok noticed the change instantly, the mistake. It was a weakness in their carefully lain foundation, and now it lay exposed, discovered. He turned the egg over in his hand.

The Siren raised her eyebrows. "He's escaped, hasn't he?"

Narrowing his eyes, Nozrok gave a low grunt as he made his decision. No more questions. He took the egg in both hands and broke it over his knee. The dense shell cracked in two, golden liquid oozing richly as he handled it with expertise. Not a drop spilled.

The girl's face instantly turned to utter terror. He could smell it in the air, thick and cold, like the wind licking the cliffside or a stone raking over wet skin. The aroma pulsated from her. She shook her head violently, pushing herself against the wall as if she could melt into it.

"*NO!*"

She screamed the word over and over again, growing shrill when the lamplight glinted off the substance approaching. Liquid gold descended upon her. Searing, suffocating, devouring pain shot down every vein, nerve, bone, organ in her body. Fear coupled with it caused the gold to expand. The smell became sweet and intoxicating in his nostrils. He smirked with pleasure.

She had not screamed for Jack in months.

Chapter Thirteen

Sticks and Stones

May Break My Bones

The next day was another hard run through the woods. A dhole was quick to skitter out of their way—the rams didn't seem to mind plowing through anything in their path. Their gate was faster than a horse, but rougher to ride. Trees sped by in a blur. Squirrels yapped angrily after them when rudely disturbed. It was a miracle they didn't leave any roadkill. If they passed any giants, they traveled too quickly to notice.

There were very few things Jack was aware of that anchored him to reality when his mind wandered: the coarse scruff he held onto beneath the reins, the tight hold of Red's arms around his middle, and the looming mountains that overpowered the horizon.

At first, the range appeared like a steady grey sky somewhere beyond the trees. But as they rode on, the blockade became more distinct in its solidity. His vision blurred before he could make out its height. The range stretched as far as the eye could see, a slab of impenetrable rock. Jagged openings distinguished individual peaks, yet they were so close and steep that even from ground level—*especially* from ground level—the mountains seemed impossible to pass.

These were the terrible mountains they headed towards. No wonder this was the wall between giant and belowlander.

Jack had no desire to see the other side.

Long ago, he and his friends had been discovered by a team of belowlanders who had been observing their exploits for some time. Among them was a gruff warrior called Cat who disliked them on sight. Her counterpart Bleddyn was the likeable one, the one Jack wanted to impress, the one who convinced them to work with the belowlanders for a *noble cause*. Treasure hunting turned to a heist with purpose. They stole the harp. After that, their hitlist grew. In the end, it was Jack's drive to prove himself that earned his name. Bleddyn led him right to it.

That man was the first to leave when asked for help. The belowlanders blamed Jack for his untimely death.

By the time the sky's color faded, the rams had reached the edge of the mountains. Rain fell steadily on his skin. An eruption broke overhead.

"It's the mountains," Brann muttered, staring up at the sheer cliff before them. "They sound like thunder when rock falls within."

Somehow, that failed to be reassuring.

Slipping off his ram, Harry announced, "We'll rest here and pick back up in the morning. It's too dangerous to enter this late."

They were really selling the place.

Spider built the shelter and Brann somehow managed to start a fire—neither seeking assistance. Alice began pestering them with questions about the belowlanders, which Spider tended to ignore and shoot warning glares at Brann when he tried to answer them. It didn't slide past Jack's notice that she had a strategy in her asking. She wanted information about resources, behaviors, numbers. Anything to do with potential foreign aid was indirectly posed. Alice was a diplomat fishing for any chance of alliance in war. And she was especially curious about witches.

"Witches?" Brann made a face. "No such thing."

"But you battle giants every day. You don't see the magic in that?"

"The only thing with power is gold."

Suffice it to say, she didn't get much further than that.

Hands in his pockets, Jack left alone to stare into the mouth of the mountain pass. It rumbled inside like a growling stomach. He wondered if it would swallow him whole if he stood close enough.

So, this is where it's been, he thought to himself. *One of the greatest kept secrets in Giant Country...*

It was bigger than he'd imagined.

Jack sighed. The truth was that he didn't know what lay on the other side of the pass. At least in the giants' fortress he knew what to expect. This was uncharted territory. His anger boiled for the belowlanders nearly as much as it did for the giants, anger at what they convinced him to do for so long, anger at their deception, anger at their betrayal.

Why the devil would Harry go back to them? Did he feel obligated to settle a debt for his rescue? It had been a year. Surely, he would have paid them back tenfold by then. Why stay?

"Want some company?"

He turned as Wendy sat beside him, not bothering to wait for a response. Jack smiled softly. She always felt comfortable to be around, like they could sit for hours and say nothing at all. He remembered the first time they met back at the Facility: the ceiling fell on his bed—or at least a piece of it. He'd never seen Kai jump so high in shock. By the time they had processed what happened, Jack recalled looking up at the circular hole above where large brown eyes smiled down at him. She waved, and like an idiot, he waved back.

"Shall we have an adventure?" she had whispered to them mysteriously.

Jack had made eye contact with his roommate whose fists were still tight by his sides. With a shrug, he'd crawled into the tunnel. Jack followed that stranger into an adventure that changed him forever.

Now, Wendy sighed contently by his side. She shifted into a more comfortable position, never minding the mud and rain or how her curls frizzed from getting wet. Nothing seemed to bother her. Sure, she became more worried than a mother hen when someone got mauled by a cougar or forgot to eat breakfast. But it was like things just rolled off her shoulders, on and off again, ready to take the next stone thrown her way. Jack admired that.

Completely casual, she voiced, "Do you want to talk about it?"

A small laugh huffed in his throat. Sometimes he wondered if Wendy could read minds. "Talk about what?"

"Anything. Whatever's bothering you."

"You sound like my mother."

This time, it was Wendy who huffed a laugh. It was moments like this that reminded him how much older she really was.

"You could talk about what happened back at the fortress," she suggested. "Harry doesn't exactly strike me as a recently escaped prisoner. What happened?"

Images flashed through his mind: eyes shot through with gold, a friend he'd thought dead betraying him without reason. The feeling was like a punch in the stomach. Both of his friends had sided with his enemies.

Jack shook his head. "I'm not ready to talk about that."

"Is there anything you do want to talk about?"

"I'm not sure."

She waited a moment, letting the rain fall on her eyelashes. "Why are you called *Giant Slayer*? Even Kezia called you as much. Or, where are the children here? I didn't see any back at the fortress."

Shoulders tensed. "Please, don't ask me that."

Wendy refrained from asking questions then. Slipping her hand in his, she leaned into his shoulder. He could feel the gold thick inside, aching. But Jack rested his head on hers and let Wendy sleep against him.

*****

Seizures came in such intensity and irregularity that she didn't have time to brace herself before the pain contorted her entire body. It never stopped *hurting*. Jill was used to it, but there was only less pain and beyond pain now. She couldn't remember what it was like without agony. That was a time outside the reaches of her imagination. Gold was her reality. No relief. Always pain.

123

Muscles tightened again. Her body was forced into gruesome figures. She wanted to yell, but all that came out were gargled gasps, her voice strangled out of her.

Time passed in throbbing heartbeats.

The seizures dissipated to muscle spasms, but the burning compression lingered. Everything choked: her mind, her breath, her body. She was swallowed up in devastation as her plights shot through her head like the effects of electrocution. Guilt ate at her insides, a parasite she deserved.

Jack.

That look on his face, the hurt and confusion… She betrayed him. And now, she realized it was for nothing. All this time cooperating with the giants, telling them her secrets, telling them *their* secrets; it was all under the false impression that she was protecting her brother.

But Harry escaped. She was the fool. Who knew how long the giants had kept up this charade.

Pain solidified inside her, another layer of gold in her veins. It made her bleary, aching, but bearable. Jill wiped her brow and stared at her moist hand, realizing that she sweated blood and gold. She rubbed it between her fingers. The dim light reflected off gilded crimson. She hated it. Did they really desire the giants' treasure once: the riches, the glory, the adventure?

Careful what you wish for…

The ground trembled as giants passed nearby. Their increased security was clear enough by the footsteps and voices that passed the chamber routinely. The disturbance sent pins and needles down her side. Weakly, Jill sat up to listen. Giants never realized how much their voices carried.

What she heard caused ice to slip down her spine.

An eruption ignited again inside of her, the seizures returning full swing. She forced herself to push past it, to grab onto those words, to send her mind racing despite the gold eating away at her bones.

Because this changed everything.

*****

Harry promised it would take one day to cross the pass.

It took three.

Rain pressed on the entire time, making the stone slick and sending debris down the cliff face. The path led them upwards. Consequently, the drop to their left quickly became a cataclysmic ravine that echoed with thunder and unseen rockslides. Jack was beginning to wish this secret pass had remained a secret.

As if to prove his point, ahead of him there was a shriek of rock as a ram's hind leg slipped with a jolt. His stomach lurched. Alice screamed as she fell backwards toward the steep expanse. In one swift motion, Harry snatched her arm in a wet clasp, his grip bruising but firm. She groaned, managing to lock hold of his arm with her free hand. The ram kicked its leg in midair until it found a foothold and pulled itself back up again, allowing its riders to right themselves again. Relieved, Jack released the breath he'd been holding.

That was the closest call of the day. There were inevitably more slips, but as it only resulted in Red's hold around him tightening, Jack didn't mind so much.

They spent the first night on a narrow ledge when it got too dark for the rams to travel. Jack didn't sleep a wink.

Something about the wind whistling through the endless drop below didn't sing him into a slumber the way it did for Wendy. No one could understand how she managed it. Even the next morning as the mountain goats picked their way along the pass, Kai would look back at him to affirm that she was still sleeping peacefully against his chest. She woke up perfectly rested a few hours later.

Rain descended in heavy sheets the second day. Ledges here were spotted with grass and clay, providing better friction for hooves. Jack and Red took up the back of the pack. There were less slips, but they were blinded by the downpour.

A rip and roll quaked in his eardrums louder than thunder. Butting their heads back at the noise, the rams surged ahead anxiously. Jack looked around for the sound's source but couldn't see a thing through the curtain around them.

Ahead of them, Brann shouted, "What is that?"

"I thought you were supposed to know these things," Jack shouted back, voice drowned in the storm.

Red's arm shot up, pointing, her breath hot on his neck. "Rockslide!"

Pebbles littered his face as he looked above. The mountain began to shake. Heart speeding, Jack urged their ram to go faster. Debris showered down on them, larger stones trying to trip them up and bruise their bodies. He heard the boulders bounding down the cliff but didn't know where they were aimed for.

"*Come on!*" Jack exclaimed, digging his heels into the ram's sides.

The avalanche of mud and stone exploded behind them. Red screamed. Her arms were suddenly gone from his middle. Breath hitched, Jack shot around and latched onto her blindly. Mud and rock dashed against his face, his arms. He yanked her towards him, keeping her from being swept away. He didn't let go.

Skittering forward with such force away from the rockslide, their ram had to pause to rest for a good while before it could continue after the others. Jack breathed heavily, arms still tight around her. She leaned against his shoulder with eyes closed, catching her breath. Wet strands of hair hung over her face. He pressed his head to hers. Thank God she was alive.

They were completely covered in mud, blinded by the rain, but he did his best to look her over without releasing his hold. Her blouse was completely shredded down the back. Whipped with gravel, her flesh was completely inflamed and tender. The only spot undamaged was where his arm wrapped around her, his skin pressed against hers. He didn't bother investigating his burning arm.

"Here," Jack said, reluctantly pulling away to take off his jacket. Gently, he covered her bared back with it.

"Is it bad?" she asked shakily. Bottle green eyes rose to his. He brushed the mud off her cheek, streaking it more than wiping it off. Rain streamed off his nose.

He offered a smile. "I think you'll live, Rubes."

She nodded—he could tell how she tried not to wince. When he turned forward again, he felt her press her face against his shoulder blade, locking her arms around his middle. He struggled to focus on the road ahead. The rain irritated his raw arm.

Somehow, they survived until that evening when Spider found a cave in the mountainside, stable and dry: two things they'd been lacking all day. They decided to stay for the night.

As soon as they entered, Spider clutched her wrist with a curse under her breath. Wendy made a beeline for the woman, insisting that she bind her injury properly. Spider looked about to protest before her ram nosed her arm and she jerked away. Wordlessly, she nodded in consent. It didn't long for Wendy to fashion a proper brace and sling for her.

Jack slipped off their ram to help Red down. Surprisingly, she didn't argue as he gently took her under the arms and lowered her to the ground. By then it was hard to ignore the stinging down his arm. He did so anyway.

"What hurts?" he asked in concern.

"Left shoulder, leg," she swallowed, "and all down my back."

Before he could offer to help, Wendy appeared beside him. "I'll take it from here. In the meantime, you get Kai to look at that arm. Make sure you clean it."

She pulled Red away to take care of her wounds. Jack's gaze followed.

He didn't even notice Kai come up. "What happened?"

Jack looked down at his arm, the skin sandpapered all the way to his knuckles with debris. "Eh, it's just a scratch."

While Kai tended to Jack's arm, Wendy went to roll up Red's trousers to inspect the damage. She flinched so hard he almost jerked forward himself.

"Alice, get those boys to look away," Wendy huffed, hands on her hips. Jack wasn't sure what she meant until she ordered, "Red, take them off."

Neck hot, Jack forced himself to focus on his own injury. Kai was meticulous, using his wet sleeve to wipe out the gravel and mud. He wasn't the gentlest of nurses. He rubbed at black spots until he was certain they were bruises, and his fingers were too large to painlessly remove splinters. By the time he was done, Jack's arm was as scarlet as a glowing tomato. He smiled in thanks as Kai bandaged him up.

A muffled scream burst behind him. Jack whipped around instinctively, earning a slap up the back of his head from Alice. Though he looked away, the image lingered: Red hugging her knees to her chest with her shirt stuffed in her mouth, bare back towards him, the skin lashed and inflamed. Nothing had looked serious, though based off his own injury he could imagine the sting. Hopefully she would heal quickly.

He caught Harry staring at him curiously. Confused, Jack made a face. Harry winked back at him.

When Wendy allowed them to turn back around, they finished tying up the rams and divided up the last of their provisions. Nothing like boar jerky and wild peas for dinner. Jack noticed Red was wearing his jacket again to cover her destroyed blouse. He decided it suited her better.

That night was the first time he was able to sleep in the mountain pass.

The rain lightened by dawn, and they were on the path again by early morning. Vultures circled overhead, waiting for someone to fall into the ravine below. Their presence was discomforting. But as footholds crumbled underfoot and the rams found it more difficult to find a safe path, Jack supposed the scavenging birds had good reason to loiter.

He didn't notice the end of the pass ahead until it was late afternoon and he finally caught sight of the sun. His stomach knotted. Surely nothing good awaited beyond that opening. Few belowlanders would know his face, but one look at the gold in his eyes would raise suspicions. Overall, he didn't know what to expect.

Harry looked back and locked eyes with him. Jack knew he was supposed to trust him; he felt it deep in his gut. Ever since they were little, they followed each other into any situation, even if that often landed them into trouble. Harry was two years older, Jack was two times faster, and within their friendship they'd never had reason to distrust the other.

Until he told Harry his sister was dead.

That was the first time he didn't believe him.

Now as Harry led them forward out of the mountain pass, Jack's jaw fit together firmly, unsure if they would ever regain that blind trust again.

Chapter Fourteen

What Little Girls Are Made Of

According to witnesses, the Siren had been shouting it all day.

"I want to speak with Nozrok!"

No one could get her to shut up.

It was too early to give her another injection, and frankly she shouldn't have been able to lift her arm let alone scream coherent demands. Her body was becoming tolerant. They would have to up the dosage.

Yldaa came to him in a frenzy, completely infuriated by this sudden turn in behavior. The prisoner had blandly refused to talk to her. She wanted Nozrok. Only Nozrok.

Fists clenched to his sides, the Giant King made his way towards the prison tower with the flustered giantess on his heels. Posted at the door was the giant Gath, an eyepatch now over his empty socket. He bared his wrists grimly before following them into the chamber.

The girl was sitting cross-legged on the table, patiently waiting. The only signs of her internal pain were the pulsing veins in her neck and the way her left hand periodically curled grotesquely in muscle spasm. Nozrok glared at her apparent ease. He knew instantly that every brick in the foundation they'd built, every blossom of fear they cultivated, it had all crumbled. This girl was all that remained.

"How dare you?" Yldaa hissed, furious as she leaned over the girl. "You think you're so entitled as to summon the Giant King like a common dog?!"

"And yet," the Siren said evenly, head cocked, "he came."

Rage festered inside. "What is the meaning of this?" Nozrok growled.

The girl shrugged. "I just wanted to talk about certain things that have recently come to my attention."

"Watch your tongue, you insignificant speck," Yldaa snapped. "Unless you're begging for another injection."

The Siren ignored her. "I want a new deal."

Something about it made him choke in cruel amusement. The absurdity, the audacity, the hilarity of this situation; what vermin thought they could plea with their trappers?

"A new deal?" Nozrok rumbled.

Infected eyes stared at him, unfazed. "Things change when you find out you're dying."

His stomach tightened, nostrils flared. Even Yldaa could say nothing in the face of this.

The girl huffed a humorless laugh. "I should've known sooner. All this time, I could've called the shots. But it's too late now for many things. And you can't give me another dose without risking it ending me. The gold is killing me too fast—I can feel it." Her shoulders seized as if to prove her point. "You can't control me anymore. You can't control a *dead girl*."

132

The silence thickened around him. Nozrok could smell no fear, not even a trace of it. She was never supposed to know until it was too late. But why did she have to find out now of all times?

But the Siren wasn't finished. She was gaining her confidence, fear shed like a second skin. "If you want my help, I want a new deal. Luckily for you, I've saved information worth your weight in… *gold*."

"*Why, you little—*"

"And you'll tell us willingly?" Nozrok questioned warily, cutting off Yldaa's outburst.

She shrugged. "For a price."

"What do you want? Your freedom?"

The girl actually laughed at that, gold streaking down the sides of her face. "Not my freedom. It's too late for that. We all know that because of this bloody gold I can't leave this country. And because I've helped *you*, the belowlanders would kill me on the spot."

"You're dying anyway."

"But this way I can die for something."

"What do you want?" Yldaa snapped, agitated.

"If I help you," she demanded, "no harm can come to Harry or Jack. They are not to be killed or injured or imprisoned or harmed of any kind—not by any giant's doing."

Nozrok worked his jaw in silent fury. "And if we don't accept your terms?"

"Then good luck finding the belowlanders, learning their tactics, or retrieving your precious harp and crown when I'm dead."

Yldaa ground her teeth. "You said you didn't know anything about those."

"I know more than I let on. I'm stubborn like that, even—" Her head writhed to the side, silencing her with a muscle contraction in her neck. The light reflected off her eyes when she recovered. "Do we have a deal?"

There was no choice. If there was any chance of retrieving the harp and crown, Nozrok had to take it. He nodded in agreement.

"Say it," the girl ordered.

"May gold eat me from the inside out should I break our agreement," the Giant King stated, a growl in the back of his voice. "No harm will come the Giant Slayer or Silver Blood by my or any giant's doing, just as you said."

Her expression darkened in suspicion. "Swear by the gold in your blood."

Yldaa nearly destroyed her on the spot. Nozrok grabbed her arm to stop her. To swear on the gold in his blood was the most binding oath a giant could make. The gravity of this request, it would prevent him from satisfying his revenge. But the harp…

Gritting his teeth, the Giant King rumbled, "I swear by the gold in my blood that no harm will come to the Giant Slayer or Silver Blood by any giant's hand."

The Siren gave a sigh. "Alright, I'll tell you everything I know."

*****

The village was larger than Jack imagined it to be. It was positioned a good distance from the mountains, dense forestry at its back and rolling hills to the right. A breathtaking view of the sea stretched out to the left; a sea of clouds instead of water. It felt like the end of the world.

Fenced off properties and patchwork crops increased the closer to the woods he looked. It was the front of the village, the part closest to the mountains that held the main hub of buildings and alleys. Even at this distance, Jack could see the chaos of battle training for man, woman, and child. The clamor of blacksmiths and machinery pounded through the rain's patter. They remained unnoticed as they approached. He wrinkled his nose at the stench.

Within the final leg of the journey, alarms erupted as if they'd set off a tripwire. Jack wondered if it was too late to turn this goat around. But there was nowhere for him to run to. Not this time. So as the group neared the village, Jack dropped his gaze and shook his wet hair over his brow. Too bad it wasn't long enough to cover his eyes.

Red's arms tightened around him for reassurance.

They slowed to a trot as belowlanders crowded before the village entrance, weapons drawn and at the ready. The crowd quickly surrounded them, and the rams reared to a halt. On impulse, Red went to reach for her bow. Jack stopped her grimly. They couldn't afford a fight yet. But Kai also appeared ready to take out his sword should the need arise.

"What's this?" Harry asked in confusion, eyebrow raised.

It took a moment more for the crowd to still. Spears and blades aimed at the center. Tension shifted around them, between them, flooding over the company in waves. It was as if the belowlanders didn't care that there were at least two of their own within the circle they encompassed. Harry was growing more agitated.

"*What's this?*" he questioned again, louder.

One person waded through to the front of the crowd to address them. "This is what happens when you return from the giants with more strangers than you left with, Silver Blood," growled the hard-looking woman. A thick scar split her right eye from her lined forehead to her hollow cheek. She had coarse grey hair, a permanent frown, and masculine features. What's more, this was the only belowlander alive that Jack knew on this side of the mountains.

"They're friends," Harry argued. "They can be trusted."

"Says who? You?" the woman scoffed, unamused. "You haven't been here long enough for anyone to take you at your word."

"Cat, this is ridiculous," he huffed. Jack noticed how Harry never bothered to mention that he'd worked with them for two years. "Talk to the Fiddler—"

His spine snapped straight.

"My judgement isn't enough for you?" Cat narrowed her eyes. "In case you've forgotten, Silver Blood, there is only one with authority over mine."

"Fine, I'll talk to the Fiddler myself." Harry slipped off his ram and pushed his way through the crowd, shouting, "I don't want anyone to move until I get back!"

There was no argument. Soon, the mountain goats settled down and Brann began to catch up with some friends of his in the crowd as if this was a regular occurrence. Spider, being the ray of sunshine that she was, just sat there looking very annoyed that she had to be associated with the rest of them.

The general, Cat, made no attempt to mask her accusing one-eyed glare. It shot daggers down his neck. Jack looked away, hoping she wouldn't recognize him. Seething anger churned in his stomach. This was the woman who had been in the group that recruited them, the one who never wanted to deal with three foreign kids, who was always arguing with Bleddyn about his decision to take them on. No doubt she was pleased when he'd given the order to retreat and abandon them to the giants. He was also certain she held Jack responsible for Bleddyn's fall.

Harry returned before Cat could guess his identity, instantly barking orders like he owned the place. "We need food, medical attention, and some bloody time to breathe. After that, the Fiddler wants a chat. He's pronounced—and hear this, folks—that until further notice, my friends are to be treated as guests by every one of you trigger-happy prigs."

Unsurprisingly, that caused a bit of an uproar. Many were indifferent, lowering their weapons and exiting the scene. For those who remained, they protested in fervor. Cat merely scowled.

Raising his arms, Harry shouted above the crowd, "Are you protesting against the Fiddler's orders?"

The crowd died down in uncomfortable compliance.

"I thought not." Harry grinned as took the reins from Alice and led their ram away. "But don't fret, friends. You can break their bones for bread as soon as the Fiddler gives the word. I always thought that was the giants' job, but don't let me spoil your guilty pleasures."

Alice turned back to Jack with a look on her face that questioned whether they chose the right person to vouch for them.

After leaving the mountain goats at the stables and seeing Spider to the infirmary, they followed Harry down the length of the village. Brann soon departed, assuring them that he wouldn't participate in tearing them to pieces if the Fiddler changed his mind. How generous of him.

They were at the far end of the village between dingy town and patchwork crops. Harry stopped before a house constructed of mismatched materials: a solid stone foundation, large glass windows, brick walls with wood and iron accents, and copper chimneys that coordinated with the greened copper door. A small garden grew in the front yard, and three miniature Shetland ponies were fenced in the back. Jack could hear the gears inside from where he stood.

"You'd better wait here while I make sure it's alright to let you inside," Harry advised sheepishly. "This isn't exactly my house."

Raking his fingers through his shaggy wet hair, he disappeared inside. Jack and his friends waited awkwardly in the rain. Passersby stared at them, but they were few. The mud was getting slippery underfoot.

Soon, they could hear muffled voices inside, rising in tension. Jack shifted uneasily. Things weren't sounding too great, though nothing was discernable until a singular voice cut through the door.

"*... Honestly, Harry, what were you thinking?!*"

Jack flinched, growing uncomfortable.

The copper door swung open, the voice going on accusingly, "You can't just leave them out like animals while it's bucketing down! They're bound to catch a—" The woman cut herself off as soon as she saw them standing there soaked to their socks. Immediately, she broke into a smile and ushered, "Don't just stand there. Come in, come in!"

Behind her stood Harry who cringed when the woman shot a glare at him.

"You heard the woman, friends," he said with mild amusement. "You'd all better get inside."

Jack followed Kai's example of nodding in thanks to the woman as he stepped in. He didn't know what to think of her. Dark blonde hair was messily tied back. Knowing brown eyes made him nervous under her gaze. She wasn't much older, maybe five to seven years—pretty, though worn from hard labor. Rough hands, wide hips, and grease stains. By the way he was looking at her, Harry must have thought she was the most beautiful woman in the world.

So, that's what changed.

"Friends," Harry announced, wrapping an arm comfortably around the woman's shoulders, "this is Liesel."

"Yes, yes," Liesel feigned annoyance, tucking a stray hair behind her ear with a little smile. She had a pleasant lilt in her voice. "I can introduce myself, thank you."

The shout of excitement behind them made Jack nearly jump out of his skin. When a small child zipped past, his heart about stopped. Harry grinned, stooping to meet the three-year-old upon impact.

"Hey there, Blue!" Harry scooped the boy up, tossed him in the air. "How's your horn playing? Have the ponies been dancing again?"

"A little," Blue admitted, pushing his yellow curls out of his eyes. "Tom tried, but he... he doesn't do it good."

"We'll have to teach Tom a little more, get those ponies dancing," Harry suggested.

"Yeah, I," the kid was still getting used to his words, "I thought that, too."

Shaking his head, Jack went to say something when another little boy appeared. He was maybe a year older than the other one, with muddy brown hair and a purple stained mouth. Smiling shyly, he tottered over. Harry ruffled his hair affectionately.

Is this even happening right now?

Liesel put her hands on her hips suspiciously. "Tom, have you been in the plumbs again?"

The second kid leaned against Harry's leg guiltily. Harry clasped his hand over the boy's mouth to hide the evidence.

"No, of course not!" Harry insisted. "Tom wouldn't *nearly* be so careless as to pull that trick off again without washing his face first."

Tom giggled behind Harry's hand.

Pressing her lips together, Liesel tried unsuccessfully to look unamused. "Come on, let's get you cleaned up." She took Tom's hand to lead him along, but she turned back to address her guests, "You must need food and rest. Make yourselves at home."

Harry set Blue down so he could scurry off after his brother. When he caught Jack gaping, he frowned. "What?"

Blinking out of his stupor, Jack coughed awkwardly. "Are they… yours?"

Harry couldn't contain the laughter. "You haven't been gone *that* long, friend. They're Liesel's. The father was killed by giants before Blue was born."

Something like relief eased his shoulders. He wasn't sure he could handle any more surprises. "Right. Sorry, it's just you and Liesel seem… close."

"I should hope so. She's my wife."

That slapped him in the face. "Your *what*?"

"My wife. Well, actually, my wife-to-be. Small details. I get carried away."

A confusion of emotions toiled around in his head. Of course, he was shocked. Completely. No doubt about that. But there was sadness, too; disappointment that he'd missed out on so much time with his best friend. The time between them was wider than he could've ever imagined. He was happy—of course he was happy—for Harry and that he'd managed to find more than a scrap of joy in this world after everything they had gone through.

But how could he have moved on so quickly? Jack still suffered from the mental scars those years in this country had dealt him. Everything in him wanted to move past it, forget about the gold in his blood. He'd tried that before. But ignoring the problems didn't erase them, and now he knew he had to settle them before he could move on.

Had Harry settled with his demons? Was that why he could be so at ease, so stable?

So there it was, that little spot of envy amid all the chaos in his mind.

The image of Jill's gold infused eyes flashed behind his eyelids. Gritting his teeth, Jack wrestled aside his thoughts and followed the others out of the entryway.

Chapter Fifteen
Weeping for a Loved One

They only got a bite to eat before they had to return to face the Fiddler.

Jack had never faced the man behind it all, never met him, didn't know what he looked like. But he'd heard the stories: A man who failed to defend his king, who lost his ear and fingers, who couldn't hear the same after the incident. They claimed he was the only one of three defenders who survived the ambush. He'd singlehandedly defended the belowlanders during their great exploit for justice, which was how he became their leader. But he never claimed the title of king. Jack didn't like the man already.

Mud squished under their feet. The rain was hardly noticeable anymore, like it melted into the scenery and was as inevitable as the sun. Jack followed close to Harry, the others behind him. The roads were practically empty now that the excitement had died down. Those who remained eyed the group warily as they passed, like wolves watching sheep, ready to pounce.

Red elbowed Jack and whispered, "There's a man who's been following us since we left the house."

Jack followed her gaze. A hunched man openly stared at them from the lamppost. Grey hair hung in wet strands, uneven eyes gleaming putrid green on the left and murky brown on the right. His nose was beaky and broken. Jumbled yellow teeth were visible due to his lopsided underbite. The rest of him was concealed under his cloak, but it was obvious something was off about his shape. A similarly misshapen cat sat at his feet, its jagged tail twitching.

"That's Crooked," Harry informed, voice low and rumbling. "He lives outside the village, keeps to himself mostly. I'd avoid him if you can. They say his mind is as twisted as his body."

Beside him, Alice frowned at the man. Perhaps she recognized the look of madness about him. Perhaps she saw something else. Either way, Crooked scrutinized them as they trumped by.

Whereas most houses this deep in town were squashed together in tall apartments, the Townhall stood apart from the rest near the stables. This was white wood and iron binding, a massive box with round windows and turning gears that could power the entire village. They stomped the mud off their boots before entering.

The room flickered with electronic lights. A fire in the hearth provided warmth, and there beside it waited Brann and Spider. They looked up when the six of them approached. A chill shot down his spine when Jack noticed that Cat had decided to join the party as well, her damaged eye gleaming in the firelight. One look at her and he instantly knew she'd recognized him.

Jack couldn't help but notice the small similarities to the giants' fortress here: the gears, the mixture of materials, the displayed weaponry, the raw precious stone over the refined. It was a mockery, a poor replica. But it was too close to flattery.

The Fiddler stood tall and lanky beside an intricately carved table of metal and wood. He had a large nose, hollow cheeks under high cheekbones, and a receding hairline. Everything was sharp, skeletal. His right ear was shredded to nothing. A scar knotted down the side of his throat. Only a nub remained of his thumb, and his ring finger was completely missing from his left hand.

The Fiddler looked at each of the newcomers in turn with eyes like polished mahogany. He lingered on Jack, revealing nothing. Jack met his gaze evenly, steely. Giants were the ones who could smell fear, but he wondered if this man thought he could see it. Jack only knew one person who could, and this guy wasn't nearly so pretty.

The Fiddler broke their stare.

"You completed the mission?" he questioned Harry, ignoring the others' very presence.

In response, Harry tossed his incredibly large satchel onto the table. It landed with a loud *thunk*.

"They expected us to go after the goose," Harry explained. "They weren't wrong, but we noticed that *this* held some importance to them as the goose and harp. When Nozrok ordered extra guards for his bird, we saw the perfect opportunity to snatch this right out from under his nose." He chuckled to himself. "Quite literally, actually. They were a little too preoccupied by another coincidental distraction."

The Fiddler pulled a bit of the object out of the bag. Jack scowled. Before them was revealed a great ring of iron laced with sapphire and gold. He'd only ever seen the crown encircling Nozrok's brow. How did Harry manage to get his hands on it?

"Would you care to explain what else you dragged back with you?" Cat spoke up bitterly. "You have brought strangers—"

"Jack is my friend," Harry cut in firmly. "And these are his friends, which makes them my friends. And I don't leave my friends behind when they need help."

The words made Jack cringe.

"Besides," he went on, "Jack knows more about the giants than anyone. He can be a valuable—"

"You ignore the fact that he is the *Giant Slayer*," Cat hissed, her one eye fixated on Jack menacingly. "We have worked with him before, as we worked with you. We do not need you to remind us of his usefulness."

The Fiddler turned his attention to Jack, still failing to address him directly. "And how is it that the Giant Slayer has returned with four other companions?"

"An old man gave them a lift," Brann spoke up with a proud grin. Spider rolled her eyes.

"And where exactly did you find them?" the Fiddler questioned, staring right at him as if he wasn't there. This was really getting on his nerves.

"The fortress," Harry informed.

"Why were they there?"

"I'm sorry," Red spoke up in exasperation, "but this is ridiculous. If you're going to continue this charade, at least have the courtesy to ask it directly—"

"I asked a simple enough question," the Fiddler cut through evenly with a stern authority that made Red clamp her mouth shut. "Whether Silver Blood or the Giant Slayer answers is of no difference to me."

146

Seething, Jack clenched his fists but did not respond.

Harry shifted to look at him quizzically. "What were you doing out there, friend?"

"I went to find you, but instead I..." His voice broke, eyes fell. The strange heat was returning, like the walls were pressing in, like he'd swallowed hot coals for breakfast and they weren't agreeing with him.

"Did you find something?" Harry pressed, interest spiking.

Jack worked his jaw, haunted by gold infected eyes. His voice came out low, "I want to talk to you in private."

"Whatever you have to say, friend, you can say to everyone here."

"I would prefer—"

"Jack," Harry sounded concerned, using the same tone with him as with the new kids back at the orphanage, gently coercing them to speak, to feel comfortable. He'd never used it on Jack before. "If there's anything you found out about the giants, just tell us."

"You can trust us," the Fiddler added.

That made the coals inflame.

"*Trust you?*" he snapped. "Really? Last time you asked us to trust you... There's no bloody way—"

"Jack, please," Harry interjected. "Now is not the time."

"Then when is the bloody time, Harry? When are you ready to realize what they did to us?"

"You are bringing up completely unrelated subjects."

147

"It's all related! Don't you understand? It's all some messed up puzzle machine, and *that's* the guy pulling the levers."

"I think you're confused."

"I think you're ignorant."

"If one of you doesn't quit your bickering, I'm going to cut someone's tongue out," Cat interjected harshly.

Harry sighed, calming down. "Would you please just explain yourself?"

Everything raged inside, tasteless and hot. "Fine!" Jack threw his hands in the air. "Jill is alive and working for the *blasted bloody giants*."

He didn't wait for a reaction. Turning on his heel, he stormed out of the Townhall and slammed the door behind him.

They found him in the stables, pacing and pulling at his hair like he was going crazy. It was only the four of them. Jack felt like his head was about to burst.

"Jack," Red spoke behind him. "Why didn't you say anything?"

I don't bloody know, he wanted to shout to the heavens, because he felt like the most clueless bloke in the world right about now. Saying it out loud made it real. It meant he had to face it, had to figure this out head on. Nothing to hide or ignore or postpone when it all lay out there for everyone to see.

Not only had he abandoned Harry, but he'd abandoned Jill. He was the one who told everyone she was dead. He was the one who left her body lying there on the floor, bleeding and broken but alive. So, what the devil was he supposed to do about it? And that was the part he found so difficult to face: not only the reason behind Jill's actions, but how was he going to fix this?

There wasn't one scenario that could take it all back.

"If you had told me…"

"If I told you what?" Jack snapped. "That Jill was alive? That she looked me dead in the eye, told me to leave, and sounded the alarm? What bloody good would it have done if I told you?"

"What bloody good came of keeping it to yourself?" Red snapped right back.

"I'm not the one who keeps all the blasted secrets."

"Seems like you're getting bloody close."

"*Håll truten!*" Kai cut in, placing himself between them. That was one Swedish phrase Jack recognized: *Shut up!* He used to hear that often.

"Red." Icy eyes narrowed at her. "Put a muzzle on it." He'd learned that one from Jack.

Her fists clenched at her sides. "I don't appreciate—"

"Muzzle."

She gritted her teeth, but didn't protest.

"Jack," Kai averted, "you know better."

"Oh, do I?"

"Nothing has ever gone well when we keep things to ourselves. If we keep secrets or can't trust each other, none of this works."

"Fine! Now you know about Jill; what else do you want to know?" Jack asked, raking his fingers agitatedly over his scalp. "Do you... You want to know why I'm called *the Giant Slayer*? Why I hate the belowlanders so much? Why they don't trust me after everything I've done for them? Why there aren't any *children* in the fortress? They tricked me into killing..."

His voice broke.

He squeezed his eyes shut, trying to block out the ghosts of their screams. There it was again: the crushing, burning, choking tension filtering through his lungs. Jack opened his eyes. Harry stood in the stable doorway, watching. He didn't care. He'd never told Harry about what happened, not really, not the truth.

"We caught the attention of the belowlanders shortly after Harry killed the treasure keeper," Jack began, speaking low, looking directly at Harry. "We were caught up in the idea that we could help them, make a difference, join the fight against the giants. And we did. We stole the harp, Jill earned her name, we pulled missions left and right.

"I was soon asked to find a way to destroy the torturer: Galigantus. He was preparing prototypes for a war machine that could scale the mountains. It was like a massive slingshot. These weapons were stored in a training facility, so I was told—a place where soldiers were made and taught to track fear like bloodhounds. Once I killed Galigantus, I was supposed to raise a signal so the belowlanders could help ransack the place."

He remembered the brutality, the challenge. This massive murderer before him, whom Jack had before seen in action, had fallen through the floor by his own machines of destruction. It wasn't his blade that ended him, though he could've done that easily. It was what happened next.

Swallowing through his tight throat, Jack continued, "I never made the signal. When I found the war machines, I fired them at the support beams and brought the whole building down. It killed everyone else inside."

"Which is why you're called the Giant Slayer," Alice muttered, the gears in her head ever turning.

Jack nodded. He never turned from Harry. "I was small enough to squeeze out of the rubble. As I escaped, I realized what was really in that building." Fists clenched, he kept on, "They told me they were soldiers. *Murderers.* They never bothered to mention they were kids. They were all *kids!*" As he screamed it, tears leaked down his face. Everything burned like the explosions, choked like the dust, crushed like the building on top of him. "Galigantus was using a school as his cover, a guaranteed defense. But the belowlanders didn't care. They tricked me into killing them, *all of them.*"

"Why'd you never tell us?"

The others noticed Harry now, leaning against the wall with arms crossed.

Anger had dissipated. All that remained was this anguish, this thing so close to fear that Jack began to wonder if it was. This hurt.

Wetting his lips, he responded with a humorless smile. "That all happened right before my blood got an upgrade. I'd earned my name. They captured me, tortured me, and by the time I got out it didn't matter. Giants, belowlanders, there's hardly a difference except one wants to destroy me and the other thinks they can still manipulate me. Well, I'm sure several of these guys want to destroy me too."

Frustrated, Harry cursed under his breath. "If I'd have known—*gah!* We never would've gone after the goose, and Jill..." He cursed again, his gaze meeting Jack's once again. "Is it really true, Jack? Is she—?"

"She's alive," he interrupted. A knot formed in the back of his throat. "She's more infected than anyone I've seen."

"*Blasted bloody—*" He passed a hand over his face. "All this time... Tell me everything."

Though it pained him to recall it, Jack did his best to describe what happened in the torture chamber with Jill. He recited every word, detailed every symptom. It only seemed to reveal yet again how little he actually knew. Why did she turn him in? How damaged was she after over a year of punishment? But Harry listened intently with the others. Jack couldn't tell if he would burst in anger or break down in sorrow. Either way, his friend looked about like a bomb with a shortening fuse.

When Jack finished, Harry's jaw clenched so hard that the vein in his neck seemed about to pop.

"We knew... that someone was working for the giants, leaking information," Harry said slowly as if the wrong word would break him. "I never would've thought it was..." He swallowed hard, changing the subject. "Come on. Liesel will have food ready and insist you'll stay with us."

Turning, he left without a word, walking like a ghost in the moonlight.

At the house, Jack watched Harry stand alone in a room, so many words lying unspoken between them bare at their feet. All of that heavy tension fell away as Harry dropped to his knees, utterly broken. Jack knelt beside him. He was breaking but not shattered. Every breath was a struggling attempt to keep from falling apart.

I promise I'm a happy person.

But not tonight.

Not tonight.

He expected Harry to say something, to shout at him for convincing them to climb that blasted beanstalk in the first place, to question how his sister would ever betray them, to demand the giants pay for their cruelty, to accuse the belowlanders of their deception and disloyalty.

Yet from the anger and hatred and betrayal, it was deep sorrow and utter regret that won out in the end.

"I failed her," Harry muttered. His voice held more pain than any amount of poisonous gold could inflict.

A tear like broken glass slipped down Jack's nose. "We both did."

Harry buried his face in his hands and wept.

Chapter Sixteen

She Shall Have Music

Wherever She Goes

It seemed that only three of those who traveled through the mountains were able to wake themselves in the morning. Wendy had slept with ease during the journey, so she didn't need the extra rest. Kai slept in but decided to investigate the village alone that morning. She wondered if Gerda was on his mind, if he could feel that they were so close to reaching her. Maybe he needed to clear his head.

As for Alice, well, she seemed to be needing less and less sleep with little apparent side effects. It was like her mind was always spinning now. Sleep was just another distraction.

The two met Liesel and her boys in the kitchen where she'd prepared a hearty breakfast of sausages, fried tomatoes, eggs, and a potato pancake she called *boxty*. She explained that Harry, too, was still dozing in the boys' room.

"Seems they're completely knackered," Liesel said, getting Blue to eat his tomatoes, "the poor things."

"Did Harry tell you, then?" Wendy asked.

She nodded grimly. "Aye, he told me. They're a tricky lot on the other side. How that girl lasted this long is beyond me."

"Mam," the boy, Tom said enthusiastically, sitting on his hands, "I'm after eating my breakfast."

Wendy smiled. It had been a long time since she'd been around children this young. Certainly, there were some Lost Boys who appeared this age, but their minds were older in most ways. Michael had a son like this: young and innocent.

"Get your things then, darling," Liesel prodded her son, who tossed his dishes in the sink before he scampered off. Blue was still picking at the remains of his tomatoes.

As Alice and Wendy helped her clean up the kitchen, Liesel asked, "Would you care to join me in the village today while the others are resting? I'm going for the messages after dropping Tom off for training."

"Errands?" Alice affirmed, tying up her boot laces.

"Aye. I'm to pick up cockleshells, find more ingredients for dinner, and take a gander at getting new clothes for the rest of you. Best not to leave you in rags that barely fit." Liesel winked at Wendy. It was true, the clothes she'd loaned from the gypsies were baggy and now filthy. Not to mention Red's blouse had been completely shredded in the mountain pass.

"I'd be happy to join you," Wendy replied.

Alice agreed as well, seemingly anxious to take a look around the village.

"Mam," Blue spoke up, pushing his curls from his forehead. "I... I'm after breakfast, too."

"Doesn't look it to me," Liesel said casually, wiping off the countertop.

"But I... I am."

"What's that staring at you on your plate, then?"

155

"I *am* after eating."

"He's not one to let up, is he?" Alice voiced jokingly.

"He's learned too much from that snoring eejit in the other room," Liesel grumbled, a sparkle in her eye. "Blue, eat your tomatoes or I'll make certain you're cleaning up sheep dung all day."

"Mam..."

"Eat."

Quickly, Blue scarfed up the last of his tomatoes and ran off before his mother could change her mind. Liesel chuckled once he was gone.

Something about it made Wendy's heart ache with an emotion she had no name for, as if she was missing something she never had and would never have. The Lost Boys called her Mother. That was all she really needed. But then there was *this*. She couldn't have this.

With a pleasant smile, Liesel turned to the girls, "Sorry, you'll have to brace yourselves for the horn. He's rather proud of it. Now, we'd best crack on, lots to do."

*****

It was completely absurd. The plan the Siren proposed to them, it could either save them or destroy them. Nozrok knew there was no other option. They would die anyway if they did nothing. The goose would perish, the eggs would diminish, and another outbreak would wipe out their entire race. There could be no other way.

"I know what you're thinking," Yldaa spoke, her voice like a thorn in his side.

He did not answer. He knew every counter she was going to pose, every weakness in this plan, every risk. He did not need her to speak them, but he did not quiet her.

"No giant has ever survived crossing the mountains."

"That we know of," he rumbled. "There have been plenty who've tried."

"Yes," Yldaa agreed with a snarl. "Outlaws, traitors, gentle giants who forget who the real enemy is. They're the ones who had nowhere left to run. Gutless—"

"Desperate," Nozrok corrected. He'd banished giants to the mountains who reeked with fear, shook down to their knees, begging him for forgiveness. Then there were those who went with head high, not a whiff of fear on them. "And we all know that *desperate* giants can be far more capable than anyone can imagine."

"You're willing to risk giants' blood on the word of a belowlander?"

"Just because no one has returned does not mean that no one succeeded."

Yldaa scoffed, throwing her hands in the air. "You sound like a knobby-kneed old crone spitting about moving rocks. Giants living in the mountains? It's a fairytale! It's impossible."

"We have no other choice!"

She quieted, grinding her teeth. No matter how much she protested, she could not change the fact that there was no other way. The Siren had given them their only chance. His hands were tied in this.

Still, she huffed, "This is madness."

Nozrok rubbed his chin, blue and brown eyes on the dying goose. "No. It's desperation."

*****

Tom raced ahead of them excitedly while Blue stayed behind, holding his mother's hand and dragging her along. Just as warned, he was tooting his little brass horn the entire way. Liesel attached a funny looking muffler to the horn's bell when they approached the crowded part of town, changing the sound to avoid annoying passersby. The strained elephantine noise made Blue giggle.

Wendy felt like she and Alice stuck out like sore thumbs despite their attempts to act casual. Belowlanders stared at them as they walked by. Liesel kept on as if oblivious to the rude glares.

"Tell me," she spoke, directing Blue away from mud puddles and onto the cobblestone road, "how'd you come to know Harry? Did you grow up in the same orphanage down below?"

Wendy shook her head. "No, Jack's the one who grew up with him. The rest of us only met him the other day escaping the fortress."

Liesel laughed at that. "Why am I not surprised? That's just like Harry: going on about family friends like he's known you for donkey's years." She shook her head amusedly to obliterate any notion that she could be upset. "Sorry, don't mind me, I'm only codding with you."

Tom slowed so they could catch up to him, beaming. He was standing next to a sun worn man with a cart full of produce.

"Could we get some plums, Mam?" he pleaded, eyeing the fruit hungrily.

158

Liesel shook her head. "We have some already, darling. Or we did until someone decided to stick his thumbs in them before I could make a pie."

Sheepishly, Tom wrung his hands. He was still eyeing the plums, though.

"Best listen to your mum, lad," the older man said, a gleam in his eye. "Don't you worry, though. I'll save you some in case she be changing her mind." He winked at the boy, who perked up at the prospects. "Are you off for training, then?"

Tom nodded enthusiastically.

"Do they have you fighting, yet? Sturdy lad as you are."

Liesel lightly nudged Tom on to answer the man. "Nah, not yet. I take care of the tools."

"A fine job, then. We all start somewhere. What name are you aiming to choose when you grow up?"

This time, he brightened as before. "I want to be Mouse! Like my mam."

The man chuckled, ruffling Tom's hair. "That's it, lad. Keep that up and you'll be getting your plums for certain."

Prompting her sons forward, Liesel smiled in farewell to the man. She managed to plant a kiss on Tom's head before he soon trotted off to join the other boys filing into the training yard.

Wendy cringed at the sight.

It was a space in the middle of the village, a square bordered by a market, with the battle training as the spectacle. Children trained on ground level with wooden swords and stunted arrows. Teachers scrutinized them with

159

a harsh eye. The smaller ones, like Tom, were put to work with supplies and equipment, cleaning, fashioning, and toting them to those who practiced in the square.

On platforms above were older kids, teens and young adults who fought so violently she wondered if the aggression was genuine. Medics stood at the ready, always at work. Those who taught these were like dictators to militia, as if training them to kill for sport rather than survival.

Wendy was no stranger to seeing children in battle stance. But this felt different. It tightened her stomach and chilled her spine. Maybe she was in no place to pass judgement. Yet what lay before her was an army of children, and she knew in her heart this was not the same as children who could defend themselves. What's more, the Lost Boys were barely children anymore. Inside they clung to childhood and childish tendencies, but they were remnants, shadows, never the man but not quite the boy.

These were just children. Children learning how to kill each other. Children learning to take down giants.

Liesel was looking at her knowingly.

Wendy turned away.

"Come, best not to linger," Liesel prompted, taking Blue's hand while he blew his muffled horn.

At the market, Liesel bought ingredients for stew and *colcannon*—a dish with potatoes and kale. She steered them to a small shop by a woman called Madame where they found themselves surrounded by fabrics and garments to choose from. As Blue played with the shopkeeper's son, Lane, they set about finding clothes that would fit the five of them. When Wendy raised a concern about cost, Liesel shrugged it off.

"I've built up enough interest that it shouldn't be an issue," she explained. "I've spun threads, I've fixed gears, I've looked after Lane now and again. The least they can do me for is trade in a few sturdy clothes. Now, take this: it matches your eyes."

Wendy took the deep blue tunic in her hands, marveling at its durability and softness. It came with a dark brown leather vest that buckled down the front, and they paired it all with comfortable leggings and thick boots. She was just glad these would all fit her.

They fashioned Alice with a plum skirt that was shorter in the front, a tough vest, and light blouse. Her boots laced up her shins over wool leggings with hidden pockets. Miniature gears decorated her leather gauntlets. She claimed it was practical and flattering.

They chose for the others with care. Alice prided herself on the burgundy getup she picked for Red, complete with a deep wine-colored hood. For Jack, they avoided anything remotely gold. The most difficult task was in finding a jacket they could both agree would fit over Kai's shoulders. Liesel grabbed an extra shirt for Harry.

Before they left, Wendy had to pull Alice away from the hats. She stared at them with a strange look on her face. "Shame," Alice muttered, "they aren't very good."

Carrying their clothes out, Liesel led them to their last stop away from the hubbub of the town. Blue was dragging his feet until he was allowed to blow his horn without the muffler.

Alice elbowed Wendy lightly. "Seems we're the talk of the town."

Wendy followed her gaze where a shady group of belowlanders stood outside a smithy, stealing glances at them as they passed. It didn't bother her so much, being the subject of common gossip. Back home in London, she couldn't escape it. She never grew up in the way her brothers did. That kind of thing was hard to explain away, even harder to hide. Once her father chased away a reporter, and another time John had to keep a scientist from sneaking upstairs to discover her. Michael was the first to lie about her age when he brought a girl home to meet the family—he claimed she was his *little* sister. Soon Wendy hardly left the house unless it was to Neverland. By then there was no limit to the theories surrounding why the Darlings' daughter wasn't seen in public anymore.

Strange how even after everything, they wouldn't believe her explanations. Perhaps when she saw them again…

"Sorry, but it is relieving," Liesel admitted, cutting through her thoughts. "They've finally found something better to blather on about than me."

"You?" Alice questioned in surprise.

"Aye, there've been a rake of rumors floating around about me." She shrugged. "Not that I've helped any. I've got a rake of things to rumor about. Trying to avoid them is like feeding biscuits to a bear."

"What exactly is there?"

"I'm the widowed mother engaged to a man who was considered an untrustworthy dosser this time last year. My husband died before I discovered I was pregnant with my youngest. And here's the kicker, when I had the opportunity to kill a giant," Liesel adjusted the bag on her arm, "I didn't."

Like the giant and the bear, Wendy thought suddenly. He'd had every opportunity to kill her after crushing the metallic bear. Yet, he didn't.

Squeezing Blue's hand, Liesel led them through an alley towards a part of town where the houses did not squish together so much. Alice was right at her heels.

"But your son said he'd change his name to *Mouse* one day like you," Alice spoke with a frown. "I was told you didn't change your name unless you killed a giant."

Liesel smiled. "That is the name I would've chosen if I could. But I never killed a giant. They used to call me a sympathizer because of it."

"Giants can't all be monsters," Wendy insisted.

Liesel cast her a look out of the corner of her eye. "Oh?"

"They can't all be monsters," she repeated, and now more than giants came to mind when she spoke. "You can't judge a species as evil simply because their leader is cruel. They're like humans."

"Giants are not humans," Liesel said firmly though not unkindly. There was a warning in her eye, as if Wendy was beginning to cross a line. "You'd do well to remember that, especially here."

The small house they stopped before was practically all steel bound glass windows, with a copper roof and brick foundation. The walls were swallowed up by wisteria and ivy. Silver bells blew in the wind from the porch. Beside the house, a magnolia tree shone like a thousand copper

163

pennies, its flowers almost plastic in their shimmering setting. They passed through the gate easily.

"Liesel, my lovely bell heather!" exclaimed a hook-nosed woman with papery skin and knobby hands. She emerged from the house with arms open wide, garlic strung around her neck.

"Ms. Marie," Liesel greeted with a smile as the woman kissed her cheek. "These are friends of Harry's."

"What precious pansies." Ms. Marie petted each girl on the cheek sweetly. Much to Blue's distaste, she pinched his ear with a fond chuckle. "Come, come; I have your cockleshells inside."

The old woman took Blue by the hand and hustled the rest of them in the house, ducking under overhanging grapevines and basket gardens. Alice almost knocked her head on windchimes. Inside, the house was just as filled with greenery. Plants hung from the rafters, vines crawled up the walls. There were succulents in the windowsills and flower pots lining every surface like pretty ladies all in a row. It was like living in a garden.

"I took the liberty of adding a few more lovelies that would make beautiful colors for your dyes," Ms. Marie went on, stepping around a family of mushrooms growing from the floorboards.

"Ah, you didn't have to do that," Liesel insisted.

"I know it! You're the only one around here who spins half-decent threads. May as well make the colors pretty," Ms. Marie rambled, disappearing around the corner to fetch her wares. "Madame won't weave or sew with anything else, she told me. Her clothes wouldn't hold a candle to the rest without you. Seems that tittering parsnip has some sense after all."

Liesel raised an eyebrow. Blue looked up at her as if requesting permission to call his older brother a *tittering parsnip* now.

Looking around, Wendy wondered how one woman could take care of so many plants. Freshly harvested onions and asparagus lay in bundles beside her, indicating more of a garden was somewhere behind the house.

"So, what's the story with the wool?" Ms. Marie's voice carried through the house. "You know Madame, always badgering me about hogwash like that. I tried to tell her the bloke saved your life, but she must want it straight from the roots."

"Didn't we just see this woman?" Alice asked softly to Liesel.

She shrugged. "Madame is a natural gossip. She'd never ask a direct question; rather use a squealer."

Ms. Marie appeared with a basket of overflowing plants and shells. "What was that, bluebell?"

"I was just telling them about Shep," Liesel covered easily.

"Right, the bloke. Dreadful thing, isn't it? Being a hermit."

"For most, but I'd wager he wouldn't be one if he didn't prefer it."

"Right, right. Even so, never talking to anyone, keeping to themselves, never being seen." She made a face and shook her head. "I couldn't stand it. Here you are, then."

165

Ms. Marie handed over the basket while Liesel inspected the contents curiously. Satisfied, she hooked it over her elbow.

"Thank you kindly, Ms. Marie," Liesel said, moving Blue away from the long ferns. "We'd best crack on."

"Oh, don't mention it," Ms. Marie chuckled, managing to pinch Blue's cheek once more. "Do tell your other little sprout *hello* for me."

Liesel assured she would as she led the girls out the door, her son at her heels. Wendy looked back just as the woman disappeared behind clusters of Spanish Moss. Quickly, she followed Alice outside.

"I am curious," Liesel spoke as they neared the fence. It took Wendy a moment to realize she'd averted to talk to her. "Even after escaping the giants' fortress, you believe in some humanity in them. Why?"

Alice was ahead of them, walking with Blue who was anxious to reach the gate. Her head was tilted, as if only half listening to the conversation behind her.

Wendy sighed, thinking back on when the shepherds were laughing with each other, running with their flock, carefree and happy. There was the giant who saved her from the bear, something in his eyes that wasn't quite humanity as it was indifference, tolerance, like he was tired of fighting. Somehow, she had seen that look before.

Pondering, Wendy answered in a backwards way, "I don't think I trust feuds anymore. They are bloody and blinding with hate and ignorance. Those who don't want to be part of it are sucked in against their will. Any who oppose the feud is labeled a traitor, while any who do nothing is labeled a coward. Even after you recognize how wrong it is to generalize an entire people as an enemy, you can never quite banish that bitterness deep within. It's poison."

Liesel looked at her for a long time, expression unreadable, hand on the gate. "You have wise words," she spoke with suspicion lurking behind her voice. "You have given me much to think about."

Wendy frowned, wondering what she meant by that. But Liesel merely kept on without another word on the matter. Blue blew his horn fervently the whole way back.

Chapter Seventeen

I Told My Love a Story That Has No End

By the time Jack finally woke from dreams he could not remember, it was nearly dawn. He felt refreshed if not slightly disoriented. Soon, he realized that was because he'd missed an entire day yesterday by sleeping. He couldn't remember the last time he'd slept so long.

The woman, Liesel, Harry's fiancé, she discovered he'd awoken first and instantly hastened him into a closet sized room at the back of the house. Jack didn't know what to do except rub the sleep from his eyes while he listened to her instruct him on how the strange room worked. Pipes ran up the copper walls, a lever adjusted the temperature, and a switch made water fall from the spout above. She gave him soap, a towel, and a bundle of clothes with the prompt demand to clean himself. Then she was gone.

Jack quickly burned himself, jiggling the lever desperately until the falling water cooled over his skin. This was easier than a bath, but the thing was dangerous. He felt that at any moment he would slip and slam his head against one of those pipes. It was like being a bug in a sink.

When he was sufficiently cleaned, he dried himself and changed into the clothes he'd been given. His shirt was dark green, a shade that reminded him of the ring around bottle green irises, and leaves were impressed into his umber waistcoat. The trousers had a detachable outer pocket at his thigh. Leather and brass bracers strapped securely around his forearms. It felt comfortable, durable, and all together befitting.

Following the smell of hot food, Jack found the others in the kitchen. Kai, Alice, and Wendy were all properly washed and newly dressed as well, shifting down the benched table to make room for him. Red was nowhere in sight.

On the table, Liesel placed a steaming plate filled to the brim with sausages, marmalade toast, potato hash, and fried eggs. "Eat up while I get you some tea," she stated. It was as if the woman never sat down.

As Jack slid in next to Kai, he felt strangely wary at the ease of this scene. It was so homey, almost normal. He expected to see the English hills rolling out to Offa's Dyke beyond the window, the Welsh forest far beyond. Liesel looked at him as if she'd known him forever, as if he was already a brother-in-law. He didn't know what to make of it.

"She stepped out," Kai said, giving him a sideways glance, "to clear her head."

Jack nodded, shoving food in his mouth to avoid responding. His ears felt hot. Last he'd seen Red, he had snapped at her when she was only trying to help. He said things he didn't mean, things he wished he could take back. It didn't feel right leaving things so unsettled.

The two little boys tottered into the room to join them at the table, forks at the ready to gobble up their expected breakfast. Harry was right behind them, hair wet, shirt fresh. There was not a trace of sorrow on him from the other night.

"Morning, friends!" Harry greeted with a broad grin, snagging a sausage from Jack's plate. Liesel only just had time to set down the teapot before Harry took her around the waist and kissed her on the mouth. She hit his nose with a sugar spoon.

"Stop acting the maggot, you big eejit," Liesel said with a laugh, turning away to get her grimacing boys their breakfast.

Harry winked at Jack, amused.

It was all so natural.

There was only one thing missing.

"So, friends," Harry said, taking a bite of stolen marmalade toast, "shall I show you around, then?"

"Most of them have seen it all already while you snored the day away," Liesel stated, practically throwing a plate of breakfast on the table for Harry. "Now stop swiping all their food and eat your own scran."

He obeyed, ruffling Blue's curls as he sat beside him.

Though Jack hadn't been one of those who had seen the town, he did not disclose that to Harry. He had no desire to be shown around. It would be too easy to run into Cat or another belowlander who held him responsible for the late captain Bleddyn's death; or the Fiddler would try to get him to divulge whatever knowledge he had about the giants. He knew it wasn't wise to make an enemy of the Fiddler. Still, Jack wasn't going to give him the time of day if he could help it.

With breakfast finished, Harry proposed that the little ones show off their talented dancing ponies to their guests. Blue and Tom got so excited that they nearly shoved their chairs over as they ran off to get their horns. Tom quickly returned though to ask his mother permission to be excused, which she granted.

A knock sounded on the door and Harry disappeared to answer it.

Kai offered his seat to Liesel so that she would finally eat her own breakfast, gathering up the abandoned dishes to wash them in the sink. Jack stood to join him.

"Does Tom have to go back for training today?" Wendy asked, making him wonder what he'd missed from yesterday.

Kai tossed a wet rag at him, the thing slapping him in the face as he caught it. Jack scowled at his friend's pleased smirk.

"I only let him go three times a week," Liesel responded with a sausage in her cheek.

"Oh?"

"He'll be working with me today on a wee windup toy he's been putting together. He's doing a savage job of it, too." She paused as if to take a sip of her tea, but then thought twice on it. Something in the way she said what came next made Jack's ears prick. "I want my sons to learn to make something, not just destroy."

He wasn't sure what she meant by it, but he recognized the passion in her voice, the edge that indicated how much she tried to hold onto her statement and make it true. He decided that Harry made the right choice in falling for Liesel. Not that he ever needed Jack's approval on who to marry. Still, he wouldn't mind calling her family one day.

Blast it, did I just sign up to be an uncle? Jack laughed to himself, but the thought didn't trouble him as much as it amused him. *Uncle Jack* did have a nice ring to it.

While Kai finished washing the dishes and he wiped off the countertop, Harry returned with a drawn look in his eyes. He shrugged with a lopsided smile. "Guess the boys will have to go on without me. That was Spider with a summons from the Fiddler."

Liesel nodded. "You'd best crack on, then. No use keeping him waiting."

"No kiss for me then, love?"

"You already claimed the one. We'll see if you deserve another later."

Harry leaned over and clasped Jack on the shoulders. "I think I've got a chance, friend," he whispered good naturedly.

Patting him on the back once more, Harry turned and left with a brief farewell. Jack wondered what the Fiddler wanted with Harry now.

They soon followed the kids outside where the miniature Shetland ponies were kept. Blue played his horn proudly. All three creatures came to his toot, wagging their heads to flip their manes around. The boy laughed, changing the melody. Jack wasn't sure if it was due to the song itself or the noise in their snouts, but the ponies actually did rear up and kick their front legs in the air like a dance.

Wendy seemed particularly fond of the boys, encouraging Tom as he struggled to do the same trick as his younger brother. Two of the ponies were circling each other now. The third sniffed at Tom's horn curiously. Its lips curled over the end and nearly tore the horn out of the boy's hands if Wendy hadn't snatched it.

"Can we speak, *bror*?" Kai asked subtly beside him. By the tone of his voice, Jack wasn't sure if he wanted to take him aside to condemn him or have a nice little chat.

Jack shrugged, stepping away from the house and their friends to a small workshop that branched off the stable. They could see the others from there but couldn't hear them. The ponies were jumping now.

"What is it?" he asked, afraid of the response.

Kai raised his icy eyes to his. "What are we doing, Jack? It's been six days."

"Six days since what?"

"Since we had a plan. Since we knew what we were doing here."

Since we left the fortress, Jack added. *Since we found Harry… Since I found Jill.*

He dropped his gaze. "I know."

"Do you? Lately it seems you've forgotten why we're here. Why are we *here*?" Kai's arms extended to the village, to the house pieced together with so many materials, to the dancing ponies, to the towering mountains. It was nothing against Liesel and her kids, Jack discerned, or even the city itself. It was the purpose of their being here to begin with that Kai questioned.

Jack rubbed the back of his neck irritably. "I'm not sure."

173

"You need to decide," Kai stated firmly. "Do we go back for Jill? Do we attack the giants? Do we recruit the belowlanders? Or do we use that pocket watch to get back to the real war that's going on?"

Thumping his fists against his sides, Jack didn't know how to respond.

Kai sighed, and for once in a long time, he seemed tired. The stiff posture, the confident stance, the hardness around his brow, it all fell away so all that remained was exhaustion. He was tired of fighting. He was tired of this hunt, this chase, this... whatever *this* was.

Thinking back on the scene they'd left with Liesel and her children and Harry, with the natural ease they had, the hominess and family; Jack wondered if Kai felt the same longing for that kind of peace and happiness as he did. How much Kai must have wanted to take Gerda away, back to Anders where his mother and grandmother still waited, where they could be a family and have a half dozen beefy little Swedes—because Jack had no doubt that any of Kai's spawn would end up nothing less than impressive or strong.

But Jack didn't know if he could imagine himself there. It was too fantastical to be real. Better to stick with Uncle Jack for now.

"You need to decide," Kai repeated, breaking through his thoughts. "We are here for you. I cannot decide for you." He scratched the scar on his jaw. "And go make peace with Red. Whatever is happening with you, it's not worth losing her."

Jack nodded in understanding.

With that, Kai left him alone.

Something twisted in his gut, making him uneasy. Jack wished he could fix everything, wished he could call his best friend back and say that he had the solution at last. But there were too many broken things he didn't have the knowledge or the skill to fix. Jill waited in a cell with gold chewing her insides. Gerda probably waited in an ice prison in an entirely different world. There were hundreds of kids crushed to death under a fallen building, and there was a man who used to laugh splattered on the floor. He couldn't take it back. He couldn't fix it.

He had to make a decision.

He went to find Rubes.

Alice felt compelled. Compulsion and impulsion seemed to mix themselves up under her skin more often recently, itching, enticing. She couldn't put a finger on it, and her curiosity was too strong to fight against these new flights of fancy. She just went along with it.

While Wendy remained outside with the boys, Alice followed Liesel upstairs into her workshop. Instantly she felt as if she'd stepped into the inner workings of a clock managed by a spider. Gears of all sizes lined the walls in interlocking harmony. Pullies bridged the ends of the room, running yarn of all colors between them in a rainbow web. Finer threads twirled and twisted into loops. Finished spools traveled down shelved conveyor belts, dropping into massive baskets.

"I repurposed it after my husband died," Liesel explained when she noticed Alice gawking. "Used to be for his tinkering. He liked to bite more than he could chew, and this helped us get things done when the Fiddler was prodding at his heels."

"It looks like a clock," Alice voiced.

Liesel smiled at that, hands on her hips. "Aye, that it is. Once you get the tick-tock down, most anything is easy enough to figure out how it's pieced together. That's why he designed it to look this way, save for the irony."

"Irony?"

"They called him *Clock*," she said, emphasis on the fact that it wasn't what she called him. But Alice saw the other irony, the unspoken one that lurked behind such a name. He was the clock who ran out of time.

Pricks shot up her fingers. She couldn't tell anymore if it was Remus' fault for the sensation or if it was a touch of her own. Her hands balled into fists, nails digging into her palms until she was certain this feeling was hers, relaxing when she realized Remus would feel it too. A sharp pressure passed down her thumb slowly, painless, an acknowledgement of their connection. The message warmed her insides. It was nice being reminded she wasn't alone.

While Liesel went to feed some ingredients from Ms. Marie's supply into a mechanism that pumped and expanded, Alice felt something fuzzy on her tongue. It turned out to be a question. "Why would you change your name to Mouse?"

Liesel laughed to herself, dusting off her hands before grabbing an apron off the wall. "Because of the stories," she spoke as she worked. There was a passion behind her voice, an excitement that lit up her eyes and made her seem ageless. "Who is the one who cares for the

176

less fortunate? Who frightens the great elephants? Who saves the brutal lion? Who beats the clock *every single time*? It's the mouse who works behind the curtain, making certain there is some light in this world even in the smallest yet most important of ways. Listen close enough to the tales and you'll notice. They are the friends to the friendless, the hidden rescuers, the fearless adventurers. And they don't bother about drawing attention to themselves. That's the kind of person I want to be—that's the kind of person I want my sons to be, if not better."

"Is that the kind of person your husband was?"

Liesel was wrenching tight a loose screw on the machine she tampered with, the one which mixed her dyes. Standing straight, she dug her fists into her hips. "My husband was a brave man in his own way," she stated, not defensively but in pure honesty. "He was brave in the shadows where no one could see."

"And Harry?"

"He isn't afraid of being seen."

Alice cocked her head thoughtfully, deciding she not only liked the woman but something in her gut trusted her as well. Which is why she broke all stipulation behind Jack's warning of the belowlanders' longing to escape, taking out the silver capped pocket watch and presenting it to Liesel. "Can you show me how this works?"

"How'd you find me?" Red questioned without turning.

"I followed where the sheep were running from," Jack quipped as he approached.

"There are no sheep around here."

"Exactly."

She shook her head with a twitch of a smile. "How'd you really find me?"

"I can't go giving up all my tricks," he teased, not bothering to tell her how he'd been walking up and down this rugged coastline for hours trying to find her after Brann suggested that this was a prime location to clear one's head. Luckily, the man was right.

Without asking, Jack sat beside her on the pebble beach. The wind blew wisps of vapor from the cloud sea into the air. They sat a good distance away from the edge, but even here the cool moisture dampened their skin in a fine layer. A cool gust nipped his ears.

Red was looking at the strangely shifting clouds, but his gaze turned to her. Wet strands of hair framed her face, escaped from the braid that hung over her shoulder. Her hands were dirty and roughened with scabs. Though her new hood covered it, she still wore his jacket.

Jack shifted, wondering what to say. He'd rehearsed the apology over in his mind while he looked for her, but it was all petty hogwash. Anything half decent had vanished from his mind. How could he admit how sorry he was that he'd yelled at her, that he hurt her? The guilt of it made his insides ache. Nothing sounded right.

"Rubes?"

She looked at him, bottle green eyes impossible to read. His throat tightened. He refused to look away.

All embellishments vanished until there was nothing left but the apology. "I am so sorry," he said, voice raw. Before she could respond, words started tumbling out in a rush, "What I said the other night, I didn't mean... I never should've said what I said, and I know that I should've told you about what happened in the chamber, and it wasn't fair that I—"

"Jack." His name in her mouth made everything stop. "You were right."

He blinked. "What?"

"You were right," she repeated, as if that explained everything.

Feeling like he missed something, Jack asked carefully, "About what?"

"You shouldn't have said what you did," she shrugged, looking back at the sea of clouds, "but you were also right in what you said."

He wasn't sure what kind of reverse psychology she was pulling, but Jack felt completely at a loss. He waited silently, hoping she would explain.

"I do keep a lot of secrets," Red confessed with a deep breath that clouded before her. It was like she was wrenching off armor, something painful and heavy that weighed her down, but removing it left her vulnerable. Jack could see the struggle she was undergoing behind her eyes. He didn't want her to feel like it was a risk with him, to shrug off the secrets, to leave herself unprotected. But he understood it was hard.

I keep secrets, too, he thought to himself. *I just ignore them until I run headlong into them.*

Red looked at him as if he'd spoken aloud, and for a moment he wondered if perhaps he had.

But she looked away again, bracing herself for a jump. "I never told you how my parents died."

"I figured it was one of the forbidden questions."

179

She huffed something close to a laugh. There was a raw light behind her eyes, familiar and different all at once, and he suddenly felt as if he knew what would come next. Carefully, Jack put his arm around her shoulder as she crumbled. Her eyes squeezed tight, head bowed, tears spilling. Sometimes the weight of what's remained unsaid can crush you before it falls from your grip. He held her tighter.

"It's the stars, isn't it?" Jack whispered gently. "The story wasn't theirs, it was yours."

Pinching the bridge of her nose as if to stem the tears, she dipped her chin.

"You don't have to tell me."

Red raised her head like she'd emerged from drowning, eyes bright, rose blotches on her nose. The worst of it was over, the terror before the plunge. "It was a bomb," she said, simple and heavy all at once. "It was my fault. It was an accident, but it was my fault."

Wind picked up, dashing his hair aside. The clouds were stirred up like foamed cream. Red closed her eyes to it and let out a sigh that released tension all down her spine. There were no more tears. She settled against him, his arm still around her, and it felt right.

"Shall I tell you a secret, now?" Jack asked softly, almost wishing she wouldn't hear him, but she did all the same. His throat swelled. Red looked up at him.

"I didn't always hate them, you know," he began slowly, easing it out. "When the belowlanders first convinced us to join them, I was all for it. Their leader was happy as a dog, brave and daring, took us in under his wing. I wanted to impress him. I wanted to believe I could

180

trust him. I guess that's the soft spot for orphans, eh? We're so hungry for a father that we go blind."

Suddenly he could see it clear as day: Bleddyn laughing over another day's adventures, slapping Harry on the back, howling at the disapproving look Cat shot him. There was Jill sitting with legs crossed, shaking her head in amusement. He remembered that was the first time they'd considered the possibility of staying. They thought they'd found something home didn't provide. But it was a dream, nothing more.

"What happened?" Red asked.

The memory fell away.

"When we asked for help getting Jill back, Bleddyn was the first to leave," Jack swallowed the bitter taste in his mouth. "I went to confront him. The other belowlanders had gone ahead, Harry was behind me. There was this split moment where we were alone on the wall, and I—" He passed a hand over his face. "I don't know what happened. I don't know if he slipped or tripped or…"

And then her hand was in his, fingers entwined securely.

He took a shaky breath. "They blame me for his death, especially Cat. They think I pushed him."

"Why don't you explain otherwise?"

"Because they wouldn't believe it was an accident," Jack said softly. "And I need to believe it was an accident."

She squeezed his hand, and he knew she understood. Taking her lead, Jack released a tense breath into the wind, and with it he released Bleddyn and his laughing promises, and the fall that would no longer haunt him. It wasn't that he felt lighter afterwards. But breathing came easier, as if a barnacle had been scrapped from his ribs.

"We're a little messed up, aren't we?" he spoke with a huff.

"I've met worse," she responded.

"I know. I almost feel bad for Alice—you know, since she's supposed to be the crazy one."

"Wendy's been a kid for fifty years."

"Fifty? You think that's how old she is?"

"Just a guess."

"But then there's Kai, if you really want to talk about secrets. The guy is either a tightlipped enigma or has very few words to spare."

"How much do we really know him?"

"Shrouded in mystery, that one."

She laughed, unable to keep it up any longer without cracking. Warmth filled his chest. There were those eyes again, those eyes that made his stomach twist in knots and his breath catch in his throat. For a moment he could forget about everything beyond this beach in this moment, and it was just the two of them feeling a little more normal and something close to free.

Chapter Eighteen

Hush, Little Baby, Don't Say a Word

Alice couldn't sleep. Something kept her awake, some patient pest in the back of her mind that told her to wait. The lights were out, and her friends' gentle breathing filled the room. But the sky was grey, a refusal to blacken, like even the night knew now was not the time for sleep.

The pocket watch ticked against her chest pleasantly. Her thumb stroked its silver cap. She hadn't understood everything Liesel showed her when she'd pried open the watch, and frankly neither did Liesel. Gears spun with indiscernible purpose. There were small switches that didn't belong, and nicks where things could slide into place differently. It was a puzzle, spinning in an unknown dance to a song only it could produce. Alice drank it all in, even if she didn't know why yet. It was important. She felt it in her bones.

When a figure appeared over her, she wasn't surprised. It was as if this was the thing she'd waited for.

"*Pst.*"

Alice looked up at the figure, focusing on the features that caught the faint light. "Liesel?"

"Yes, now hurry up and put on your shoes before I regret this."

Doing as she was told, Alice watched Liesel warily as she went to wake Wendy who only needed a touch and a look to wake up and understand the need for silence. It was strange. None of this surprised her but unfolded in a story she felt she'd read before. Even as they passed the others without waking them, she did not feel the need to question it, because it all felt right and sensible. How very curious.

Liesel hustled the two outside, a silhouette in the dim light. Clouds blanketed overhead. The sky was holding its breath for this, waiting for the climax. Strapped to a boxy wagon with strong wheel were the three Shetland ponies ready to go. Liesel took a leather strap in one hand and a crook in the other, and without a word of explanation, she slapped the ponies' rumps to get them going and started up the hill away from the village. Wendy gave Alice a confused glance. She merely shrugged, the only answer she had, and together they followed the woman over the hills between the forest and mountains.

The hills swelled and sank before them until the village lights disappeared behind them. Rock formations obscured the terrain. Alice wondered if they'd fallen from the mountain, tossed aside like apple cores and orange peels. At least they provided enough cover for Kai. She wondered if anyone else noticed that he was following them. It all made perfect sense, really.

"Where are you taking us?" Wendy voiced at last as the shadow of the mountains grew larger beside them.

"I'm due to pick up wool," Liesel explained, nudging the ponies along. "With the cold coming, threads will be in high demand."

"And you decided to make the trip at midnight?"

"Aye, sometimes it's the best time to get things done."

They had entered a dip in the mountains where the cliffs towered endlessly above them, surrounding all sides but behind. Here, Alice felt small enough to fit through a keyhole.

"Why bring us?" Wendy asked, oblivious to the most pressing of curiosities. But maybe Alice was the only one who heard it: the clicking, the grinding, the hum deep in the mountains. It reminded her of the old giant's words of haunted stone. But these weren't ghosts.

"I've been thinking about what you said yesterday," Liesel confessed, leading the ponies to a small spring to drink, "about feuds and giants."

The sound was louder now. Wendy turned to Alice, a sign she heard it too. But Alice was focused on something else. The mountains were moving. Something inside her gut waited patiently to see what would come out of them.

"It reminded me of my own suspicions," Liesel continued. "Perhaps they're not all as bad as we've been taught to think."

Loose stone skittered down the cliff face. Tremors traveled up her shins. The mystery of the mountains revealed itself so naturally to Alice that she felt she'd known it all along.

"It's a machine," she whispered in awe.

A massive hand grabbed the edge of the dark opening.

Liesel craned her neck expectantly. "It's alright. They're friends; you can trust them."

Following the hand came the rest of the giant, a hesitant frown on his face. Faint light shone off deep brown skin and an oil black beard. He sat on the ground before them as if to prove he meant them no harm, the mountain opening at his back.

Stepping forward, Liesel introduced, "This is Wendy and Alice." To them, she said, "This is Shep."

"The hermit?" Wendy asked, piecing things together from their time with Ms. Marie.

"Aye," Liesel nodded, amused, "the mute hermit. I call him Shep."

Alice very much doubted he was a mute, but she didn't argue. She just hoped Kai was hiding himself well.

*****

Toog clutched the edge of the cliff and watched the scene below with toiling rage in his gut. Two days of crossing the mountains, battling its mysteries, undergoing its dangers, losing a fellow giant each day in crossing: it all led him here to the most disturbing scene he had ever before witnessed. Not only was there a giant living in the mountains—a mere ghost story until now—but this giant, this *traitor*, was interacting with belowlanders without hatred or weapon on hand. The impossibility of it made his bones chill.

Beside him, Gath scrutinized the sight as if questioning the vision in his remaining eye.

"Is that...?"

Toog grunted without pealing his eyes from the scene.

"But it can't... It doesn't make sense."

186

"Are you going to stop bumbling like a cracked crow, or should I relieve you of your tongue as well as your eye?"

Gath scowled, but did not respond.

From behind, a giantess joined them, dark skin dusted grey from journeying the mountains. "Do you recognize him?"

"He was banished years ago," Toog growled, recalling the treacherous shepherd who spent days under interrogation and torture from the late Galigantus after his conspiracy was discovered. The giant confessed to sparing and even saving over a dozen belowlanders over his life. He was in his youth then, but now he was grown. "He's supposed to be dead."

"What in iron, stone, and clay..." Gath mumbled, daring to peak further over the edge.

Silently, they watched as the traitor removed the sheepskins from his belt and carefully piled them in the belowlanders' cart. Toog felt his blood boil. Not only was this traitor engaging with belowlanders, but he was trading with them. It was unnatural, deceitful, cowardly. If he was not so strongly bound by the orders of his king, Toog would have leapt from this ledge and torn the traitor limb from limb until he was nothing but an insignificant stain on this barbaric rock. But his orders stayed him and controlled his festering rage.

"Can we use the rat to our advantage?" Toog questioned the giantess in a low rumble.

"Already done," she replied. "A simple game of cat and mouse. Gave him enough incentive to send the message tonight."

"They're leaving," Gath voiced.

Toog looked over the ledge again as the belowlanders left the hidden alcove with cart filled. The giant below waited until they were long gone before standing.

Gath spoke again, a breath in the wind, "What do we do?"

The mountains moaned and ground and moved to close behind the traitor as he disappeared into an unseen path. Stomach clenched, Toog settled his decision.

"See that the rat gets through," he told the giantess as he pulled away from the ledge. With a grunt, he indicated that Gath should follow as he picked his way down into the ravine and entered the passage through the mountains. The traitor was far ahead in the darkness. Toog stalked him with bloodthirst in his mouth.

*****

Jack jerked awake with the memory of blistered hands and Nozrok's voice lingering beyond his nightmare. A full moon shone brightly through the window, silver light pooling over the floor. His heart settled as he realized where he was.

Red was curled in a ball beside him, far enough from him not to be questioned, yet close enough to feel her body heat. Determination seemed to keep her asleep. He felt the urge to brush the hair out of her face but refrained himself. The light made her eyelashes shine blue.

Taking a deep breath, Jack looked away.

Gold shadows flicked behind his eyelids. His skin felt clammy. The air seemed too still, suffocating.

As if afflicted with fever, he stood quietly to avoid waking the others and stepped outside.

The wind rustled his hair and the stars winked down at him. He thought about what Kai had told him that day, how he needed to figure things out, make a decision. But he felt completely lost. The obvious thing to do was to take the pocket-watch-express out of there and go face off this Master Puppeteer. Kai would finally be reunited with his fiancé—or, *almost* fiancé. Everyone would be happy. And he wanted to go. He wanted to finally find this devil who ultimately caused him so much pain, who forced him into this impossible situation. It was the right decision, he knew it.

Then there was Jill. A friend, a traitor, a prisoner, a victim: he didn't really know what she was. But down in the pit of his stomach, he could not let go of the Jill he knew. No matter how much gold coursed through her veins, no matter how twisted her mind might have become after a year of torture, she was still his Jill. His oldest friend. His family. He couldn't just abandon her, not again. Nothing made his stomach turn more than the thought of leaving her again.

Groaning in frustration, Jack ran his fingers agitatedly through his hair and looked up at the sky. He wondered if his parents were watching him from up there. Did heaven have windows? Could they see everything he had done, everything he had become? Did they know what he had to do? He longed for them to tell him what to do. He didn't want to make this choice.

Softly, he closed his eyes and whispered, "What do I do?"

Pain split through his skull as something crashed into the back of his head, throwing him to the ground. Stars were everywhere now, his vision swimming. The thing was on top of him, holding him down, the cold steel of a blade flat against his throat. Ragged breaths huffed on his face. Blinking away the dizziness, Jack focused on the misshapen face of his attacker. He recognized the man instantly.

"Let me go!" Jack croaked, gut clenching.

Crooked pressed the knife harder beside his Adam's apple. "Silence, or I'll cut your throat out."

"What do you want?" He flinched as the blade bit his flesh.

"Listen, Giant Slayer," Crooked hissed between jumbled teeth. "The giants demand you return their crown and harp to them at the Well within five days."

"You dirty backstabbing traitor," Jack growled. "You're working for *them*?"

That earned him another sharp nick. Blood tickled over his neck.

"Five days to reach the Well with the crown and harp," Crooked sneered, eyes ablaze. "In exchange, they'll give you the antidote for the gold and release girl."

He nearly choked. "Jill?"

"They'll kill her if you fail. Come alone."

Crooked stood with the knife out before him should Jack made any sudden moves. But his limbs had numbed and his mind was racing, trying to make sense of it all.

"You have five days."

The man's foot smashed into his stomach, knocking the breath out of him. Ringing deafened his ears. Clutching his abdomen, Jack gasped for air that stubbornly refused to come. By the time he recovered, Crooked had long disappeared into the swampy shadows of streetlamps and cobblestone.

Chapter Nineteen

Ladybird, Ladybird, Fly Away Home

The belowlander called him Shep, the mute hermit, the giant who saved her life. Their connection had grown over three years, a silent friendship in their nook of the mountain. He would bring her wool. She would show him how to make metal come alive. Perhaps one day he would tell her his name when it was not a danger to be spoken by humans.

Tonight, the carefully built relationship had reached a new step: She brought others to meet him. It was progress that sent hope coursing through his veins, and his head swam with the peaceful future that was sure to follow when he entered the heart of the mountain.

This was the greatest secret in the country.

Warm light swallowed him as he stepped from the tunnels and entered the hollowed peak alive with activity and machinery even giants struggled to understand. Gears stretched up the rock walls like algae, in constant motion. He often wondered if this was the very center of it, the battery for the whole moving mountain range. It was also his home.

Exiled giants flooded the broad expanse like a market square. Lamps stood erect where they had tapped into the strange power in the mountain's ore. Craftsmen labored, some returning from work across the range, others bartering their talents for goods. Shepherds came here to sheer their flock, but most would make rounds through the tunnels. Farmers were devising efficient ways to produce food from boxed gardens. Families filtered through at least once a day, as this was the main hub of society for the nocturnal outlaws.

They were a community bound together with a common dream.

"Balthaz!"

He turned at the sound of his name, offering a smile. There was comfort in hearing his true name. "Ajaal."

Ajaal was younger and taller than him, copper skinned with curly black hair and a short beard bound with brass rings. His eyes were still bright despite hardships he'd gone through—hardships most everyone here had suffered.

Good, Balthaz thought to himself, *we need those with bright eyes to remind the rest of us to hope.*

Clasping his forearm in greeting, Ajaal asked, "You met with the belowlander?"

"Aye," Balthaz responded, finding difficulty in containing his excitement. "She brought friends with her this time: two women."

"Were they afraid?"

"I could not smell it."

Ajaal's smile broadened in enthusiasm. "This is good, isn't it? She's beginning to trust you enough to bring others to meet you."

"Or it is them who she trusts to bring," Balthaz added. "Either way, it's progress."

"Have you spoken to her yet?"

He shook his head. "It's safer for the both of us. If my name were to slip into the wind and catch Nozrok's ear, everything we've built will be wasted."

"At least you're making headway with the belowlanders."

"One belowlander."

"One can change everything."

Eyes slightly narrowed, Balthaz wondered at that. Those were his words, his ideals. It was what he'd convinced himself long ago when he first began to meet with Liesel, what he encouraged the other giants to hold onto when spirits swung low in their hidden haven.

Sometimes it could only take one human and one giant to form the foundations of peace.

Perhaps it was true. He hoped it was.

It was the other side of the mountains that worried him. Nozrok and his followers would never soften their stone hearts to the idea of peace with the belowlanders. It was too barbaric a prospect for them. Hatred ran deep in their bones. Balthaz was afraid they would have to bathe in blood to obtain peace before this was over. If he could control it, he would never let it come to that. But if it came, as he dreadfully suspected, every giant in these mountains must all be willing to fight for it.

His spine pinched at the nape of his neck. Turning, he searched for the eyes he sensed, but there was no stranger in this expanse. Agitation crept down between his shoulder blades.

"Have there been new exiles found?" he asked.

Ajaal shook his head. "There hasn't been word of any sent, so no search parties have gone out. Why? Did you see something?"

No, he hadn't seen anything. But he was increasingly becoming aware of an odor creeping into his sinuses he had not smelled in years. Not fear. But close.

A frown began to pull Ajaal's face in. "Balthaz?"

Unsettled, he said carefully, "We should inspect the mountains. I'll lead a group out at dawn; will you come?"

Ajaal nodded without second thoughts.

"Rest, then." Balthaz patted his shoulder, leaving the young giant as he noticed the child barreling towards him from across the expanse. Worry seemed to vanish instantly.

She collided into him with a joyful squeal. "Baba!"

Balthaz picked her up easily, and she threw her arms around his neck. He laughed at her excitement. "Soon, my diamond, you will be too big for me to carry."

Giggling, she twisted her black braids through her fingers. Scars marred her cheeks and under her ears, evidence of the Children's Plague that their kind suffered from. She was one of the lucky few who survived without the aid of the golden eggs. He called her the strongest gemstone he knew, the one that shone brightest after enduring such terrible pressure. Squeezing her tight, Balthaz kissed her cheek.

"Are you leaving again, Baba?" she questioned with a tone she'd learned from her mother.

"Not until dawn, Almasi."

She dropped down and took her small hand in his, leading him through the bustle of nocturnal giants where her mother waited for them expectantly.

He had no time to look behind where shadows lurked in shifting tunnels.

Toog still could not believe what his eyes perceived.

Giants in the mountains.

And this giant, this traitor whom they've followed silently through grinding mountain passages, he was pulled away by his child to his wife—a giantess Toog did not recognize. The giant kissed her, earning a slap, a smile. The child did not act ashamed or surprised. It was too casual and yet so revolting. How could such a treacherous cuckoo end up in such content? His stomach twisted into a knot, unsettled.

"To think that all this time…" Gath marveled beside him, keeping his voice under his breath. "How could so many giants possibly stay here completely undetected?"

"Perhaps not so undetected," Toog grumbled. "Perhaps these vermin are in league with the belowlanders."

"That's impossible."

"As impossible as giants living in the mountains?"

"The belowlanders could never side with a giant, not as a whole anyway. It's not some myth come to life—it's completely impossible."

His voice was wearing on Toog's nerves. Nails dug into the rock. He wondered if a few damaged gears would cause the entire mountain to crumble over them.

Gath continued, wondering aloud, "Maybe they're a rebellion biding their time until their numbers grow just enough to overthrow the King."

Toog frowned. "That's the first idea you've had without sounding entirely brain damaged."

"What's more," he ignored the comment, "we're helping them do it."

The words set off a ripple in his mind. With every criminal they exiled, the number of hidden rebels increased. An uprising was imminent. Who knew how many more giants waited in the mountains beyond the tunnels that branched from this hive? They were supplying the enemy and they'd been none the wiser for it.

Backing away into the tunnel's shadows as it again began to move, Toog growled, "Come. We must inform the King."

Chapter Twenty

Down Came a

Blackbird

Jack had five days. Five days to decide if he would take the deal the giants offered, an opportunity he detested yet knew he would seize. He'd bring them the harp and crown, if he could find where they were even kept. They would release Jill and the antidote to the poisoned gold in his blood. Somewhere, he sensed a trap. Nozrok could very well be trying to deceive him. Or perhaps the old fool was lying about the offer to begin with.

But it could be true. Despite the risks, the potential benefit was too great. That was enough for him.

He had five days.

If this was going to work, he had to be cleverer than the giants he'd face.

It was hardly dawn when Jack concluded that he had to act swiftly, venturing into town with the hood drawn up over his head. The sky was leaking. Mud sloshed over the cobblestones. Those lamps which had swallowed Crooked now glowed hazy in the grey morning as some early risers wandered the streets. He passed tall apartments of different materials, all bland in comparison to Liesel's house. The sound of machinery pricked his ears. He couldn't escape that inevitable *click*. It reminded him of the prison tower.

Jack found the stables easily. Musty heat enveloped him as soon as he entered. Mountain goats turned their enormous heads his way, staring at him with slit eyes. On the chair before him, Brann jerked awake. He suddenly realized he hadn't thought this through.

"Giant Slayer?" Brann asked groggily, eyes narrowed as he processed the scene.

Jack wanted to convince him that this was all a dream.

"What are you doing here?"

"I'm, uh," he thumped his fists against his thighs, "investigating."

"*Investigating?*" Brann's forehead scrunched up.

Jack tightened his lips and nodded with as much casual enthusiasm as he could muster. "Yep."

"What for?"

"Well, you see," he fumbled, realizing it was too early in the morning to make up any sensible lies quickly, "I have a plan."

"For the Fiddler?"

"Yes!" He leapt at the opportunity. "I have a plan for the Fiddler, and I need a ram to do it. But, see, I wanted to assure myself that we have the right resources for my plan before I propose it to the Fiddler. And that is why I am here. Investigating."

Brann nodded, though he seemed to struggle making sense of Jack's words. "So, that means you're going to join us?"

His stomach clenched. With an absent shrug, he said, "I have a plan."

The prospect of him joining the belowlanders' cause seemed to thrill Brann, for he instantly perked up, fumbling out of his chair. "What all do you need to know?"

Jack blinked, hesitated. "I mean, what all can you tell me?"

A lightbulb went off above the man's head. Excitedly, Brann showed him around the stables, introducing him to the best of the rams, showing him the tack and double-saddles, explaining how the animals knew by instinct how to cross the mountains. The double-saddle was designed as a failsafe in case something happened to another ram or they picked up strays.

When Jack asked if he would demonstrate how it worked, Brann said modestly, "Sure. Muffet can do it much better and faster than I can, but—"

"Muffet?"

"*Spider!*" he suddenly exclaimed. His face dropped like he was afraid the Ray of Sunshine would come barging in at any moment because he used the wrong name. When she didn't show, his shoulders relaxed. Calmly, he beckoned, "I'll show you."

Jack watched carefully as Brann saddled one of the mountain goats, paying special attention to where the supplies came from and what all was needed. He thought he could remember how it worked. He would have to do this himself later—he had no intentions of attempting to ride one of these beasts bareback across the mountains.

When Brann finished, Jack thanked him for the lesson. He helped put away the tack and saddle, then left the belowlander with a grin that dropped as soon as he stepped outside in the rain. Jack sighed. Now came the hard part.

He had to talk to the Fiddler.

"I'm glad to see you've come to logic and morality," the Fiddler said, pouring himself a glass of wine dark as blood. Jack's nose twitched involuntarily at the sight. Wasn't it a far too early to drink? It was hardly dawn. When the Fiddler offered him a glass, Jack declined. Alcohol never agreed with him.

"What is this valuable piece of information you're finally willing to disclose?" the Fiddler asked.

Glass met lips and the bloodlike liquid slid into his mouth. Maybe it was the man's nonchalant demeanor that made Jack's skin crawl, or the way his flat eyes analyzed him like still brown waters where sharks lurked beneath the surface. Either way, it set his alarms blaring with distrust.

Jack worked his jaw. "It's about something you've been after for decades."

The Fiddler swallowed, gaze narrowed in interest.

"The goose," he went on. "You haven't managed to get it yet."

"We've had difficulty making headway since the last setback," the Fiddler admitted.

Jack bit his tongue. Because Bleddyn's death, Harry and Jill's capture, and his own disappearance definitely classified as a *setback*.

He forced himself into complacency. "But that's because you've been focusing on the wrong endgame."

The Fiddler rubbed his chin with his good hand, the crippled one folded across his chest. "You have my attention, Giant Slayer."

None of the belowlanders knew the giants the way Jack did because their methods have always been militant. In the beginning, he only sought treasure and adventure. This landed him in many of the wrong situations at the right times, and before long he'd acquired ample information about how the giants worked and lived. Jill was curious, and Harry was indifferent, but Jack had been fascinated. The tables had turned quickly to horrified.

"As children, giants are prone to a plague that very few survive from," Jack disclosed slowly, watching the Fiddler intently. "The only cure is the golden goose eggs, which can heal most anything for giants. The eggs are lifesavers, but not entirely essential. It'd still cause a whopping kick to the knees if the eggs suddenly stopped rolling in. And there's only one gold-laying goose."

"Without the goose," the Fiddler pondered, "there would be no eggs, save for their stores."

"Without the eggs, more than half of the giant population would be wiped out."

"And with this intriguing information, what exactly is it that you are proposing?"

Jack hesitated, the weight of his unspoken words choking him. There was a lie somewhere in what he planned to say, but what would this man do with the truth he heard?

"Don't capture the goose," he spoke evenly. "Kill it."

The Fiddler didn't respond, his stare steadfast and unyielding.

Jack continued, "The harp, the crown; they mean nothing. They're just trophies that will be nothing but trinkets collecting dust in the end. But kill the goose and you'll bring the giants to the ground."

The wine glass was placed carefully on the metal and wood table. Scarred fingers traced its rim. "And you're willing to help us achieve this?"

Resisting the urge to grind his teeth, Jack nodded curtly. "I can."

Having downed the last of his wine, the Fiddler stood silently. Jack's fists pressed against his sides. Surely this was what the Fiddler had wanted to hear: that he would help them, that he could send a blow deep enough to forever damage the giant species. He could sense the interest despite the man's steadiness.

Hopefully the Fiddler was unaware that he held the giants' demise in his possession already. No bird could last long without her song. Jack had stolen that a long time ago.

The silence buzzed, and Jack began to wonder if the Fiddler was far cleverer than he had anticipated.

"Your assurance to aid our cause is encouraging," the Fiddler finally announced, turning to him. "I'm certain you will prove more than valuable to us."

Jack suppressed a snicker.

"As for this information, it is enlightening. But I have it in good faith that if you can so resolutely assure me that you can successfully get close enough to kill the goose, then you can just as successfully get close enough to capture it and bring it here."

His stomach tightened.

The Fiddler massaged his crippled hand, thoughts formulating some mute song in his mind. "You never know when such a rare animal could prove useful."

Useful. There was only one use for such a creature in the hands of the Fiddler. Golden eggs were weapons to humans exclusively. Jack didn't want to think about what the implications meant to have something so poisonous in this tyrant's possession. His distrust heightened. All Jack could do was shrug as if it was neither here nor there to him. But his imagination had taken root. How many belowlanders would drown in gold if they opposed the Fiddler's reign? A giant could heal its own kind with the eggs, at least. A belowlander would destroy it.

"You know," the Fiddler said, jerking Jack from his shadowy thoughts. "It's always fascinated me, this gold. How can it be so destructive for us yet have such healing properties for giants? It manipulates us, leaving its mark no matter how much is infused. Your eyes," he lifted an arm, "they're the obvious sign. Like a brand shared only by the victims of such torture. Silver Blood's are the same, as were those of my predecessor. But only the blood reveals how poisoned you are."

Jack gulped, discomfort increased.

"Silver Blood's is only just tainted—orange, as if gold and blood mixed but neither takes over the other." The Fiddler turned, a dagger of stone and bronze extended toward him. "Would you mind? I'm dreadfully curious."

His gut clenched in repulsion. For over a year, Jack had avoided seeing his blood. Every injury he met with a blind eye, never looking too close for fear of what he might find. What right did this crippled dictator have to ask such a thing? Those flat brown eyes regarded Jack as if he was some strange and monstrous specimen of the human race. Was this what Red felt like when anyone wanted to see the Wolf emerge? Were they both something unnaturally beyond human?

Jack shook himself. He was getting distracted. Gritting his teeth, he reminded himself that he couldn't afford confrontation right now.

Resisting the urge to flinch, Jack took the dagger and drew the blade across his palm. He grimaced, much to his irritation. The Fiddler didn't seem to notice. Squeezing his hand into a fist, blood dripped to form a small puddle on the table's surface.

Jack didn't want to look. Hopeless ignorance wanted to assure him that it wasn't so different than before. There was no gold, though he felt it weigh him down. There were no side effects, though the gold almost killed him before. There was nothing binding him to this country, though he'd felt its pull ever since he'd left the first time.

Inevitably, his resistance didn't matter. Jack saw the blood on his palm fall from his wrist to land on wood and metal. His heart sped. He felt like he was about to vomit.

Veins of gold swam through dark blood, swirling together like water and vinegar. They did not mix. He couldn't tell which substance had the upper hand.

The Fiddler's voice pounded like static against his ears. "Some say the giants can smell gold in the blood as they can smell fear. Some say they can track it."

Jack tried to steady his breathing. He couldn't tear his eyes away from his stained hand. *Snap out of it*, he thought harshly, pleading.

"Mere superstition, of course," the Fiddler continued smoothly. "But many go to great lengths to dispose of a threat even if only for superstition."

Jack frowned, pulling himself from the murky shock in his mind. "Are you threatening me?"

"Threaten?" The man raised one eyebrow as if the accusation offended him. "I am simply informing you that rumors are powerful things. The ones that hold even a drop of truth are the most dangerous."

So, the Fiddler meant to control him with blackmail. A rumor that could light like a wildfire and cause the belowlanders to swarm. But Jack was already living under the belowlanders' rage because of Bleddyn's death, and he was not afraid. The Fiddler had no power over him.

"You will meet me later to further discuss these plans, yes? Assemble a team; get you adequate supplies."

Jack nodded mutely.

"Good." The Fiddler opened his hand, a permission to leave.

After leaving the Townhall, Jack looked up at the sky in frustration. All that and he wasn't much closer to finding out where the harp and crown were. Except they were somewhere in that building. It was the only clue he had to go on.

"You're feeding biscuits to a bear if you think you can find the icebox down there."

Jack hit his head painfully against the countertop, nearly toppling over a stack of pans. Beside him, Liesel stood looking down at him. He was hoping he'd have another hour before anyone started waking up.

She cocked her head. "I take it you're not joining us for breakfast?"

Guilty, his ears grew hot.

She narrowed her eyes at his makeshift bundle in his lap, the supplies thrown into a knapsack, the napkin for provisions. "Hm."

"I wasn't meaning to steal anything," Jack hastened.

"No, of course you weren't. Just my food and whatever else you've got there."

A moment passed. The back of his neck itched, and his ears rang. But Liesel only stared at him undeterred before she took a thickly padded bag from a cupboard above and began to carefully pack it with provisions. The icebox was across the room, the latch hidden where tiny hands couldn't reach. Jack sat there dumbly until she spoke again.

"Should I expect another visit from the Fiddler today?"

He frowned. "Another?"

"Aye." She folded some bread rolls into a handkerchief to stow into the bag. "He comes around here every now and again since my husband died. He's convinced that I can take up my husband's work and old projects, weapons and black powder, theories he never got around to finishing. If you're doing what I think you are, then that'll probably mean another visit from our esteemed leader. I'm cut to the onions having to feign the clueless widow. But I'll keep it up as long as I have to."

Jack blinked, trying to make sense of the stream of words. "What does that mean?"

"It means the Fiddler wants a bomb," Liesel said over her shoulder while she found a container for the leftover *colcannon*. "And I refuse to cooperate."

His frown deepened. "Why are you telling me this?"

Liesel sighed, palms pressed against the countertop. Exhaustion clung to her shoulders. Jack wondered why she was helping him. If she knew what he was up to, would she let him go?

Slowly, Liesel lowered herself to his level and touched his face with a calloused hand. His breath hitched at the gesture. His mother used to hold his face like this, just by the neck, thumb stroking the spot just behind his ear. Liesel's hands were rougher, but the touch was familiar. His spine trembled.

Shining eyes pleaded with him. "I hope you know that not all of us agree with him."

Jack's throat tightened. He thought of how Liesel sent her son out to training three times a week, how soon the boy would be taught to destroy, and then little Blue would join his brother on the training grounds. He wondered how she felt about following the Fiddler's orders – did they get her husband killed? And there was Harry, and this bomb, and the grease stains on her shirtsleeves… She had the opportunity to aid the battle, yet she held herself back. Would explosives end the fighting or merely worsen the casualties?

208

She was still looking at him. He nodded to show that he understood, or at least he was beginning to.

Lips pursed, she dropped her hand to squeeze his shoulder. "Now, what is it you're after?"

*****

Something about the dawn sent the shadows in an uproar. They stretched long and thin, shrinking back from the blazing light even as the storm clouds threatened the horizon. Birds scattered to the clouds screaming warning. The earth rumbled in mass marching. It was enough to quake the trees, but the mountains remained oblivious.

Toog's message had come from a blackbird in the middle of the night. Response was swift, thriving off rage. Never was an attack less imminent.

The giants were moving.

They were heading for the mountains.

Chapter Twenty-One

The Cow Jumped Over the Moon

Morning had broken by the time Jack found himself in the Townhall once again, poised in the rafters, waiting for the Fiddler to finish his daily composition.

Music vibrated in sweet melancholy, strings singing imperfection. The Fiddler was half-deaf and crippled. His song betrayed a former talent, but at least he was still lost in some musical reverence that kept him from seeing Jack above.

Hands fumbled. The bow screeched across the violin strings. Jack held his breath as the Fiddler dropped his instrument in frustration. Silence rang in his ears. Finally, the Fiddler gently placed the violin in its velvet case and abandoned the room, locking the door behind him.

Jack released the breath he'd held, carefully lowering himself to the floor. It was a long drop, but he landed on his feet in a crouch. Figures. A perfect landing for once with no one around to see.

"You know, I will tell them you've gone," Liesel had warned him after explaining where the harp and crown was hidden. Her husband had designed the secret entrance in the Townhall, and Jack strongly suspected that she also had a hand in its construction.

"That's why I haven't told you where I'm headed," he'd responded. He tried not to think about his friends sleeping in the other room, about what they would do when they discovered him missing. But he had to do this alone. If they followed him… Well, hopefully this would all be over before they caught up.

In the Townhall, Jack found the latch hidden beside the fireplace, just where Liesel told him. The wall tugged open into a door, a closet with moneybags piled in the corner. It was a ruse. The real treasure lay underfoot.

"May the road rise up to meet you." Liesel had kissed his cheek in farewell, pressing the bag of food in his arms.

He'd squeezed her hands, trying to convince himself he was doing the right thing, trying to make her understand. *"I'm going to fix everything."*

"Ah, but darling, you don't have to."

Darkness swam before his eyes. Before he could change his mind, Jack lifted the sheepskin rug from the ground and opened the trapdoor to reveal a winding steel staircase descending to blackness. Liesel had said there was another exit down there, so he let the wall seal behind him and the trapdoor close above.

Warmth surrounded him, a musty aroma stinging his sinuses. A heavy noise, swinging, hit his eardrums. Liesel had explained the heavy chains that controlled the backdoor. It would lead to the stables where his supplies were stowed.

Jack removed the torch tied to his belt and lit it quickly, blinking in the sudden light. The basement was large, rectangular, walls lined with gold, silver, and jewels.

Hay sprinkled the floor. He suppressed the urge to stuff his pockets with coin. This wasn't a treasure hunt anymore. After everything, look at where the gold led him. He had to let his hatred overcome his longing. Taking a deep breath, Jack continued his search.

Chains ran across the ceiling in a pulley mechanism, attached to a small portcullis raised over a dark tunnel. A cool breeze filtered through. If he stuck his head inside, he could see the morning light at the end of it, greyed by the clouds. Hopefully there weren't any guards stationed on the other side.

He turned back to the room, torch raised. It didn't take long before he discovered Harry's satchel with the crown still inside, the bundle leaning against a smaller object covered by a blanket. Jack hadn't seen the harp since he'd stolen it. Despite himself, he was afraid to touch it even though he knew it wouldn't sing for him. The harp mourned the goose as it was likewise missed. Neither thrived without the other. Even so, Jack hated touching the harp's gilded soundbox and aching strings. It emitted a sorrow that washed him in guilt.

Quickly, Jack managed to strap the satchel securely to his back, the crown more cumbersome than heavy. At least the harp was small and would be easy to carry under his arm.

The noise changed from swinging to snorting, jammed in rhythm. His stomach tightened, blood chilled. Liesel didn't say anything about something alive being down here.

Slowly, Jack held his torch outstretched and narrowed his eyes. Bulking movement shifted in the shadows. Blasts of wakened breath sent gut churning fear deep inside him.

"Of all the blasted bloody things," Jack hissed, gooseflesh itching down his arms, "it had to be a cow."

Leaden horns curved into lethal points from its skull, a gold hoop gleaming through its nose. Knotted muscle splashed in onyx, powerful hooves sharp and heavy, drooping eyes shining in morning haze. The bull was half his height, but that did nothing to calm Jack's dread.

Fighting paralysis, his nerves urged for fight or flight. The waking bull was still making sense of its surroundings, fumbling to its feet. Silver coin scattered at its step. The bull's eyes zeroed in on him at last.

Jack's mind raced. He only had the crown. The tunnel gaped open behind him, easy to follow. Then there was the harp beside him, the bull, him, the bull…

The bull bellowed, shocking him into action. Jack threw the torch, snatched the harp, and ran. Hooves clambered against stone. Ducking into the tunnel, Jack yanked the chain on the wall free. He saw the bull charge, heard the clanking portcullis give, then all light flicked off as the abandoned torch sputtered out.

A crash jarred his very bones. He fell back on his butt, breathing doubled with his speeding heart. Beyond his feet came a snort, a frustrated moan, the rattle of horns against iron. Jack heaved a sigh of relief.

He hastened to his feet, fully aware that the noise could've easily alerted the Fiddler. Quick, he hustled out of the tunnel with the harp hugged close. He couldn't stop shaking. Maybe it was irrational, but cows like that always brought back bad memories. These moments made him want to run far away. But he never really knew where he wanted to run to.

Sunlight washed his skin as he exited the tunnel. More miniature cows stood lazily to one side of the small pasture while the back of the stables stood opposite. Cautious, Jack made his way inside. Rams' heads swiveled to regard him with squashed pupils. He greeted them with a distracted wave.

He found his supplies where he'd hidden them: the knapsack, Liesel's insulated bag, a crossbow, and a spiked staff. Selecting a mountain goat, Jack repeated everything Brann had shown him about saddling it, strapping the harp and bags on in a secure web across the saddle's second seat. Satisfied, Jack hopped on himself and made his escape.

It was safer to leave out the back, away from the hubbub of the village in the morning. He rode over the pasture, beyond the main gate and its guards, charging for the mountain pass with nothing but the road ahead on his mind. He was going to get Jill back. He was going to make everything alright.

Clouds rolled in overhead by the time Jack and his mountain goat entered the pass. Suddenly, the earth rumbled in terrific destruction and rock rained down from the peaks. Sheets of stone slid down into a black chasm. Rubble dusted the air grey. It was too late to turn back, and Jack had to hold on for dear life while his ram cantered on. The chaos couldn't be natural—there was no storm to provoke this. Something was wrong. But he couldn't control it. He could only press forward.

Chapter Twenty-Two

Lavenders Blue,

Dilly Dilly

No giant was immune to fear. They were trained most of their lives to suppress it, to extinguish it, even to cause it in the most excruciating of ways. But anyone who claimed such mastery over fear that they never felt it at all, they were either liars or fools. The Giant King would say that everyone had their breaking point. Balthaz knew fear existed even in its suppression.

He'd smelled it in the depths of the prison tower where giants were kept underground away from sunlight, surrounded by iron and stone, dripping in trembling chains, bathed in filth and decay. He'd smelled it by the bed of his sick daughter, the Children's Plague wracking her body with indescribable pain, fear moldering from his wife as she wetted Almasi's cracked lips, fear chewing his insides in his utter helplessness. He'd smelled it from refugees, cliff's edges, and skirmishes between giant and belowlander alike.

But Balthaz had never smelled fear like this. Cold, hollow, dead. It coated his throat like dust, weighed his heart like a stone.

Only that morning had he set out with ten giants down the shifting passages. When the thunder sounded behind them and the mountain screamed in pure agony, they had pressed against the walls afraid the tunnels would fall in. Rock rolled in. Metal moaned in the ore. It took too long for the mountains to settle, the ten giants waiting in the following silence until Balthaz started back from where they came.

Gears creaked, sluggish in rotating the tunnels. By the time they returned, the stench of fear overwhelmed his sinuses. Dust still blinded the expanse in grey, but the wreckage lay stark before them.

The mountain peak had collapsed. Bare sky stretched overhead, white light filtering into a tomb.

Others arrived from surrounding passages, joining in mute horror as the giants began to uncover the bodies. Ajaal found the first survivor. Balthaz found the second, a child too shocked to speak or cry. The third died soon after he was retrieved from the rubble. They were the only ones found alive.

Balthaz kept on, barely aware as scouts arrived with news of the invasion. Not a war, but a massacre. Vain hope pressed him to keep sifting through the debris, hope that he wouldn't find familiar faces among the bodies. It's what kept them all going, what made the fear thicken. But as more victims were uncovered, carried, lain side by side for later burial, everyone found someone to mourn for.

Faces swam together leaving Balthaz in a dull haze. He'd left his family that morning, kissed his wife and daughter goodbye, saw Almasi waving to him as he'd gone. Could they have escaped? Perhaps they went to visit another settlement, away from here, before the King's army rained destruction upon this place. But he found giants who'd been here when he left: shepherds, farmers, peddlers. He even uncovered, much to his distress, one of Almasi's playmates crushed by the fallen web of gears.

The wreckage was dense, the casualties endless. Sifting through the rubble, Balthaz froze when hair brushed his hand. Ajaal came to help uncover the giantess, unfamiliar, pebbles falling from her mouth. All color had been drowned in grey. Grimly, Ajaal carried her away, the brightness in his eyes dimming with each corpse they found.

Alone, Balthaz passed a hand over his face in exhaustion. His stomach ached. He stood, stretching out his spine, looking around. The two survivors were being tended to, the child asleep in the older giant's lap. Balthaz wondered if they knew each other before the collapse or if now this tragedy would bind them forever.

Someone shouted his name, a giantess with olive face streaked in dust. Breath rushed out of him. Balthaz stumbled forward, trying to process what he was seeing. The giantess stood before the uncovered forms of a mother curled around her child as if trying to shield her from the mountain falling over them. It was them. His wife's body was crushed around their daughter hugged close to her chest.

Terrible trembling seized him as Balthaz fell to his knees. It couldn't be true. Everything in him willed them to move, to wake up. He wanted his wife to slap him for kissing her, wanted Almasi to run into him in her full-force embrace. Hands shook as he reached for them. He brushed the hair out of his wife's face. Tears dropped on Almasi's cheek, leaving dark trails. He held them both, completely broken, sobs overtaking him though neither answered his cries.

Storm clouds rolled in overhead.

The mountain grieved.

Chapter Twenty-Three

There was a Crooked Man

Red woke when the windup mouse rattled off the shelf and the earth quaked under her palms. The rumbling stopped soon after she sat up. Every muscle ached. The full moon made the Wolf harder to contain and made rest difficult. Yet the rising sun and empty room proved she'd overslept.

Dressing quickly, she stepped outside where she found Wendy standing with Harry and the two little ones, all staring out at the mountains. The road filled with people likewise looking.

Red frowned. "What is it?"

Wendy turned her head in concern, pointing. "There's smoke, there. Something must have caused the earthquake. An eruption?"

"Maybe it's the giants," one of the boys said in awe.

"The giants?" Harry raised an eyebrow. "What makes you say that, Tom?"

"Maybe they climbed the mountains," Tom explained.

"Or broke them," Blue offered.

Red crossed her arms, trying to see the damage in the distance. "Can that happen?"

Harry shook his head. "No, the giants are far too cautious to try and breach the mountains. Any who try to cross them disappear, killed. It's probably just some eruption, like she said, or a bad rock slide. They happen now and again, though none this bad."

"Do you think the pass is intact?" Wendy wondered aloud.

His brow furrowed. "I hadn't thought of that. I should probably make sure someone's sent out to check on it."

"I'll do it!" Tom exclaimed enthusiastically, followed by Blue.

"Maybe next time," Harry said, ruffling Tom's brown locks. "Alright, lads?"

Blue pouted, but Tom followed Harry back into the house with a resigned look on his face. Wendy was still staring at the mountains, frowning.

Red stood beside her. "What's wrong?"

"Nothing," she replied, "it's just, I don't know. Something about it doesn't sit right."

The smoke billowed from the range, rising into the grey clouds above like dust on the wind. Red had never seen a volcanic eruption before. She still wasn't sure that was what she was seeing now. There was no ash, no lava, and the earthquake lasted all of a few seconds.

She sighed, tucking her jacket tightly around her. "Where's Jack?"

Wendy shrugged. "He may be upstairs with the others. I haven't seen Liesel either, though the boys mentioned she'd gone out to fetch a few things."

With a nod and a final look out at the mountains, Red turned back inside. Wendy remained on the porch alone.

The stairs led to a spacious workshop, gears silent and pullies still, but thread ran overhead in an intricate web. Alice stood drawing on a bare wall, arms white with chalk. Kai sat on the floor watching designs unfold with lists and lines bridging names together. Red frowned at the chart. On one side was stacked enemy names across from a list of allies. She didn't recognize some of the names: *Häxan* and *The Tainted* under enemies, *robbers* and *People of Earth* under allies. Between the lists floated two titles with question marks like uncertain entities: *giants* and *Frost*. Above was a rough sketch of an open watch, arrows pointing to gears, question marks gracing the ends, worlds scrawled around in a circle: *Wonderland, Neverland, Enchanted Forest, Giant Country, Realm of the Snow Queen*. Now Alice was working on a different chart, a marked line. She was frantic, beaming.

"There are patterns; do you see the patterns?" Alice asked over her shoulder. She'd drawn a long line ticked with years and names. A timeline.

Kai narrowed his eyes. "Wendy was first targeted, then Red, then Jack, me, you… It's like where the watch has taken us."

"Exactly!" Alice jammed her chalk beside each name. "Neverland, Forest, here, and the Snow Queen's Realm is due next."

"What about Wonderland?"

"We didn't use the watch to get there." She pointed to the biggest name on the wall. "That was all Anne Christiansen."

Kai scratched his jaw. "But didn't you go to Wonderland before, when you were ten? That would mean you were targeted just before Fang started hunting Red."

"Well, I never said the patterns were perfect," Alice huffed. "Some pieces are just harder to fit."

"Maybe it's less to do with a pattern and more to do with who presses the button on the pocket watch," Red spoke up still struggling to make sense of all the chalk scribbles. "What is all this anyway?"

Alice wrote a quick note about the button. She barely turned her head. "If we figure out the key to the Snow Queen's plan up to now, then maybe we can figure out how to stop it."

"And the key is?"

"*Why us?*"

Red sighed. She wasn't sure how important all this was. It seemed like chasing rabbit trails to her, pointless. But Alice was fixated on it, that much was clear by the marks all over the wall. She wondered how much Kai followed along with it. Maybe he was ready to listen to anything that would mean saving Gerda.

"Do either of you know a ginger haired boy?" Alice asked suddenly, turning now to face them. Shadows crept under her eyes. "Freckled, tall, sharp features. I don't think he spoke English."

Kai shrugged. "No one you haven't met already."

"Me neither; why?" Red frowned.

Alice pushed her hair out of her face. "Back in the Forest, Kezia accidentally showed me two faces before she started on about the battle with Carabosse: Lupa, who helped me figure out who the Master is, and a ginger haired boy. Maybe he knows something."

"Or maybe he's just another face," Red offered. "Maybe he's not important."

"Everyone's important. Trouble is trying to figure out why."

Crossing her arms, Red scrutinized the lists. "Why do you have the giants up there? Jack told you they wouldn't associate with a foreigner."

"I have reason to doubt that."

"Because you think you know more about giants?"

"Because I think giants know more about giants. And Jack is biased."

"And you aren't?"

"I'm terribly biased," Alice admitted, "but also curious. I don't believe we know everything, which is why I'm still asking questions."

Red rolled her eyes. She was growing tired of this; the path forward was clear enough now. They knew who was hunting them, who her forces were, where she was. They knew what they had to do: stop the Snow Queen, rescue Gerda. But Alice wasn't satisfied with that. There were always more questions, more puzzles. One day she would have to learn that sometimes there were no answers, and life was exhausting looking for answers she could never find.

"Have you seen Jack?" Red asked, returning to the reason she came up here in the first place.

Kai craned his neck around to look at her. "I thought he was with you."

"I just woke up. Wendy hasn't seen him either."

"Did you check with Harry?"

"He's downstairs with the boys."

Footsteps pounded rapid-fire against the stairs, and Wendy burst into the workshop out of breath and frantic. "Liesel just got back," she exclaimed. "She says Jack's gone."

Red's stomach cinched. As Kai got to his feet, Red slipped past Wendy and flew down the stairs and outside where Liesel stood by the door. She heard the others follow close behind.

"What do you mean Jack's gone?" she asked.

"He left this morning," Liesel responded. Dark blonde strands fell over her face, brow knit with concern. Her gaze kept straying to the mountains where the smoke was thinning now. "He wouldn't say where he went."

"Why didn't you tell us sooner?" Red's fists clenched at her sides, itching, anxious.

Liesel raised her filled basket. "I figured you'd mean to follow, so I went to fetch provisions when the ground started shaking, and I hurried back here."

Before Red could push for more details, Kai shouldered past her and set off purposefully across the road. A lingering form on the other side started hastening away. In an instant, Kai charged and slammed the man against a lamppost, a shower of droplets falling from the impact. Red blinked, stunned as she recognized the twisted old man from their first day in the village. She jogged over to Kai as he pinned Crooked firmly to the iron pole. A cat fell from his cloak with a yowl.

"What did you do, old man?" Kai hissed, so close to the man's beaky nose he could've bitten in off.

Crooked stretched lined lips over jumbled teeth in a grin. "I don't know what you mean."

"You know what I mean. You think I haven't seen you out here watching the house all morning?" Kai clutched the man's collar with both fists. "What did you do with Jack?"

"What's going on here?"

Harry's sudden interjection was trying Red's patience. She saw Crooked's twitchy eyes, that smug grin relishing in holding knowledge he wouldn't share. Just before Harry could catch up to them, she grabbed the awful cat by its scruff and held it out at arm's length to avoid raving claws. Crooked cried like a crow. Kai held him tighter.

Behind her, Alice and Wendy approached with Liesel who held her to boys close to her sides. Harry kept his distance, taking in the scene. The cat wailed, struggled, but Red refused to release it. She glared at Crooked and let the threat sink in.

"They took my cat," the man sputtered. "Said they'd kill her if I didn't give him the message."

"What message?" Kai pressed.

"Who are *they*?" Alice added, speaking up behind.

The cat hung limply now, tail twitching, growling from the depths of its chest. Red didn't move an inch.

Crooked licked his lips. "A giant, it was a giant."

"That's impossible," Harry protested sharply. "No giant would dare cross—"

"*Håll truten!*" Kai hushed, agitated. Icy eyes bore into the old man. "The message?"

His Adam's apple bobbed, mismatched eyes still trained on his feral cat. Without batting an eye, Red drew a knife and held it aloft towards the creature. The cat hissed.

"Five days," Crooked spurt. "Five days to reach the Well with the harp and crown—"

"You bloody traitor," Harry growled, jaw clenched.

Kai cut him short, "What else?"

"In exchange, they'll give him the antidote for the gold and they'll release the girl. If he doesn't show, they'll kill her." Crooked finished his recitation with a cruel sneer. "It seems the Giant Slayer can be bought."

Red was just about to gut the blasted cat when Alice spoke up, "How long ago did you give Jack the message?"

"What does it matter?" Red shot.

"When did you tell him?" Alice pressed, ignoring her.

"Midnight last night," Crooked shrieked when Kai gave him an enticing shove.

"Including today," Wendy caught on, "he still has the five days to reach this… Well."

"That gives us four to catch up," Kai deducted before releasing the old man. "*Sticka!*"

Crooked stumbled, gasped, then was thrown into the ally as Harry crushed him against the wall. In her surprise, the cat was able to twist out of Red's grasp and scamper away.

"How did they get to you?" Harry demanded, violent in comparison to Kai. "How did they get here?"

Crooked shook his head, sniveling. "I don't know."

"You expect me to believe you?"

"I told you everything I know."

"HOW DID THEY GET HERE?!"

"*Harry!*" Liesel's sharp voice visibly cut through him like a knife. She stood in front of her boys, throwing Harry a warning glare. With a scowl, he let Crooked go. The man shuffled away after his cat in the shadows.

Red's face grew hot. "What are you doing? Why'd you let him get away?"

Liesel eyed the small crowd forming across the way watching them from a distance. "He's only a messenger," she insisted coolly.

Harry shook his head in frustration. "*Blasted bloody messenger.*"

Clenching her fists, Red wanted to hit something— preferably Jack. What was that idiot thinking? After everything that happened yesterday, everything they talked about, he still left without them. He was probably trying to keep anyone else from getting hurt. It was something she would've done. The fool.

"How did…" Harry was so furious he had trouble speaking. "How was a giant able to surpass the mountains? They've been bloody terrified of them for eons."

Kai and Alice exchanged a look. Red's anger dulled with confusion. Did they know something they hadn't bothered to share with her? What with their chalk lists and their questions, did they know something about the giants? About Jack?

"What about the harp and crown?" Wendy spoke up, looking between Harry's fluster and Liesel's calm. "If the giants demand an exchange, then what about Jack's end of the bargain?"

Harry shook his head. "That daft ox must've gone empty handed. He couldn't have found where they're hidden. Maybe he's trying a bluff or…"

Liesel pursed her lips, looking away guiltily.

Harry's face blanched. "You didn't."

"I didn't know he was going to take them straight into Nozrok's manky hands," she argued.

His hands flew to his head. "Well, what did you think he was going to do?"

"Not this, I can assure you." She crossed her arms, holding her ground, clearly still aware that they were out in the open and causing a scene. "Quit acting as mad as a box of frogs. It's not like I sent him gallivanting into a bear trap."

"No, but if he went after the harp and crown, he's just as likely to be dead or dying as he is on his way to the Well. And even then, who's to say the earthquake didn't make the passage cave in on him?"

"What are you blathering on about?"

"It's a trap, Liesel," Harry exclaimed. "The crypt is guarded now since you've built it, and I know how Jack feels about bulls."

Red's stomach tightened. Jack's parents had been killed by a cattle stampede. If she ever encountered the thing that killed her parents, she wasn't sure how she would react. She'd probably freeze. It wouldn't end well to freeze in the face of an armed bomb, or a raging bull.

228

Harry turned on his heel to take off into the village, but Kai caught his arm and held him back. "I don't believe it," Kai rumbled. "Jack's not dead."

"How would you know?"

Eyes darkened. "I know."

Tension stretched between them in their locked glares. Red felt like she was on the verge of plunging into an empty void. But the longer they waited, the further away Jack could be traveling. Or the longer he lay bleeding out in a crypt.

"We have to check," Harry said at last, low and decisive.

"And if we find nothing?" Kai questioned, a dangerous growl in the back of his voice.

"Then I'll take the lot of you to the Well myself."

"You'd best crack on, then," Liesel huffed, "before the storm hits."

Red followed her gaze. Billowing grey clouds covered the mountains, rolling towards them in a great mass. Light flashed inside. If Jack was out there, they'd never catch up.

Rain pelted down on him from an unnatural angle, daggers in the wind trying to push him back. Jack could hardly see the pass. It was all looming shadows and shades of darkness. Lightning lit everything in harsh reality for split seconds before leaving spots to blind his vision.

His ram was resilient. When it started to stop, Jack nudged it on and it obeyed. The animal probably thought he was an idiot. This was not prime weather for travel. He should've considered the impossibility of finding shelter when he couldn't see anything. But he had to remind the ram that this was an urgent and last-minute journey, and that complaining would get them nowhere. It was a long journey ahead. They would take things step by step.

Parts of the path were obliterated by storm and rockslide. At these points Jack was most grateful for the ram. Carefully, it picked its way across unseen ledges and footholds, smugly shaking its head when they'd crossed safely. Jack determined he had a very prideful ram.

Time waxed and waned. He wasn't sure if they'd been battling the storm for minutes or hours. An entire day could've been wasted in this endless storm. He anticipated finding a cave or overhanging where they could rest like last time, but either no shelter came, or they'd obliviously passed them all.

Wind relentlessly beat against him. Debris caught in the gale and slashed his skin with the rain. The ram bowed its head, bracing against the wind rather than bullying through it. Jack didn't argue. One small misstep could send them reeling backwards. He tightened his legs against the ram's sides and prayed they wouldn't blow away.

The gust passed, making the storm seem calmer than before. With a snort, the ram continued on.

They pitched forward. Jagged cracks shot through the mountain face as the ground dropped from beneath them and then caught itself. Mud and stone roared in teeth-rattling cacophony. Jack latched to fistfuls of the ram's scruff in both hands. For a brief instant the ram stood frozen in panic. The rockslide tumbled below, jarring the loose slab they stood on. The ram surged forward, scrambling, jostling. It was all Jack could do to hold on.

The slab jerked down. His insides plummeted, overcome with the weightlessness that comes before falling. Terror kicked in.

The ram suddenly locked into place, jolting. It scrambled to get its hind legs up on the ledge where it landed, managing to get a foothold beneath one hoof. Before Jack thought to climb up on the ledge himself, the ram found footing and shakily pulled them both up. Apparently, it decided that was a good time to rest.

Heart speeding, Jack let the aftermath of the situation wash over him. He'd never felt so completely helpless. His life lay in the hooves of this mountain goat now. Bending over, he buried his face in the ram's wooly fur and decided to call it Gruff.

Chapter Twenty-Four
Star Light, Star Bright,
First Star I See Tonight

It was midafternoon by the time they'd discovered the crypt with nothing but treasure lining the walls and a grumpy bull pacing the floor. No harp, no crown, and no Jack. Kai wanted to head instantly after Jack, but scouts had already been sent to assure the pass hadn't collapsed from the earthquake, and Harry insisted on speaking with the Fiddler first. It seemed like a waste of time. The storm had reached the village with harsh rains and strong winds. Trying to catch up to Jack before he reached this Well would be hard enough without the delay.

The Fiddler wouldn't see them until evening. At that point the scouts had returned with reassurances that the pass was damaged but still intact. Red and Alice stayed with Liesel and the boys at Ms. Marie's house, as it was a safe place closer to the Townhall, while Wendy and Kai went with Harry to meet the Fiddler. As soon as the scar-faced general Cat let them inside alone with the Fiddler, Harry anxiously stepped forward.

"Jack has gone," he said in even urgency.

The Fiddler's flat eyes narrowed only slightly, otherwise unfazed. He leaned against the hearth massaging his crippled hand. "I only just saw the Giant Slayer this morning."

"You did?" Wendy spoke up, hopeful, revealing a kind of desperation Kai tried to conceal.

"He came before dawn to make a deal and discuss a plan of action."

Kai frowned. What kind of deal would Jack want with this man?

"We need to go after him," Harry urged.

Steady, the Fiddler looked between the three of them. "Why?"

Grinding his teeth, Kai suppressed his frustration. He didn't like the Fiddler's tone.

"He's headed into a trap," Harry explained. "The giants got a message to him, and now he thinks he can save my sister and get a cure for the gold alone. We have to help him."

"Why?" the Fiddler repeated. He moved to the table now, the one carved in wood and hammered in iron, and leaned into it with one slender hand.

Harry worked his jaw. "Because I don't let my friends charge into danger alone."

"You've done it before."

"I've sorely learned from my mistakes."

The weight of bringing up Galigantus and the very thing that earned Jack's title filled the room in tight tension. It visibly set Harry on edge. Kai wondered what the Fiddler's game was. After all, surely it was the Fiddler who sent the order to ransack the school where Galigantus hid.

He had no guilt in his part of the horror. But he would prod at the Harry's guilt for letting Jack go in alone. How much of the Fiddler's power rested on his manipulation?

"He's a traitor, a deserter." The Fiddler lowered his voice, "You do realize that?"

"He's only doing what he thinks is right," Harry argued.

"That's no excuse. I will not risk the lives of my people to pursue a deserter. That includes you."

Kai's stomach tightened. "We are not your people."

The Fiddler raised an eyebrow. "No? You've only worn our clothes, eaten our food, stayed in our town."

"Only as guests," Wendy cut in, "not citizens."

"Then as a host, I can refuse your inhabitance whenever I see fit."

"No one denied that," Wendy spoke again, preventing Kai from bursting in agitation. "It's your town, your rules; we're not arguing your right as host, but we do reserve the right to leave as we wish. We're not prisoners."

"And as far as I know," Kai said evenly, "this isn't even your town. The belowlanders recognize no king who can act on such power without the people's consent. They haven't claimed an official leader since the last king died under your watch. Or so I've heard."

Wendy glanced up at him in surprise. But Kai caught the harshness behind the Fiddler's eyes. He didn't know how much his people talked behind his back, on the streets, at the market. Kai had walked around the village every day since they'd arrived, watching and listening in anonymous invisibility. Much could be learned by simply paying attention. It kept his mind sharp.

"Nevertheless," the Fiddler continued, "though my control over your actions is limited, I won't spend valuable resources and *loyal* people on one man, whether he be traitor, prisoner, gone against his will or gone of his own will. We won't follow."

Harry clenched his teeth and met Kai's eyes, Wendy standing solemnly between them. Kai didn't bother saying that he'd told him so. But he was right. The Fiddler would never do anything out of the kindness of his heart if he had nothing to gain or lose. Their strategy would have to shift.

Turning back to the Fiddler, Harry disclosed, "He has the harp and crown."

His reaction was anything but expected. Flat brown eyes narrowed in contemplation, lips in a thin line. No surprise. No rage.

Harry grew increasingly agitated. "Was I not clear? Jack is taking the harp and crown to the giants."

"Useless trinkets."

"What did you say?"

"We don't need them." The Fiddler waved it off distractedly. "All we need is the goose."

Furrowing his brow, Harry huffed in disbelief. "And who told you that?"

"Doesn't matter; it's the truth. The harp and crown were a waste."

Kai noticed how Wendy twisted her fingers painfully together as if to keep herself from lashing out. She originally came along to keep the other two in check, but now she might be just as likely to lose her temper as they were.

Glowering, Harry placed his hands gently on the wooden and metal table. The cause for his tension was clear. If the harp had been a waste of time, then Harry had been captured and tortured for nothing. Jill had been imprisoned for over a year under the giants' manipulation for nothing. Jack had been separated and suffered from merciless guilt for nothing. They all had gold in their blood for nothing.

Harry lowered his voice. "And Jack?"

The Fiddler didn't heed the ice in Harry's tone. "He made his choice. We can go on without him."

"You're a fool. Your ambition doesn't stand a chance without Jack. He's the one who got the harp in the first place."

"And you got the crown. Now they're both gone. I wouldn't hinge all success on the name of a traitor, praising his skill like a hero while he rides now to the enemy."

"You know, you're right." Harry cocked his head. "It wasn't just Jack who got you this far. It was all three of us: Jack, Jill, me. Without any of us, you'd still be cowering behind your mountains hoping the giants don't find a way past them. Now, Fiddler, your mountains have been breached. Jill is gone, Jack is gone—"

"The Giant Slayer has *been* gone," the Fiddler interjected.

"And he came back. Now he's gone again, and you're trying to tell me that we can't follow. But you don't seem to understand something." Harry leaned forward until his knuckles bleached, so close to the Fiddler he could've spat on him. "Without Jack, you don't have me."

Silence stretched thin as the Fiddler held Harry's hard stare. Kai was anxious to leave, forget the Fiddler and his belowlanders, charge after Jack. But they wouldn't get far if the Fiddler sent his followers to stop them. Time was running out. They nearly lost the day already, and the storm was getting worse.

"Tell me something, Silver Blood," the Fiddler said evenly, completely unfazed. "If you had the opportunity to turn the tables of this war, wipe out the enemy in one sweep, would you do it?"

Something about Harry's quiet shifted, breaths changing rhythm, the muscles in his shoulders frozen. Kai balled his fists so tight his knuckles cracked. Harry's sudden intrigue in the Fiddler's words could mean he'd change sides on them, something they hadn't counted on. Kai wasn't prepared to tell Jack that another one of his childhood friends had betrayed him.

As Harry straightened, the Fiddler continued, "The Giant Slayer revealed our next course of action, and now he has given us the perfect window of opportunity. The giants will undoubtedly expect a sabotage when they meet the Giant Slayer, which means they'll send a significant group to the encounter. Nozrok won't expect a strike on the fortress. We'll assemble a team to capture the goose and bring it here, crippling the giants while their backs are turned. And you, Silver Blood," the Fiddler jabbed a slender finger at him in a passion, "you are going to lead us in this great victory."

Harry's nose twitched. "You expect me to—"

"Do not be rash," the Fiddler snapped. "Think carefully about what this could mean. They won't be able to heal or survive plagues. Their population will be so dwindled that they'll never recover, and we will wipe their blight from this country once and for all. Our people will no longer *cower* behind the mountains, our children will be able to grow old without ever suffering from an abominable enemy, and the giants will become nothing but a myth that haunts our histories and bedtime stories. Just think of everything we could gain."

And everything you could lose, Kai added grimly.

But Harry's shoulders were squared, brow furrowed, head craned back. For all the stakes raised up on both sides, it all came down to who he would betray.

"I need to think it over," Harry muttered.

The Fiddler dipped his chin in acknowledgement. "I expect your answer by nightfall."

Without another word, Harry turned to leave. Kai's spine stiffened. Wendy slipped her hand into his to follow out, but she hesitated and faced the Fiddler.

"I don't doubt that you're a great leader," she said solemnly. "But I've seen the consequence of feuds, and I know that in that game, no one wins."

The Fiddler remained silent as they left the Townhouse, barely keeping pace behind Harry as they shouldered their way through the storm to Ms. Marie's house where the others were waiting for them.

Inside, tiny electric lights flickered behind hanging herbs and around flowerpots on the windowsills. The glow was like being surrounded by a thousand fairies in a house of glass and steel. Red and Alice stood to meet them, Liesel approaching quickly. In the back, Ms. Marie kept the small boys entertained by showing them how to make whistles out of reeds. The rest gathered instantly in a tight circle.

"What happened?" Liesel urged.

Leveling a glare at Harry, Kai lowered his voice, "You're considering his offer?"

"What offer?" Alice pressed. "The Fiddler?"

Harry ignored her and matched Kai's tone. "I've already decided."

"Out with it, then," Liesel ordered. "No need to be cryptic."

With a finalized huff through the nose, Harry briefly explained how the Fiddler reacted to their request and his alternate offer. Liesel's nostrils flared.

"May he be afflicted with itching without the benefit of scratching," she cursed under her breath.

"My thoughts exactly," Harry said coolly. "We need to move now for the pass before the Fiddler tries to stop us."

"You know he's already sent a team to block the pass and stables," Liesel countered. "You'll never make it that way."

Red met Kai's eyes briefly. He knew what she was thinking.

"No."

"I can get past them."

"No," he repeated, harsher.

"I can reach Jack in time," she pressed.

"We already have him to worry about. We are *not* splitting up again."

"Besides," Harry added, though he clearly didn't understand what Red was really suggesting, "you don't know the way to the Well."

"Jack does," Red argued.

"How does that help you?"

"I can catch him."

"Not in this weather; not without a ram."

"You want to test me?"

"Enough," Kai snapped firmly. He stepped close, his face a breath away from hers. "The moon's still full. It's harder to control, you said so yourself."

Red grit her teeth, lowered her eyes. "It's not so bad now."

"One bite and you end up just like Fang. You're willing to take that chance?"

She didn't respond. Kai stepped back again.

"I know a way," Liesel spoke up, eyes shifting as her mind raced. "Gather your belongings, we'll leave the boys here, and follow me. It's a long walk and we may have to make camp on the way."

*****

Ever since the giants stopped giving her injections, Jill's seizures had diminished. The pain of course lingered, heavy and churning through her veins, leaking down her muscles, seeping into her bones. She was dying. But it was bearable. And with her mind clear and wits about her, she thought ceaselessly of the week ahead and the plan she'd bestowed upon the Giant King.

Jill had chosen the Well as the meeting place not only because its positioned isolation made an ambush impossible, but because that was the place where this all began. From the Well had sprouted the beanstalk they'd climbed three years ago. They emerged from the Well and stumbled into a country that forever changed their lives. It was at this place that Jack had slain his first giant.

The memory was fuzzy, but she could still remember it. Jack had climbed the beanstalk higher to get a good look at the country from above while Jill and her brother had already stepped away from the Well and the climb behind them. When the yellow teethed giant Cormoran discovered them, she and Harry could only stare openmouthed in shock. It was Jack who saved them. He leaped from his perch onto the giant's back, kicking and punching like an aggravating rodent. He'd never meant for the giant to die. But when Cormoran made a swing for him and Jack dodged out of the way, the giant fell and hit his head smack against the Well. Jack didn't have much time to process what he'd done before they fled the scene as fast as their legs could carry them.

Harry had been so ecstatic about the whole situation, thrilled about giants in the sky, praising Jack the Giant Slayer. His enthusiasm was contagious. But Jill often wondered what Jack would've felt in that moment if they'd stopped to see the consequences of what he'd done. Seen the hollow eyes and slack jaw and pooling blood of the murdered phenomenon. How different would things have turned out for them?

Jill clenched and relaxed her hands to keep anchored in the present. Despite Nozrok's oath, she expected he would try to seize his revenge on Jack at the end of all this. The plan would change; it already had. The whole country felt the mountain fall. If Nozrok was willing to send an armada to massacre his own people hiding in the mountains, then surely an oath would do little to hinder his wrath. Somehow, she would have to use her part in this scheme to save Jack.

The Well would be Nozrok's obstacle. He would have to close the distance instantaneously to avoid Jack's escape. Jill's mind raced to figure it out.

Numbers and trajectories came easily to her, like a golden web stretching across her mind's eye. It was how she killed Yldaa's father and sister, how she felled them with a stone to the head before they drowned, how she earned her name. Of all the geometric outcomes, only a few would save Jack.

She would have three seconds.

*****

They spent the night under one of the bulking rock formations on the swollen hills while the storm raged through the darkness. Kai had to force himself to sleep. He knew Red didn't even try.

Liesel had them up and going long before dawn. Rain still hammered down, creating a shield that blinded them from the village. Mud splashed up to his knees. Alice was coated in it up to her chest, but she didn't want to talk about how that happened.

As they journeyed, Kai began to get an idea of where Liesel was taking them. He wasn't so sure he knew what her plan was.

"Where are you taking us?" Harry kept asking, hair hanging wet over his forehead. A small braid dripped water on his nose.

"Do you trust me?" Liesel would respond.

"Yes."

"Then you'll see soon enough," she answered. She hiked up her skirt and tucked it in her belt to keep it from weighing her down.

The exchange repeated over and over, with Harry's assurances that he trusted her growing more exasperated as they went on.

When they reached the cavernous outcropping in the mountainside, Kai eyed the spot where the giant had emerged from the previous night. Large rocks littered the area. Deep shadows carved into the cliffs, no doubt scars from yesterday's earthquake. Something about it seemed off, raw, hollow. Kai's stomach tightened.

"Why are we here?" Harry asked, rain running down his face.

Red frowned in confusion. He'd forgotten that she didn't know about Liesel's unusual friend. He wouldn't have known himself if he hadn't followed Alice, Wendy, and Liesel here earlier. Before things could get complicated, Kai met Alice's eyes and nodded towards Red. Getting the message, Alice pulled Red aside to explain.

Liesel turned to face Harry and asked once again, "Do you trust me?"

"Of course I trust you," he assured. "But what does that have to do with anything?"

She smiled, kissed him with a hand on his cheek. The gesture made Harry look even more confused. Then Liesel turned toward the mountains, cupped her hands around her mouth, and shouted at the top of her lungs, *"SHEP!"*

"The mute hermit?" Harry frowned.

"She may have exaggerated the term," Alice said loudly over the rain.

"*SHEP!*"

Lightning flashed, blinding for a split second. The light receded. A giant towered over them, his stooped head and shoulders forming an umbrella above Liesel.

Harry scrambled back and nearly slipped in the mud. "*Blasted bloody—!*"

"Don't be scared; you said you trust me," Liesel hastened, neck craned as she looked between the giant and her fiancé. "He's the one who saved my life."

"When your husband died?"

"He tried to save both of us."

"And I was banished for it," the giant intercepted, a voice low and rumbling like thunder.

This time Harry did fall backward into the mud. Even Liesel stood openmouthed.

"I thought you said it was mute!"

"*He*, Harry, not *it*," Liesel shot back. "And I only assumed."

Red's breath came hot against Kai's ear. "There are more of them," she whispered warily. "I don't know how many. The rain obscures the scent. They're in the mountains behind him."

"They've been waiting for us," Kai mumbled. Did they know about Jack's deal with the Giant King? Were they in on the plan?

"Why do you call?" the giant questioned, emotionless.

Liesel extended her arms. "My friends need your help."

The giant's eyes swept over them. "I know half of you. I do not know the others."

"This is Red, Kai, and my fiancé, Harry."

"Harry Silver?"

Kai's spine chilled as the name hung in the air.

"*Silver Blood* needs help from a giant?" He couldn't tell if there was humor in the giant's tone or disbelief.

Liesel glanced back at Harry. Kai watched him, hoping he wouldn't say anything stupid.

"You," Harry fumbled, "you crossed the mountains?"

The giant straightened. "I live in the mountains."

"How many are you?"

The giant was silent. He gave a sigh heavy as the wind, and when lightning cracked again to light his features, the despair was unmistakable. Kai recognized it. He saw it on Fang before being pushed into the swirling portal. He'd seen it on his mother and grandmother when they got the news that his father would never come home again. He felt it drowning him in ice when he was ripped from the woman he loved. Something desperately terrible happened here. This giant was still suffering.

"There used to be hundreds of us," the giant answered at last. "Maybe even a thousand."

Harry gawked. "A thousand giants, all this time… And you never attacked us?"

"Most of us were banished by Nozrok and kings before him because of the barbarity of our beliefs. We want peace between giant and belowlander. We question the hatred that fuels Nozrok's heart and the hearts of his followers. And most of us were caught acting on these treacherous ideas." The giant looked down at Liesel, gentle. "Many were banished for far less than trying to save a group of belowlanders and only succeeding in saving one."

Kai eyed Harry as he tried to process it all. Time wore thin. Jack was a whole day ahead of them and they had ground to cover. If Harry kept asking questions, they would waste another morning talking rather than pursuing their friend.

Anxious, Kai spoke up, "Will you help us reach Jack before he gets to the Well?"

The giant leaned back in amusement. "Silver Blood needs the help of a giant to find the Giant Slayer."

"He's crossing the mountains to bring the Giant King the harp and crown at the Well. He's got four days now. We can't catch him on our own," Wendy shouted as the wind whistled. "Will you help us?"

Rain fell harder around them. Grey dawn brightened the sky, but only enough to prove that night had passed.

In a grave rumble, the giant said, "I am Balthaz, leader of the Mountain Giants. I swear by the gold in my blood that, if it is within my power, I will help you reach your friend."

From a hidden lip in the mountainside, two giants stepped forward into the alcove. One was male with oil black hair and brass rings in his short beard. The other was smaller, a female with olive skin, black eyes mysterious, and slender hands.

"I am Ajaal," said the black-haired giant.

"I am Trell," echoed the small giantess.

"We swear by the gold in our blood that if it is within our power," they vowed as one, "we will help you reach your friend."

Liesel placed her hands on her hips with a sigh, turning from the giants to the rest of them. "Let it, quick! You don't have much time; you can thank me later. May the road rise up to meet you. Now go."

Chapter Twenty-Five

Ashes, Ashes,

We All Fall Down

The goose lay curled in her cage beside Nozrok when he summoned Uzfra into the throne room with Toog and Yldaa. They had three days before Jack was to reach the Well. His mind toiled at what lay ahead.

"The time has come to prepare the giants," Nozrok announced, anxious in announcing the finality of his plan. "In two days, I want every able giant armed and loaded with food, supplies, and weapons. Uzfra will be charged with those who remain. Take the old, injured, and sick here along with any children hidden away throughout the country. This will be fortified once we are gone and until we return."

"Yes, my king," Uzfra affirmed, baring his wrists in submission.

"For now, Yldaa," Nozrok continued, "you will choose twenty giants to stay behind protecting the fortress. Toog will prepare supplies and artillery for our journey. And Uzfra will tend to transportation for the goose and the Siren, which I will take over once we leave."

Toog also bared his wrists in submission, but Yldaa was less humbled. "Why bring an army to the Giant Slayer?" she questioned with a scowl. "Do you expect him to deceive us?"

Nozrok fingered the war hammer tied to his belt. "I do not know what to expect. But if all goes according to plan, we'll still need the army. We must uphold our end of the bargain."

At the mention of the witch's bargain, Yldaa made to protest when the goose gave a sickly honk that caused all sound in the room to evaporate. Shoulders tensed. Eyes turned expectedly on the bird. But the goose remained silent.

A grave sigh rattled his chest. Nozrok tore his gaze away. "The girl is right. This is our only chance. We must succeed one way another."

*****

Liesel stayed behind to fetch her boys and prepare the house in case the Fiddler decided to pay her a visit when he discovered her fiancé had managed to escape. She was concerned what he would find if he ransacked the house.

"More secrets," Harry had voiced, raising an eyebrow.

She'd shrugged mischievously. "I just don't want the house to explode."

Red's skin crawled at that.

Now the five of them sat on three giants' shoulders, lumbering through the mountain tunnels in inky darkness. The cold forced Red to pull Jack's jacket tight around her. She knew they traveled farther because of the giant's long gait, but the pace was tedious as they picked over debris and around collapsed walls. Heavy footfalls echoed around them. She still couldn't count how many giants fell into step behind them.

Wendy had fallen asleep, snuggly perched on Balthaz's shoulder. On the short giantess, Trell, Alice sat looking around in wonder. Wasn't she afraid of heights? The distance from the ground didn't seem to bother her now. She was probably thinking about her chalk charts and listed names and endless questions circling around in her brain like a thousand buzzing sprites.

Music vibrated in the air. Grey light swallowed them as they emerged from the tunnels into a clouded expansive room. The sky hung bare high above, a steady patter of rain falling in the storm's lull. Giant silhouettes littered the area covered in dust, some bloody. They lifted rocks and dug through the rubble blanketing the floor. Baritone voices had taken up a song here, deep and melancholy.

A giantess in the crowd raised a hand toward them in greeting and Balthaz returned the gesture.

"I have left her in charge until I return," he explained grimly as they slowly made their way across the rough landscape. "She shall take care of those who remain and those who have yet to arrive."

"What happened here?" Harry asked from Balthaz's other shoulder opposite from Wendy, looking around at the gloom. And the bodies. A pit formed in Red's stomach as nostalgia washed over her. They were walking through a graveyard.

Wendy woke with a yawn, rubbing her eyes, taking in the sight around them. From Ajaal's other shoulder, Kai met Red's eyes. *Ten*, he mouthed with a nod to the giants who trailed them. She nodded in understanding.

"Nozrok discovered our presence. He sent troops to level the mountain, the very heart of our refuge," Balthaz explained, his gravelly voice lowered to a growl. "We're still recovering the bodies."

Red's throat knotted, wanting to look away, but she couldn't. She'd seen this before. She'd done this before. A building leveled, bodies under bricks, smoke in the air. Metal tasted her tongue. Burnt flesh tinged her nose. At thirteen, she found her parents in the rubble and only two stars in the sky. She never touched a bomb again. She never took presents from strangers again.

"We were gone at the time, going in search of new exiles and checking on other settlements in the mountains. When the mountain collapsed, we heard it scream, felt it grieve. We came back to find this." Balthaz choked on his words, a break that made Red's stomach clench.

Wendy gingerly placed a hand on the giant's neck, understanding in her eyes beyond comprehension. But Red could comprehend it. They all could. Wendy watched Lost Boys come and go and never return. Alice had been in the heat of ongoing civil war. And Kai... Red frowned. She recognized the harsh steel behind his eyes, but she didn't know where it came from. Was it all Gerda? Did his love for her cause him such pain? Or was there something else, something in the Snow Queen's realm that cut him deeper than just Gerda's capture? Perhaps Red didn't know as much about Kai as she thought.

"The belowlanders are not the only ones who suffer under Nozrok's reign," Ajaal spoke, his shoulders rumbling under her legs.

Harry frowned as if trying to bend his mind to this.

Things look different through the eyes of those you once considered monsters, Red thought to herself.

Alice cocked her head. "What are they singing?"

"An ancient song," Trell answered softly. "To some it is prophesy; to others, legend. Giants have sung it for generations."

"I've heard it before," Alice pondered.

"Many remember the first part, with its rage and destruction. They forget the warning that follows because of it. Here, we take it as an urge to continue on for our cause, to stand against the rage, and from our determination for righteousness we will rise victorious even if we fall. From mourning blooms hope. It rises like the sun."

"And we along with it," Ajaal added, gentle in his own grief. But he joined the chorus in humming, the tune vibrating from his chest and through Red's body as she sat on his shoulder. She let it overwhelm her, clear her mind, bring her peace.

When the moment passed and she opened her eyes, they had long left the remnants of the fallen mountain behind. More giants than before had joined behind them.

"The tunnels are blocked from here," Balthaz informed, eyes raised to a hazy light peering through the collapsed ceiling. "We must brave the peaks and mazes above."

When they surfaced, the storm returned in a fury. It swallowed them whole, adding to the unruly chaos of the mountains' deceiving maze. Time elapsed undetected. The sun vanished, the only light being the blinding flash of lightning colliding with stone. Sharp rain swirled with bruising sleet.

The altitude caused Red to struggle for consciousness. Each breath rattled in her chest. The giants dared not climb any higher for their sake, though Wendy remained unaffected by the thin air.

Wind and rain grew into a fervor. A stone sheet was shaved off the mountainside into a sheer chasm. The swirling darkness veiled any hope of distinguishing rock from open air. Hugging the cliff face, the giants were forced to a halt.

Balthaz shouted something that was swallowed up by thunder, but the message was clear. They would have to wait out the storm and risk the consequences.

It wasn't until Gruff tumbled into the looming woods that Jack realized they'd escaped the mountain pass. He heaved a sigh of relief. Exhausted, he leaned forward against the ram's bushy neck and allowed himself to roll off its back. Wet grass welcomed him when he collapsed. Rain dripped down, the trees filtering its descent.

He knew he should keep going, knew there was still much to do. But drowsy timelessness overtook him. He heard Gruff lay down somewhere beside him, the metallic click of the crown rattling against the harp. Water fell on his face, branches waved high above him, and the gold in his blood sifted with the rhythm of its country.

"Almost there," Jack muttered. "Almost there."

With a groan, he rolled over and forced himself up, knees buckling as his feet slipped. The sky was brighter than he remembered, though he still couldn't see the sun. Gruff was ready for him by the time he walked over, eyes attentive, ears perked. Jack pet its nose.

"Come on. We'd better get going."

On cue, Gruff stood with clanking packages. Jack secured the harp and crown again before climbing back in the saddle, revealing how sore his butt was.

The rest of the ride was a blur of weaving around trees and whipping through underbrush, the terrain growing more open and still interwoven as they went. This was a place where giants could hide yet humans could become carelessly exposed.

Jack tried not to think about the friends he'd left behind, distracting himself with planning for the impending doom that lay ahead. The sky began to bleed color again. Bursting from the thicker, Gruff reared to a stop. Jack's heart pounded. All was silent. The clearing before them was the size of a giant's battlefield sloping up into one great hill where a ruined relic still stood.

They called it the Well.

It plunged straight through the heart of Giant Country.

Chapter Twenty-Six

It's Raining, It's Pouring

The Well looked naked now without a beanstalk twisting from its mouth. Jack tried not to think of when he'd cut it down, but his hands ached from blistered scars on his palms and the pads of his fingers.

Sunlight shone hazily through the blanket of clouds overhead. Gruff took him up the barren slope steadily, ears twitching. Jack slid off when they reached the Well. They were completely exposed from all sides. No giant could sneak up on him, but anyone watching could see him plain as day.

Hastily, he set to work yanking knots into place and entangling his treasures in a web of rope. He didn't bother wiping sweat from his brow.

Time passed, and the clouds lowered, covering the hill in mist. Gruff nibbled lazily at the grass. Securing the last of the ropes, Jack wrapped the end around his forearm and strategically placed the harp and crown on the edge of the Well's open mouth. He had his leverage now. He was ready to push the bundle over or save it. All that was left to do was wait.

And wait.

And wait…

Jack couldn't remember nodding off, but when the ram gave a low bleat he snapped awake. He scrambled to his feet, squinting as he looked around for danger. But the fog had thickened, and now he could hardly see ten meters in front of him.

Shifting uneasily, he double checked his knots and secured the rope around his wrist. Dew dotted his skin. His hair felt damp against his scalp. He tried to detect any tremble underfoot, but it was a fruitless attempt. Unless the giants attempted to climb the hill, he wouldn't know of their presence.

Thunder rumbled in the distance where the mountains loomed. Something caught his eye. Chills raced up his spine. He instantly poised himself by the harp and crown. "I'm warning you!" he shouted. "I'll knock it over, and you can say goodbye to your bloody golden goose."

He waited, ready. Gruff looked at him dully.

Slowly, tension left his shoulders. "There's nothing there," he assured the ram as its slit pupils continued to stare him. "There's nothing there."

He half-expected an ambush right then—just his luck—but there really was nothing there.

The day waned on. His arm grew stiff. Before long, Jack began to wonder if the old man had lied to him, that there was no deal, that the giants weren't coming and certainly not with Jill and the antidote. But why would Crooked lie? And even if he had, how would he know about Jill? Unless the giants told him, or the Fiddler, or Cat, or Brann, Spider, Harry...

He shook his head. Only the giants would've told a man like Crooked, and only the giants would have the motivation to steal the harp and crown from the belowlanders. If the Fiddler was behind it, he would've asked for the goose.

Maybe it's a set up, he speculated. Any moment now and he'll be surrounded. But if the plan was an ambush, then the giants would lose everything. Their future was literally hanging in the balance, and Jack was holding the rope.

All the same, the wait was getting tiresome.

Scuffing caught his ear, so subtle it might have been the wind through leaves. But it gained rhythm. Heart pounding, Jack's grip tightened.

Scuff, drag, slosh. Scuff, drag, slosh.

He narrowed his eyes. A hazy silhouette formed in the distance, its shape growing steadily recognizable features. Swallowing became difficult. Was this another traitor sent by Nozrok to meet him? It limped and huffed as it dragged its burden along. Gruff snorted suspiciously.

As the figure approached, he realized who it was. "Jill."

Gold-shot eyes never wavered from him as she struggled to carry the heavy bucket and walk at the same time. Jack felt frozen, like his feet weighed a thousand pounds.

Jill stopped close enough beside the Well for him to see the sheen of sweat on her brow, but far enough away that they couldn't touch each other. She lowered the bucket to the ground. Whatever liquid it contained sloshed violently over the lip.

Catching her breath, she almost smiled. "Jack."

He flinched back when she stepped toward him. Smile gone, her body convulsed in minor muscle spasm that passed quickly. He knew his reaction hurt her, but he couldn't tell how he felt now that she was here again.

"You work for them," he stated. It was no longer a question.

Briefly dropping her eyes, she cringed at his accusation. "If nothing else," she said, voice strained, "you must understand that everything I've done has been to protect you and Harry."

"And now?"

"Nothing has changed."

Jack shivered and looked around him. The mist was lifting, daylight dimming, but he could sense the eyes watching him. *They're here*, he deduced. If the giants knew what was good for them, they would stay away.

Jack frowned at the bucket, eying the dark liquid inside. Chest tightened. "Is that," he gulped, "the antidote?"

Jill huffed, neck seizing before she could speak. "We both know what this is."

"A pail of water?"

"A joke."

He almost laughed. Of course; he should've known no antidote existed. The gold in his blood was permanent, a stain, a wound that would never heal. Getting rid of it would be too good to be true.

"Careful," Jill warned when Jack realized how heavily he leaned against the precious bundle he'd configured. "If that goes over, you'll be dead in seconds."

Quickly, Jack tugged it back to safety, loosened the hold around his forearm, and tangled the ropes in his fingers. His brow furrowed as her words registered.

"Dead in *seconds*?"

"Three."

"How?"

Before he could react, Jill hefted the bucket and swung it with painful strength right for him, bucket crashing into the bundle and colliding with his chest. Water exploded. Breath rushed out of him. A sharp clap and swoosh hit his ear drums just before he met the ground, and all became a blur of grey sky and bruising ground, clanging metal, raging screams.

But he couldn't stop tumbling.

*****

Nozrok gave the signal as soon as the Giant Slayer pulled the harp and crown from danger. They'd long recovered designs for one of Galigantus' war machines, a massive slingshot more powerful than anything they'd ever invented. This was only a prototype, but it would do the job. No giant's hand would harm the Giant Slayer. He meant to keep that vow.

At his signal, Toog hit the trigger with his foot. Gears snapped. Ropes flung forward. The stone sailed just as the Siren struck, and everything exploded.

Blown back, he shielded his eyes. Air pressure dropped instantly. Wind swirled, sucking the fog away into a swirling vortex at the top of the hill.

"That devious speck," Yldaa growled beside him. "What did she do?"

Grinding his teeth, Nozrok rumbled, "She broke the crown."

The portal gaped cold and beckoning. Trees swayed on the opposite side of the clearing, and shadows broke forth from the forest. Giants raged forward. It didn't take long for him to realize that these giants were no friends of his.

"What do we do, my king?" Toog asked, poised by the now cracked slingshot.

Stomach stiffened, Nozrok looked between Jack tumbling helpless down the hill, the harp lying bare in the clearing, and the armada ready to take him down. But the crown had broken. They didn't have long.

Yldaa and Toog waited for his command.

"Get to the portal," Nozrok ordered. "I'll take care of the rest."

*****

Jack regained consciousness quickly, gasping. His head pounded terribly, ears ringing, and when he touched the back of his skull his fingers came away tainted with blood.

What happened?

With a frown, he realized the noise wasn't all in his head. He craned his neck in the grass and saw such blurry chaos above that he didn't know what to focus on. Giants surged from the surrounding forest, meeting in mass collision. Most charged for the icy light churning in front of the Well—*When did that show up?* Screams made for war erupted all around. He struggled to remember how he got there.

Jill.

He sat up too quickly. Spots swarmed his vision. Where did she go?

First he saw the harp, uncovered, shining in the moonlight. The crown had disappeared, probably fallen somewhere when the ropes slipped. He should've ties the knots tighter. Rope burns stung his forearms.

As he watched, a giant quickly scooped up the harp and wrapped it in fur before stashing it in his cloak. Jack squinted through the haze. Brown and blue eyes locked on him.

Nozrok.

Instinctively, Jack reached for a weapon that wasn't there, realizing too late that he'd left everything with the ram. He fumbled trying to get his legs under him. But gashed knees screamed in protest, and his ankle throbbed unbearably. The Giant King smiled at his feeble efforts.

Another giant slammed into him, ramming Nozrok away from Jack like an angry bear. He blinked. Was the giant trying to save him? But that couldn't...

"Jack."

He whipped around and quickly discovered his ribs were bruised. Jill lay not far from him, sprawled out unnaturally, her leg twisted gruesomely. Something about the way her body convulsed made Jack scramble for her in a panic despite his own pain.

When he reached her, he hovered over her hesitantly. "Jill?"

Her eyes fluttered, a glassy blue shining with gold. A smile twitched. "Jack."

Frozen in shock, his heart felt heavy in his chest. Sticky golden blood flowered from her abdomen. "No," he protested. Hastily, Jack pulled her to him and let her head rest on his shoulder while he tried desperately to stop the bleeding. He couldn't tell what caused this or where exactly all the blood came from. "No. Jill, how…?"

"Three seconds," she murmured, weak, wet. "I had three seconds… three seconds to…"

"Forget about the three blasted seconds. How do I stop the bleeding?"

"It's raining."

"How do I stop the bleeding?"

"I don't hurt anymore."

"Jill, how do I save you?!"

Sobs threatened to choke the words out of him. He pressed against Jill's wound in vain, metallic blood leaking between his fingers. Tears traveled hot down his face with the rain. Jill took one of his hands in her frail fingers, pulled it away from her abdomen, held it tight.

Her breath brushed warm against his neck. "I'm sorry."

Jack couldn't look at her, not like this. He refused. "You shouldn't be sorry. It's my fault, all of this."

"Jack, I…" Her voice faded, a pause stretching longer with every heartbeat.

"What?" When she didn't answer, Jack finally turned to see her, nudging her a bit. "What is it, Jill?"

Striking eyes stared unseeing into the sky as rain washed her face. Fingers were limp in his grasp. He was the only one holding their hands up now.

"No," he begged, pulse throbbing in his throat. "Wake up. Come on, you can't… Not after all of this. Jill…"

She wouldn't answer. Tentatively, he brushed the hair out of her face.

"Harry's waiting for you," Jack whispered gently. "Your brother is waiting for you, Jill."

His voice broke and every breath came shaky as crying seized him. The chaos behind him didn't end until the portal closed, taking with it all but three giants. But it all flitted without notice. Jack barely acknowledged Gruff tottering toward him before golden darkness coaxed him into unconsciousness.

Chapter Twenty-Seven

Now I Lay Me Down to Sleep

The remaining giants took them to a spot etched into the cliffs at the end of the range, hidden from view on either side of the mountains. Black sands fed into the cloud sea. Docked on the shore sat a hollowed log, left there by a giant with copper skin and onyx curls—Ajaal, he'd mentioned his name was. Now the giants stood behind near the cliffs, allowing them privacy.

Everything came by in a haze for Jack. After Harry had found him on the hillside, his friends tried to explain how they got here, that the giants who were with them were good giants who lived in the mountains. He let Wendy tend to his immediate wounds. He let these giants take him to this hidden coastline without resistance. But Jack hardly processed any of it.

Now he stood stone faced on the shore, watching Harry carry his sister forward like a babe. Tears ran lines down Harry's nose. He'd never had the chance to even see her alive again.

Wendy and Alice arranged wildflowers and grasses along the bottom of the split log like a nest, elegant and soft. Jack stood close in case Harry needed assistance. But Harry didn't struggle laying Jill down into the bed. He held a shaking hand to her face, frozen in sudden morose.

Carefully, Red placed Jill's hands over a bouquet covering the bloody stains on her abdomen. Harry gave her a nod in appreciation.

Like this, Jill could've been sleeping, at peace at long last. Someone had washed her face and hands, and her hair was brushed. Gold only shone in the flower petals and details in the log's bark. It didn't hold the poison and hatred as it might have before; now it seemed honorable if not forgiving. In the end the gold did not claim her. Maybe Jill would've liked to know that. It had overwhelmed her, weakened her, but it never conquered her.

But no one said anything like that.

Instead, after Harry pressed a kiss to his sister's brow, he signaled for Kai to take the opposite end of the log and pull it into the cloudy ocean. Jack and Harry finished it off, pushing the log in together, wading in with it. Physically incapable of continuing, Jack released first. But Harry kept on until the clouds reached his waist before he let Jill set sail alone.

Face wet and salty, Harry raised his hand in final farewell. "So long, sis. Forgive me, our next meeting won't come for a long time."

Jack watched as the mist swallowed her whole. It didn't feel right saying goodbye to the oldest friend he'd ever known. He'd done it twice now. How was this time so much harder? Fighting the lump in his throat, he wished her goodbye before she disappeared forever beyond his reach.

Alice and Kai were explaining everything to Harry and the giants, about the impending war, about the Master

265

Puppeteer, about the Giant King's alliance. It was an in-depth pitch, and Jack couldn't take another word of it.

He sat on the black beach, staring at the horizon where Jill had vanished. He hadn't spoken a word since the battlefield.

Three seconds.

He understood now. They'd found the slingshot, a prototype. Jill had always been good with aim and angles; she'd taken down two giants herself with only a slingshot and stone. The weapon must have taken three seconds to shoot. How fitting it would've been to be killed by one of Galigantus' inventions.

Then Jill got in the way.

Three seconds.

His throat swelled, eyes burning with tears. He bowed his head to his knees and sobbed without any trace of anger. There was no more anger now. It died on the hillside bleeding gold. Only sorrow remained, heavy, aching.

I don't hurt anymore, she'd said.

But he did. With every heaving breath, he hurt so bad. Jill was gone. And everything in him blamed himself. He just wanted to make things right, get the antidote, save Jill.

I'm sorry, her words echoed through his head.

"I'm sorry, too," he whispered. "I'm so, so sorry."

Like a sheet of cool water, a calm settled over him and the crying ceased. His eyes were puffy, and pressure had built up behind the bridge of his nose, but he felt lighter. There was a familiar ache in his chest where he still missed her. For now, though, he could live with that. He'd get used to the guilt, too, eventually.

Silent, Red came and sat beside him. Jack wanted to hold her close, hold her hand, let her lay her head on his shoulder. He wanted to say how sorry he was for causing the dark circles under her eyes and tension in her shoulders and the anxious way she clutched her hands around her legs and tapped her left thumb. He wanted to say how sorry he was for leaving her.

"They figured it out," she spoke at last. "Where we're headed, who's behind all this, who we're up against."

Jack knew this already, but he nodded to show he was listening.

"They're talking about how a war is unavoidable," she huffed. "As if avoiding it was ever an option. If this master, witch, queen, whoever she is—if she's after us, it'll always come down to a fight."

The wind swept past them, blowing her long hair to the side, exposing her face. His stomach clenched as déjà vu brushed down his spine, remembering when they sat together on the beach just a few days ago. He felt like so much had changed since then.

Red shivered at the chill. "I'm so tired of fighting."

Jack raised an eyebrow. "You're sure about that?"

"No," she admitted, thumb still tapping. "But I'm scared. I don't think I'm ready for this one. I don't know how this ends."

He felt the same. He wasn't sure he could survive sending off another boat to sail away forever.

"Why'd it have to be us?" Jack questioned, voice so broken he was afraid the tears would return. "We've been so focused on finding out who's after us, but... But why did she come after us?" His words hung in the air unable to continue.

Red sighed as if she'd heard the question before. "I don't know. I'm not even sure it matters anymore."

Sand skipped across the shore like coal dust. Tendrils of mist tugged to the side at the wind's call, stretched in peculiar angles. Something in the air foretold rain.

Jack closed his eyes for a moment, Jill's last words passing through his mind: *It's raining.*

"I'm sorry, Jack," Red's voice spoke gently, hesitant. "I know how much Jill meant to you. I can't imagine losing the person you love."

He frowned at her words, turning to her. Is that what she thought? Gaze downcast, she wouldn't meet his eyes.

"I was never in love with Jill," Jack said softly. "She was... She *is* like my sister."

Her head snapped up. "I didn't—"

"It's you," he interrupted, heart pounding in his chest. "It's always been you."

He waited a moment, but before she could respond, he rose to his feet and left.

"You have to admit, friends, it's a little unbelievable," Harry confessed, scratching the back of his head. "So, I can't say it'll be easy convincing people about this."

Alice shrugged as if admitting the whole thing sounded mad—and she would know. Jack himself could hardly believe the very things he'd lived through, what it all meant, what they were heading towards. He supposed he'd let Alice take charge of all the wonderings. His head hurt too much trying to keep everything straight. Better for him to take things as they came along and hope for the best.

Harry pulled a half-smile. "But that doesn't mean I won't try. Every belowlander and giant who will join will be ready whenever the rabbit comes, you can be sure of that."

Behind him, the giant Ajaal spoke up in agreement, "My people will stand with you. For our country, for our freedom, and for our peace."

"For our peace," Harry echoed thoughtfully. Letting it sink in, he nodded in resolution. "Yes, I think I can fight for that."

Jack remembered the giant who saved him from Nozrok on the hillside and wondered where he was now. Maybe he could also fight for peace, for the sake of that giant, for the sake of Jill.

At Kai's request, the giants had removed their cloaks and cut them into smaller pieces without question. Kai fashioned the pieces into makeshift coats and leggings for the five of them, assuring them that the precaution was necessary for where they were going. He secured the furs on them himself for good measure. With the padding tied to his appendages, Jack felt stiff and heavy. Kai frowned at the furs disapprovingly but gave a grunt as if this would do for now. Jack hoped the Snow Queen's realm wasn't as cold as he was beginning to suspect.

Harry shook each of their hands in farewell, but for Jack he didn't hesitate to pull him into a firm embrace. Jack clasped his arms tightly around his friend. Too much lay between them now, and he didn't know where this void came from. Maybe it was that guilt nestled inside, or the unspoken apologies.

"Good luck with the Fiddler," Jack said, pulling away.

"After I'm done with him, he may need more luck than I do." Harry grinned, but the smile didn't quite reach his eyes like it used to. "Anyway, where you're going you'll need more luck than anyone, eh, friend?"

"That's an understatement."

Harry huffed a laugh. His gaze drifted to the cloud sea behind them, a ghostly shine glazing his eyes. "It's not a game anymore, is it? No more adventures, treasure hunts."

Jack shrugged. "Depends on how you look at it."

"Yeah, I guess so." Pulled out of his trance, Harry clapped him on the shoulder affectionately. Whatever distance Jack felt between them, he didn't seem to notice. "We'll see each other again before this is over."

His eyes looked too much like Jill's. Memories of the three of them laughing over their adventures in a cave behind a waterfall flooded his mind, moments they could never have again. Still, Jack managed a smile. "I'm counting on it."

Harry gave him a last slap in farewell before turning to mount Gruff and follow the giants preparing to brave the mountains.

With a hollow stomach, Jack joined his friends around the pocket watch Alice produced.

"One realm left," she voiced, eyebrow raised. "You know who's waiting there, don't you?"

"Everyone," Red muttered.

The word weighed heavy in the air, swelling with fear and anxiety. Jack hadn't thought about the realities of what all they would have to face again—a mad queen, shiploads of rotten pirates, a ferocious pack of wolves, and now the giants. But what remained unsaid, Jack thought, that's what terrified them the most.

It's not a game anymore.

Kai grabbed the watch firmly, a growl edging his voice. "Let's finish this."

Wendy joined, then Red, both silent but determined. Jack took hold of the watch last, casting a glance at Red, hoping she would meet his eyes just once. She didn't look up. His chest tightened, festering an urgency inside that ached ceaselessly.

Kai grit his teeth and pushed the diamond button.

Chapter Twenty-Eight

Leave Them Alone,

And They'll Come Home

Ice built in shifting shards around them as the giants scuffed through the halls, expanding so they could walk with enough room to spare. The trip was a struggle as they dragged along the passionate prisoners. Only one refused to fight. Behind Nozrok, Yldaa held the rebel leader securely. But Balthaz kept on rigid, head high, like he was proud to be prisoner to the Giant King. Nozrok should've known this was the giant who led the mountain rebels. The cowardly warrior, the disgraced shepherd, the dangerous traitor who confessed to harboring belowlanders and criminals. How long had Balthaz been planning a rebellion against him?

Even as anger boiled within, Nozrok wondered if perhaps these prisoners could see reason. They were outnumbered, outsmarted, and in unfamiliar land with no allies. If giant's blood could be spared, then Nozrok could consider pardon. But only if they renounced their treacherous ideas. As for their leader, Balthaz, he would have to be broken or executed. Nozrok couldn't risk another uprising.

Approaching the hall's end, the doors stretched high and opened before the flood of giants entered the growing throne room. Nozrok narrowed his eyes. The witch sat before them, other humans standing on either side like worthless accessories.

"What do you bring me, giant?" the witch questioned, her voice crystalized. Her face glinted with ice like a second skin, an armor distorting what monstrous and sumptuous features lay beneath. Only her eyes remained exposed.

"An army," Nozrok answered.

"An army bound in ropes and chains?"

"They interceded us before we came here," he explained, tone low. "But with a little convincing, they should see reason in returning oaths of fealty to me. Even traitors, they are still giants. I will allow them the chance for redemption."

Strangely framed eyes shifted to Balthaz. "What say you, leader of the mountain giants?"

Nozrok's spine tightened at the specificity of the title. How much did this witch know?

Behind him, Balthaz straightened and spoke directly to him, "I'll never swear allegiance and bare my wrists for a giant who attacks his own kind just as the one you call *enemy* has. You do exactly what the belowlanders have done. They do it in the name of liberty. You do it in the name of extermination. Either way is massacre, but your reasons are monstrous."

Nozrok ground his teeth, fists clenched to his sides. But before he could respond, the witch spoke first, even and resolute, "Pretty words. I respect your morality."

Balthaz frowned in suspicion. One of the humans bared her pointed teeth in a pleased smile, golden eyes watching them hungrily.

273

"However," the witch continued, "until you can find it in your sense of morality to work with me, you must understand that I can't have you running loose in my realm."

Ice shot up from the ground and bound Balthaz on the spot, crawling up his arms in sleeved chains that fed into the floor. Nozrok looked back in shock to find the same phenomenon happened to the other prisoners. For the first time since he could remember, Nozrok felt tendrils of fear churn in his gut. He smelled it, too, reeking from behind him among prisoner and guard. Except for Balthaz. There was not a whiff of fear from him.

As the prisoners were taken away, Balthaz took up a gravelly baritone that spread to harmonious melody from every rebel giant with him. Nozrok's spine crawled at the tune. He knew the song well. Every giant knew the song, but this was different. This was a declaration.

"Dusk has dawned, I hear its call,
above the world I've watched it fall;
I smell blood and I smell bone,
and I smell fear coated in gold;
Grind your bread and bake their teeth,
and death will come while you're asleep;
I will rage. I will rage.
Fee-Fi-Fo-Fum
'Til the mountains crumble down,
and oceans become heaven's crown;
Land sinks low, the gold runs dry,
and when these bones rain from the sky;
'Til the giants fall to myth,
and none remains to journey with;

I will stand. I will stand.
Fee-Fi-Fo-Fum
I will stand for my homeland,
for nowhere else could bear my hand;
I will stand by friend and kin,
we share the gold under our skin;
I will stand 'til my death comes,
and as my soul greets sky and sun,
I will sing, I will sing,
Fee-Fi-Fo-Fum."

The song hung in the air after the prisoners had long disappeared. But there was another hum, quiet under his jacket, stirred by the music. He kept the harp concealed for fear of its discovery. Yldaa gave him a scowl, her anxiety becoming agitated. Keeping his breaths steady, Nozrok extinguished all fear.

"Now," the witch went on, undeterred by the song, "about the real reason we're working together?"

"Jackie's alive," Nozrok explained bitterly. "Wasn't aware of others."

"No, I didn't think you would be. At least you were wise enough to leave your *Giant Slayer* alive for now." Fury edged her voice now, sharp enough to cut diamonds. "Though, if you disobey me again you'll quickly discover worse things than death."

He glowered, but she did not acknowledge him. Despite their size difference, Nozrok was keenly aware of this witch's power over him. He could no more argue than he could rise against her.

She sat back in her fur lined throne in satisfaction. "My darlings are coming to me now to complete this game we've played for so long." A frosted finger tapped against the throne's icy arm. "I think it's about time we reach the final round."

*****

The colors were colder than usual, harsher, and the ticking came in sharp jabs at Jack's eardrums. It all vanished the moment the arrows landed on a jeweled star. Stillness overwhelmed him, a vacuum of sound and blinding whiteness that didn't dim but slowly grew form around them.

The pocket watch's face cracked. A shock like lightning shot through their hands and they each jerked back, the watch falling into the snow. It frosted over on impact.

When the cold hit, it was biting, unforgiving. Jack wished he had more coats.

Alice stooped to retrieve the broken pocket watch. Hugging herself, Wendy scooched closer to Red to keep warm. Jack shivered, blew into his hands, and looked around to make sense of this world of white. He suddenly realized two things at once: they were standing in a graveyard, and they were not alone.

Kai stepped towards the lone figure who lounged on a snow-covered headstone examining his fingernails.

"It's about time," the stranger spoke, raising crystal eyes up to them indifferently.

Fists clenched to his sides, Kai bristled. "What are you doing here?"

The young man stood grandly with arms spread wide. An icy wind rustled through his spikey white hair. "I'm the welcome party!" His smile stretched, regarding

276

the whole group. "Welcome to *Snedronningens Land*, *Snödrottningens Land, Skandinavien...* Otherwise and better known as the Realm of the Snow Queen."

Acknowledgements

Thank you for coming on another adventure with me! This book has taken longer to craft than any of the others; it's seen me through one of the busiest years of my life. I'm so excited that Jack's installment is finally complete.

Like anything, I never could've done this alone.

Thank you to my family for being the most encouraging, loving, ridiculous bunch I could ever be blessed with. I love you more than words can say, so I'll just wrap it up in a hug. These books wouldn't be the same without your honesty and insight.

Thank you to my friends, the true ones I could never live without – you know who you are. Thank you for showing me how to live unfiltered, unashamed, unafraid. I can't tell you how much this year has taught me about friendship, but I hope that it bleeds through these pages and blossoms in these characters as I hope it shines in my own life.

Many thanks, of course, to the authors whose stories make this possible: J.M. Barrie, Hans Christian Andersen, and Lewis Carrol, as well as the unknown storytellers behind "Little Red Riding Hood" and "Jack and the Beanstalk." I grow ever more in love with their classic tales every time I dive into this series. I'm blessed to shine a new light on their legacies.

I loved weaving in renowned nursery rhymes into this installment, whose writers are as conspicuous as fairytales'. From "Hey Diddle Diddle" came Cat, Bleddyn, and the Fiddler, with the Fiddler also stemming from "Old King Cole." Liesel and her first husband came from "Hickory Dickory Dock," and their children are a good blend of "Little Boy Blue," "Tom Thumb," and "Little Jack Horner." Shep and Madame were inspired by "Baa, Baa, Black Sheep," and Ms. Marie by "Mary, Mary, Quite Contrary." Brann derived from "Jack Be Nimble," and Spider from "Little Miss Muffet." And of course, "Jack and Jill" might've held the most weight in this story.

Special thanks to Kiselev Andrey Valerevich, Orla, and Facanv for the gorgeous images that make up this cover, as well as to Derek Murphy for his incredibly helpful tips on DIY book covers. Thank you to my proofreaders who find what I can't and make this an all-around better story.

And to you wonderful readers, thank you so much for all of your excitement and encouragement. I'm thrilled that you have continued on this journey with me and these characters. It means the world to me that you've chosen this book to pick up and carry with you. I hope you've enjoyed the ride!

Above all, thank you to my God who receives all the glory. I hope that everything I do ultimately points to Him. I wouldn't be here without You.

Get ready for the last adventure…

The Realms Series

Book Five

Realm of the Snow Queen

Emory R. Frie

…Coming Soon

Emory R. Frie is the award-winning author of debut novel, *Heart of a Lion*, and the Realms Series books, *Wonderland*, *Neverland*, *Enchanted Forest*, and *Giant Country*. She is currently attending Berry College to further pursue her writing craft, adding explorations in playwriting and experimental poetry to her passion. When she isn't writing, Emory enjoys watching musicals, sewing costumes, reading everything she can get her hands on, and going on adventures with her friends and family. She is captivated with wanderlust and dreams of learning to fly. Raised in Oregon, she now lives in Georgia with her family and rambunctious Scottie pup.

www.ingramcontent.com/pod-product-compliance
Lightning Source LLC
Chambersburg PA
CBHW031122210626
46816CB00016B/1895